unconditional

unconditional

HOLLY J. WOOD

OLIVE
LEAF

ISBN-13: 978-1-940427-00-3
ISBN-10: 1940427002

Library of Congress Control Number: 2013946779

Book Website
www.hollyjwood.com
Email: hollyjwoodauthor@gmail.com

Give feedback on the book at:
hollyjwoodauthor@gmail.com

Printed in The United States of America

For Steve

ACKNOWLEDGMENTS

I'd like to thank the members of my writing group. Devon Dorrity, for generously sharing his time and incredible talents by designing the cover and formatting the book. Christy Dorrity, for always having a listening ear and a never-ending supply of great advice and feedback. And Natasha Plyer, for coming up with the title, offering great suggestions, and making me laugh until it hurt. This book wouldn't have been possible without each of you.

A big thank you to Jen Hendricks for her stellar editing skills and entertaining emails. It was so nice to make a new friend along the way.

I will never cease to be amazed by Melissa Papaj and her unbelievable camera-wielding expertise. I'd also like to thank Mary Bledsoe, Kendra Belliston, Jillian Joy, and Zuzanna Ludwiczak for their contributions to the cover.

There is nothing so wonderful as having a great family support group. I want to thank my sisters Ginger and Janelle for being my sounding boards, and for not sighing when I have yet another question about my stories. Also, my heartfelt gratitude goes to my sister-in-law Kami for being at my side for every fireside, supporting me through the highs-and-lows, and for always giving me a reason to smile.

To the rest of my Rudd sisters: Jenna, Joanna, Julie, and Michelle. And my Wood sisters: Janae, Julie, Lisa, and Jackie, for reading, encouraging and listening.

I want my in-laws, Don and LuAnn Wood, to know how much I appreciate them for watching the kiddos and cheering me on. I feel so blessed to be a part of your family.

A gigantic thank you to my husband, Steve, for making it possible for me to pursue this crazy new adventure. For believing in me even (and especially) when I didn't believe in myself. Where would I be without you?

To Trevor, Lucy and Layla, for being my cutest fans and for reminding me daily of what matters most. I love you, for always.

Finally, I want to thank my Father in Heaven for His love, guidance, and goodness. This has been a fascinating journey; I'm humbled and grateful that I never had to traverse it alone.

E liza Moore, you are the girl of my dreams and the person I want to spend the rest of my life with . . . will you marry me?"

My eyes widened in shock as I looked from his questioning gaze, to the ring box in his hand, and back again.

Could this seriously be happening? A thousand thoughts ran through my mind as I stared into those eyes I'd come to know so well.

A few seconds passed and he cleared his throat, making me realize that I still hadn't answered. This was one of the most pivotal moments in my life; the moment when someone was asking me to be his wife. I'd imagined what this moment would feel like, but I'd never expected it to be like this.

I saw the shadow of uncertainty cross his face as he realized what was happening. He knew me well enough to understand the truth—that I didn't know how to answer his question.

CHAPTER

one

O kay, everyone. One, two, three . . . let 'em fly!"
A cheer rose up and dozens of cameras flashed as we launched our graduation caps into the air. We'd done it! We were official high school graduates.

Jill and I laughed as we covered our heads, seeking to evade the caps that were raining back down upon us. I stooped down and picked two of them up, handing one to Jill. She smiled as she accepted it, and then we squealed and gave each other hugs.

"I can't believe this day has finally come," I said as I pulled away from her.

"I know! I can't imagine what life will be like without seeing you every day. Even though you're leaving me behind to be a cool college girl now, you better *promise* to keep in touch. I want all the details." She grinned, arching a delicate eyebrow. "And when all those cute college guys are chasing after you, don't forget to mention that you have an adorable, *single* best friend back home."

I laughed. "It's a deal—as long as you promise to remember *me* when you're a world-famous hair stylist."

"Deal." Jill giggled and we put our arms around each other as we walked to find our families.

Jill and I had been best friends for what seemed like forever. Even though the university I would be attending was only an hour away and I was sure to see her often, I still wished that she was going with me. But when she'd been accepted to the local beauty school, I knew it was the perfect choice for her. She loved doing hair and all things fashion. Our separation was just another testament to the fact that this was the start of a new chapter in our lives. Hopefully a good chapter.

"Honey, are you sure you don't want to take Mr. Fluffy with you?"

"Mom, you *do* realize I'm going to college, not preschool, right?" I stared in disbelief as she held up the raggedy stuffed animal I'd had since birth. I turned to my sister, Courtney, for back-up.

She nodded. "Yeah. We don't want Eliza's roommates to think she's totally wacko . . . they can find that out on their own."

"Hey!" I aimed a pair of socks at Courtney's head.

"Alright then." Mom sighed and her face fell as she placed Mr. Fluffy into a box. "Farewell, little friend. I'm sure you won't take it personally that the owner you've been so faithful to throughout the years—the one you've always offered love and comfort to—no longer has a place for you now that she's grown." She sighed again as she continued to stroke the stuffed rabbit.

Courtney and I exchanged wearied looks.

"Mom, if it means *that* much to you I can take Mr. Fluffy with me." I could hide him under my bed if it came right down to it.

She looked up at me but her smile was sad. "No sweetheart, I'm just giving you a hard time. It's difficult for me to accept that you're all grown up now. I can still see you in your pigtails and pajamas, dragging Mr. Fluffy around the house." Tears began to mist her eyes and I knew she was in danger of crying again.

I reached over and gave her a hug. "I promise I'll come home often, and you can call me as much as you want. I won't be far away." My leaving home was tougher on my mom than I'd expected.

I glanced over her shoulder at Courtney. It was obvious that she was trying to mask her sadness as well. She was fifteen now and she'd be the only one left at home once I was gone. Thank goodness I'd chosen a school that was only an hour away—how would they have reacted if I'd left the state?

"Okay, girls, pizza's ready!" Dad called up from the kitchen.

"Perfect timing. All this packing has made me hungry." I broke from Mom's hug and stood to stretch my legs. We needed something to lighten the mood, and Dad's famous pizza and homemade root beer were just the ticket.

"Well, we've definitely made some good progress. It seems like we're just about finished," Mom said. She stood and surveyed the small pile of suitcases and boxes.

"Yeah, and you've saved the most important for last." Courtney held up the two items I *was* saving for last to ensure safe packing: First was the large padded envelope that contained all of Luke's letters.

Luke was my missionary and the guy I hoped to marry someday. I couldn't believe he was still writing to me. More than that, I couldn't believe that he still wrote to tell me that he *loved* me.

I had worried constantly that his feelings would fade while he was away and he wouldn't feel the same about me. But with each letter his attachments seemed to grow deeper, and so did mine. In two months (*two months!*), he would be home. My heart jumped as I realized how soon I would be able to see him again.

Cradled in Courtney's other arm was Great-grandma Porter's music box. I'd never told anyone about the special dreams that had led me to find Grandma's music box and all of the treasures it contained, but Mom had let me keep it.

"Thanks, Court." I reached out and took the items from her, carefully placing them on my bed.

"Better come and eat while it's still hot," Dad yelled again.

I was the last to leave my bedroom. Taking one final look at my stripped-down walls and empty drawers, I turned off the light and headed downstairs.

"Can someone explain the aftermath of the Civil War as outlined in section thirteen?"

I sighed as I stepped through the door and realized that I was once again late. I quickly scanned the room for a seat. This was a full class, and I usually arrived early so that I could avoid the rigmarole of stepping over people to get to a free desk. Why were there never any empty seats on the end?

I made my way up the stairs and offered quiet apologies as I climbed down a crowded row of legs, bags, and feet. I felt the heat rise to my cheeks as I sensed the awareness of eyes lingering on me as I passed.

Keeping my gaze trained on the empty chair that was now just feet from my grasp, I tried to ignore the irritated sigh from the professor at my disruption. I reached the seat and quickly sank into it, unzipping my bag as quietly as possible.

"Glad you could finally join us," a voice whispered from behind me. I turned around and with an inward groan realized I'd had the misfortune to end up smack-dab in front of Darren Fields. I'd met Darren on our first day of class, merely two weeks ago, and had spent the entire two weeks since avoiding his advances. This just wasn't my day.

I gave him a half-hearted smile and shrugged, before turning my attention back to the professor. I hoped that if I seemed absorbed enough in the lecture Darren wouldn't try to bother me again.

There was movement as the guy in the seat next to mine shifted. I looked over at him, but he had his hand covering his face as he took notes. I decided I'd better get busy doing the same since I'd already missed the first few minutes of class.

I pulled out my notebook and flipped to an empty page. I'd barely begun writing when the voice behind me whispered again, causing me to bristle.

"So, I was wondering if you had any plans for tonight?"

Before I had a chance to respond, Darren continued, "There's a new movie coming out and I thought maybe we could go see it."

Trying hard not to let my full annoyance show, I turned around and whispered, "Sorry, I already have plans." I didn't make an excuse for what those "plans" entailed, and spared the half-smile I would have offered under normal circumstances. This was the third time I'd turned him down in the past week. The guy needed to take a hint!

As if anticipating my response, he immediately volleyed back with, "Well how about tomorrow night, then?"

I fought the blush rising to my face as people around us began taking interest. "Sorry, I can't tomorrow night either," I whispered abruptly, and then turned back around, determined to focus on the class.

"Why not?"

Was this guy for real? Was I going to have to transfer from this class to avoid him? I felt my pulse quicken as I frantically tried to think of how to deal with the situation. The best option seemed to be to get up and try to find another seat, but looking around I realized the closest empty desk was clear on the other side of the room.

Ugh.

"Eliza, did you hear me? Why can't you go out tomor . . ."

Darren's words were cut short and my heart stopped as the guy sitting next to me suddenly put his arm around me and turned to face Darren. "Because she's already got a date with me, buddy, so I'd appreciate it if you'd leave my girlfriend here alone."

Darren's jaw clenched and he snorted as he looked at my neighbor incredulously. "You expect me to believe that?"

"Excuse me, Mr. Fields, is there something going on here that you'd like to share with the class?" Professor Gunner asked. Our interaction had apparently caused enough distraction that he could no longer ignore it.

"No, sir, I'm sorry," Darren replied as he scooted back in his seat. I didn't miss the scowl he shot toward the guy with his arm around me before turning to his notes.

"Well then with your permission," Professor Gunner looked pointedly at Darren and then at me, "I'll continue." There were a few quiet snickers around us before he resumed his lecture.

I was trying to process what was happening here. I avoided looking at the guy next to me, but he still had his arm around my shoulder. After a few seconds, he leaned over and whispered, "What time did you want me to pick you up, again?" He'd said it just loud enough for Darren to hear. I could barely discern the hint of humor in his voice, and his face was so close to my ear that I almost shivered.

"Uh." My mind felt frazzled. "Um . . . I think we decided on 7 o'clock," I whispered back uncertainly. I kept my gaze trained on my notebook as I tried to will the heat away from my cheeks. If I looked at him it would totally blow my cover. I'd never been able to master a decent game face.

"That works." I could tell he was smiling openly now.

I offered a tentative smile back, and then covertly glanced behind my shoulder. Darren was slumped back into his seat with a sour expression on his face. I felt a small sense of relief, but the stranger still had his arm around me.

Suddenly I wondered what new predicament I'd found myself in. Could I put on this charade for the entire class period? I was grateful that this guy had come to my rescue, but now I found myself in a whole new level of discomfort. Aside from the fact that I knew absolutely nothing about him, it was going to be impossible to take good notes with his arm around me—much less concentrate on the lecture.

As if reading my thoughts, he slowly pulled his arm away, freeing me from the situation. With a cautious sidelong smile, I wrote "Thank you" on my notebook page, and slid it over for him to see.

The corner of his mouth twitched as he jotted a quick "No problem" on his own paper.

I smiled shyly, and then turned my focus back to the professor. I pretended to be interested in the lecture, but try as I might to ignore it—I had definitely felt goose bumps when he put his arm around me.

As soon as class was over, everyone began collecting their stuff. I'd planned on waiting until Darren left to thank the guy sitting next to me.

No such luck.

"So how long have you two known each other?" Darren asked. His arms were crossed and he looked as though he was in no hurry to leave.

I felt my face flush, unsure of how to respond.

"Oh we just met the other day, but we hit it off *real* fast," the stranger said. He casually slung his backpack over one shoulder and held his hand out to me. "Ready?"

I looked at his outstretched hand, and then finally willed myself to look up into his face. What I saw made my breath catch in my throat. This guy was cute . . . *really* cute. He had light brown hair and deep blue eyes that held a spark of amusement in them. Granted, this was a large class, but how had I not noticed him before?

I felt a small jump in my stomach as I realized I'd been staring at him a few seconds longer than I should have. His hand was still outstretched.

I quickly glanced at Darren. The expression he wore was daring me to make a move. I realized that if I didn't take this path he would never stop pestering me.

Oh criminy!

I reached out and grabbed the stranger's hand. "Yep, I'm ready. See you later, Darren." As ridiculous as this situation was, I had to admit it was extremely satisfying to see the look on Darren's face: defeat. Finally!

I tried to ignore the tingling sensation in my hand as my newfound friend led me out the door and down the hallway. I hadn't felt anything close to this excitement in a long time, and it scared me.

Once we were safely out of sight from the moping Darren, the guy let go of my hand and turned to face me. He had a genuine smile and the unmistakable glint of humor in his eyes.

"So, Eliza, now that we're dating, I should probably introduce myself." He extended his hand again, but this time for a handshake. "My name's Sawyer Murdock."

I laughed and shook his hand. "It's nice to meet . . . wait—how did you know my name?"

He gestured back the way we'd come from. "Your eager fan back there gave it away."

I relaxed my brow and smiled. "Oh, right. Well, I can't tell you how much I appreciate your coming to my rescue like that. Darren's a nice guy, but he's a bit, um . . . persistent."

"Yeah, that's one way of putting it." Sawyer shook his head with raised eyebrows and I laughed. He looked at me for a moment and then grinned mischievously. "But you know, he actually did me a favor."

"He did?"

"Yep. I noticed you on the first day of class, but I hadn't gotten up the nerve to try to talk to you yet. When Darren started asking you out, I figured I'd better cut in before you gave in to his—*persistence*," he confessed with a shameless smile. "So are you dating anyone?"

I laughed. "Wow! You don't waste any time do you?"

He shook his head. "Can't afford to waste time around here. A beautiful girl like you is going to get snatched up fast. You snooze, you lose!" His energetic mood was infectious and I was flattered by his compliment.

It was obvious by his tan that he spent a lot of time outdoors. His smile carried the confidence of someone who had won over the heart of many an unsuspecting girl. It was nice to be admired by such an attractive guy, and I was almost tempted to encourage his flirting. Almost.

"Well, thanks again, Sawyer. It was really nice to meet you. I totally owe you one, so if there's ever anything I can do to return the favor, let me know." I smiled graciously at him and then turned to walk away.

"Whoa, hold on a second!" Sawyer reached for my arm and turned me around to look at him. "You never answered my question. Are you available?" His eyes searched mine and I took a deep breath, fighting to ignore how nice it felt to have his hand on my arm.

"Well . . . not exactly."

He raised an eyebrow. "Is that a nice way of telling me to get lost?"

I twisted the ruby ring on my finger and wondered how many times I'd had this conversation before. "No. It just means I'm not dating anyone right *now*, but I am waiting for a missionary."

"Ohhh, I see." Sawyer's face donned a knowing look. "That's cool. So when does your missionary get home?"

"In a couple of months." I felt the familiar, odd excitement rise within me in realizing it would be so soon.

"Huh . . . well that's coming right up." He smiled, but I caught the quick, calculating expression that played across his face. We stood there looking at each other for a few moments, neither one of us speaking.

"Yeah . . . so anyway, I guess I'd better be getting to my next class." I started to turn around again, disliking the way my heart had begun to flutter under Sawyer's gaze.

"Okay, but before you go—you know how you said you owed me a favor?" The tone in his voice made me stop in my tracks. He took a step closer, and I felt the hair on the back of my neck rise. "It's not like I think you owe me or anything, but since you were nice enough to offer—I've thought of something you can do for me."

"Of course. What is it?" I smiled to hide the nervous tingling in my stomach.

"You can keep your date with me tonight." His eyes held mischief, but also a challenge. He had me in a tough spot, and he knew it. If I refused, it would mean I hadn't been sincere in offering my gratitude.

"Are you serious?" Half of me honestly questioned whether he was joking while the other half sort of hoped he wasn't.

"Well, yeah . . . that is unless *you* weren't really serious about thanking me before?" He raised an eyebrow as he let the implication hang in the air.

I shook my head and laughed. "You are one smooth operator."

He shrugged and grinned, but there was an uncertain expression in his eyes as he waited for my answer.

I took in a quick breath to try to steady my racing heart. "Okay. What time?"

His smile broadened and I watched his shoulders relax. "We already arranged that, remember? Seven o'clock. Why don't you give me your phone number so you can text me your address."

I felt a wry smile curl my lips as I reached into my bag for my phone. I was going to have to keep my eye on this guy—that much was obvious. Somehow, though, something deep inside of me was stirring. It was a sensation that I hadn't felt in a long time.

Not since Luke had left.

CHAPTER

two

I walked back to my apartment after classes were over, still somewhat stunned over the events that had unfolded this morning. The summer heat was merciless, and my shirt felt damp where my backpack straps hit. Although I'd brought my trusty Honda Civic to college with me, our apartment was close enough to campus that I usually chose to walk.

I automatically stopped at the rows of mailboxes and pulled out my key. It was my ritual to stop here every day, just as I had at the mailbox at home every day for the last twenty-two months. I held my breath as I turned the key and opened the box, and then let the breath out in a sigh.

Empty. Again.

I tried to swallow down the disappointment as I locked the box and put the key away. Why had I expected a letter today? I knew that there was little chance I would get one, but it had been almost a month since the last letter had come and I couldn't keep myself from hoping.

Luke was serving in Mexico. Missionaries were allowed to email family, but friends (and girlfriends) had to wait for letters. Mexico's mail system was unreliable. Sometimes I would get one letter; sometimes they came in small stacks. Those were the really good days.

I hated to think about the first few months after Luke had left. I'd missed him so much I was often in physical pain, and tried to console myself by listening to our song on repeat. Before he'd left, Luke had played "The Promise" by Tracy Chapman for me on his guitar. I listened to it whenever the heartache became too intense to bear.

I was proud of him and knew that his mission was the best thing he could be doing, but that didn't make the pain any easier. After phone calls, texts, and dates, it had been hard to only have letters for communication. It almost felt like he had died. But of course, I never expressed any of my sadness when I wrote to him. I didn't want him to lose focus.

In those first few months he'd written often, judging by the dates on his letters. I'd cherished each word like a lifeline. Then, after about a year, the mail I received from him had slowed down. In the sporadic letters that came he still assured me of his love, but with them coming fewer and farther in-between, sometimes those words seemed hard to believe. At times, I even struggled to remember what his face looked like, and that worried me. I would pull out his pictures and study them until my eyes hurt. I was afraid things would be different when he got home. I was afraid we were slowly growing apart.

I walked up the stairs that led to our apartment floor. Our building had three levels, all with doors leading to an outside hallway. Our apartment was on the end of the second floor. I walked past the open door of apartment seven, and Monet Douglas stuck her head out.

"Hey, Eliza." She took a step toward me and lowered her voice, "You might want to be careful when you go in your apartment. Drew and his friends were in there a couple minutes ago."

"Oh *great*." I sighed and rolled my eyes before giving her a half-smile. "Thanks for the warning."

"No problem—I got your back." She winked and continued watching me as I moved down the hall.

I cautiously approached the door to our apartment, not sure what might be waiting for me on the other side. Still aware of Monet's gaze, I turned and said, "If I don't come back out in five minutes, send for the police."

She smiled and gave me a thumb's up. I grimaced before opening the door. Whatever I'd been expecting still didn't prepare me for what I saw: leaves. Bags and bags full of leaves covered every conceivable surface of our apartment floor.

"Drew, you're dead meat!" I yelled, even though I knew he and his friends were long gone by now.

Monet appeared in the doorframe and gasped. She put a hand over her mouth and spoke through her fingers, "Where in the world did they get all of these *leaves*?"

My shoulders slumped as I surveyed the mess. "I *told* Lacey she was asking for trouble." I waded through the foliage to get a couple of garbage sacks from the kitchen.

"What in the . . . what *happened?!*" My three roommates appeared behind Monet, hands loaded with grocery bags and mouths agape. Lacey was the one who'd made the initial outburst and I watched as her expression melted from shock to anger. "Oh it is *so* on!" she growled as she stepped across the threshold. Bree and Charlotte followed in her wake, eyes wide with surprise.

"Lacey, I *told* you we were in for it after that last prank—there was no way Drew was going to let that slide," I said as I crouched and began stuffing leaves in the bag.

Drew and his roommates had started hanging around our apartment since the second day of the semester. We were good friends with them by now, but what had started as fun pranking between the eight of us was quickly becoming an all-out war.

"How did they get in?" Lacey demanded. "Haven't we been locking the door religiously?" She threw each of us a questioning glance.

"Yes! We've all been super careful ever since they hid that rancid can of tuna fish under the bathroom sink," Bree said.

I scrunched up my nose in revulsion just remembering the smell. "Monet, did you see how they got in here?" I asked.

"No, I just saw them on their way out. From the way they were hurrying, I could tell they'd been up to something. I wish I could have caught them in the act." She shrugged helplessly and then started backing toward the door. "Good luck cleaning up the mess. I'd help, but I have a huge test I need to study for."

With that she was gone. I couldn't blame her; this was our war not hers, after all.

"Well, guys, we might as well start cleaning up," Charlotte said in her soft-spoken way. "Let's just be grateful that it's leaves and not something worse."

I looked at her and smiled. She was forever finding the bright side of a situation.

"I'll be grateful all right—just as soon as we come up with another plan of attack," Lacey said, adding a villainous cackle, which made Charlotte and I laugh.

"Oh no you don't, Lacey." Bree glared at her as she placed a bag on the floor and shoveled leaves in with her hands. "All we did was tie their front door to the railing so they couldn't get out of their apartment. No big deal. They only had to call their buddies next door to let them out. And look how they repaid us! The pranking stops *here*," she stated firmly. "Besides, we all know that you and Drew are secretly crazy about each other, and that's why you're pranking—to hide your true feelings."

"Whatever, Bree!" Lacey's face instantly reddened. She picked up a scoop of leaves and threw it at her.

"Hey—no fair." Bree laughed and then chucked a handful of leaves back. "You're just in denial—admit it!"

Before long, we were all involved in the leaf fight. We laughed hysterically as leaves filled the air like confetti and caused an even bigger mess than before. But it was worth it.

⟨✥

"So where do you think he'll take you tonight?" Bree asked. I stood in front of the mirror, applying the final touches to my makeup.

"I don't know, maybe out to eat and a movie? I still can't believe I'm doing this. He's basically a complete stranger." There was no mistaking how nervous I was. The butterflies in my stomach were so intense they threatened to lift me off the floor.

"You'll have fun, and this will be good for you." Bree put a reassuring hand on my arm and smiled. "Besides, if he's as good-looking as you say he is, there's no *way* you won't enjoy yourself. Even if he's boring, you'll be entertained just staring at his face."

I snorted. "Nice, Bree. That's real deep."

She laughed and we walked into the front room. Charlotte was on the couch studying. Lacey was vacuuming.

It had taken us over an hour to bag all the leaves and take them to the dumpster, but Lacey was determined to suck up every last shred of evidence. Drew and his buddies were coming over later, and she didn't want them to have the satisfaction of gloating over any trace of their prank.

I smiled as I looked at my three roommates.

I'd been so nervous to start a summer semester, mostly because I didn't know any of the girls I was sharing the apartment with. The only thing I'd known was that they were all LDS, as the ad stated. I couldn't believe how well I'd lucked out. From the very first day, we'd all hit it off like we were lifelong friends. Lacey and Charlotte were in their second year, so they shared a room together. Bree and I shared the other room, and this was the first semester of college for both of us.

Charlotte, Bree and I were all from Utah, and Lacey was from Nevada. Our personalities blended well together. Although we usually stayed up into the wee hours talking and laughing (often causing me to be late for my first class), these past two weeks had been some of the most fun of my life.

Lacey turned off the vacuum; apparently satisfied she'd devoured any miniscule leaflet that dared to remain behind. I went into the kitchen for a glass of water, but almost dropped the glass when I heard a knock on the door.

"It's *hi-im*," Bree whispered in a singsong voice. Lacy and Charlotte grinned at me. I placed my glass on the counter and tried to act natural as Charlotte answered the door.

CHAPTER

three

Is Eliza here?" Sawyer asked. Charlotte nodded and opened the door wider, inviting him to come in. I walked into the front room and Sawyer grinned as soon as he saw me, the whites of his teeth a stark contrast with his tan skin. He was wearing dark jeans and a light blue polo, which complemented his eyes and skin tone.

I introduced him to my roommates, noticing the quick glances they gave me. They obviously agreed with my opinion that he was more than slightly good-looking. Bree stood directly behind him and gave me a huge, cheesy grin and two thumbs up. I had to look away to keep from laughing.

"So, you ready to go?" Sawyer looked down, his eyes locked on mine.

"Yeah, I'm ready." I smiled at him, and then turned to my friends. "See you guys later. Don't forget to interrogate Drew about how he got in here today." I looked specifically at Lacey.

"You got it." She winked as she closed the door behind us. I could hear their muffled giggles as we started down the hall.

"Your roommates are cool," Sawyer said as he pretended not to hear the giggling. "What was that 'interrogation' business all about?"

"Oh, there are just some guys we're in the middle of a prank war with. They got into our apartment today and dumped leaves all over. We don't have any idea how they got in." It helped calm my nerves to keep talking. I'd been on a lot of dates since Luke had left, but none of them had made me feel this unsettled. *What was wrong with me?*

Sawyer chuckled. "I saw some guys on campus that were asking the grounds keeper if they could have the leaves he'd just bagged from an old tree. I thought it was pretty weird, but it all makes sense now."

"Aha! I'm sure that was them." I shook my head and smiled. "Lacey is already scheming about our next prank. I'm a little scared to see what she comes up with."

Sawyer held the door open for me. "You'll have to point them out to me sometime so I can tell you if I recognize them."

I nodded and climbed into the passenger seat of his shiny black Audi. His last remark had caused a little thrill to rise inside of me. It held the subtle implication that he wanted to hang out again.

I watched him circle in front of the car as I buckled my seatbelt; trying not to gape at the leather interior and high-tech control panel.

"So how do you feel about fried chicken?" Sawyer broke through my thoughts. He put the car in drive and pulled out of the parking lot.

"I'm a fan," I said, relaxing into a smile. I was starting to feel more comfortable around him.

"Glad to hear it, 'cause if you'd said you were a vegetarian I would have felt bad about the chicken I slaughtered for our picnic tonight."

Eww! "Did you just say 'slaughtered'?" I stared at him with my mouth hanging open, but his face was serious.

"Yeah, didn't I mention that I live on a farm? I told my parents I had a hot date, so they told me to take Ol' Henrietta out to the chopping block—this bein' a special occasion and all." He added a slight, country twang to his tone as I continued to stare at him, wondering if he was indeed serious . . . or sane.

"So where is this farm of yours?" I crossed my arms, unsure if it had been wise to go on a date with someone completely unknown to me.

"Just a few miles outta town. I'll have to take you there sometime. Ma and Pa would sure like to meet you."

I caught just the slightest twitch at the corner of Sawyer's mouth. He was being careful not to make eye contact.

I relaxed my shoulders a bit. I was pretty sure he was putting me on, so I started to drill him about farm life. He answered every question with ease until we pulled up to our destination: a local pond, with picnic tables and a walking path along the shoreline.

Sawyer walked around to get my door. I looked over at the pond and smiled as I saw that the sun was setting over the horizon, casting a golden hue across the water. It was a perfect summer evening.

"We can sit at one of these tables, or I brought a blanket if you'd rather eat closer to the water," he offered as I climbed out of the car.

"Let's sit by the pond, that way we can see the ducks and swans better."

"Sounds good to me." Sawyer went to the back of the car and popped the trunk. He reached in and I watched intently, half-expecting him to pull up a limp chicken by its claws. "Well, here she is—Ol' Henrietta!" Sawyer emerged from the trunk holding a red-and-white-striped KFC bucket.

I tried to keep a straight face as I pointed an accusing finger. "I *knew* you weren't serious. That was totally cruel—I almost believed you!"

He bent over and erupted with laughter, taking several moments before he could speak. "You should have seen the look on your face!"

"Seriously, I cannot believe you would pull something like that when I don't even know you." I stood with my hands on my hips and tried my best to look severe, but the sight of him laughing finally caused me to break down. I giggled in spite of myself, and walked over to take the bucket from his hands. "Here, I'll take *Henrietta* for you."

Sawyer stood upright and gave one final chuckle before trying to look penitent. "I'm sorry, Eliza, I couldn't help myself. You seemed a little nervous when I picked you up and I wanted to lighten the mood. Will you forgive me?" His blue eyes held a charming gleam that was hard to resist.

"Oh, I guess so," I sighed in playful annoyance. "As long as you promise not to make up any more stories. When you talked about slaughtering animals I was afraid I'd gone out with some kind of psychopath serial killer."

"I'm sorry; I can see how that could freak you out. No more stories, I promise." Sawyer gave a slight grin. He made a scout's honor sign and I giggled again. His eyes seemed to light up each time I laughed.

He reached into the trunk and retrieved a worn quilt and two old-fashioned bottles of root beer. "There's a spot over by that tree—what do you think?"

I looked over to where he was pointing and noticed that it was a ways off from where most of the other people were gathered. "Looks good to me."

We set up our picnic beneath the gently swaying branches of a tree. The conversation flowed naturally between us. I learned that Sawyer was from Sacramento (*not* from a farm). As I'd suspected, he was a returned missionary and had served in New Zealand.

He was the oldest of three kids, and he was majoring in Biology. This was his second-to-last semester, and then he planned to attend medical school. It was his lifelong dream to become a heart surgeon.

"So now that I've talked your ear off," he smiled, "tell me more about you."

"What do you want to know?" I smiled back at him.

"Everything." The sun had set long ago and it was getting dark, but I could still see the intensity of his eyes as he studied me.

"Well that could take a long time," I teased. He nodded and then waited for me to continue. I told him about my family and then more about my roommates. I explained that I still hadn't decided on a major yet, and that I was getting my generals out of the way until I figured it all out.

"That reminds me," I said. "If you're so close to graduating, how come you're in my history class?"

"Ugh," he groaned. "I didn't realize I still had that general to fulfill. I wasn't excited about being in a class that was mostly full of freshman . . . until I saw you, that is."

I was grateful that the darkness hid my blush as he leaned back on his elbows and continued, "So you just graduated from high school, huh? I must seem like an old man to you."

I scoffed. "Yep, you're practically ancient. How old are you? Twenty-two?"

"Actually, I'm almost twenty-four."

"Oh." I paused, "Well then I probably seem like a baby to you." I gave him a half-smile, expecting him to tease me again, but his eyes were serious.

"Not at all."

There was a moment of silence between us that felt super-charged as our eyes locked. I felt my heart speed up and suddenly I was desperate to change the subject. I cleared my throat and glanced away. Both arms were behind me and I was leaning on them for support, so I tilted my head back and looked up at the sky. "Look at all those stars!" I exclaimed, truly excited by the sparkling array above us.

Sawyer looked at me for another long second before gazing up to the sky as well. "Yeah, it's awesome to be away from the city lights. You can see the stars much better out here."

Most of the people at the pond had left by now. I could hear the hypnotic sound of crickets as the waves lapped gently along the shore. We were both lying on our backs, with Sawyer's arm only inches away from mine. He pointed out several constellations, and then suddenly he leaned up on his elbow and looked down at me.

"I'm taking an astronomy course right now and I have access to the telescope. Do you want to go on campus and check it out?"

"Yeah, that would be cool." I raised myself up with my elbows behind me, and suddenly my face was mere inches from his. I held my breath as he looked down at my lips, and then back to my eyes. I knew he was thinking of kissing me, and with an electrifying jolt I realized that I wanted him to.

However, in the next second, he stood and held his hand out. I felt disappointment seep through me, and then guilt for feeling disappointed. *What was I thinking?* I had never kissed anyone else while Luke was away—I hadn't even come close to wanting to. For what felt like the hundredth time tonight, I wondered what was going on.

I took Sawyer's outstretched hand and allowed him to pull me up. We threw away our trash and then folded the quilt. Sawyer tucked it under his arm, and then offered his free hand as he led me to the car. Without thinking, I took it, telling myself it was so I wouldn't trip in the darkness . . . but I wasn't fooling anyone.

As we walked back to the car, I looked up at the stars and found the one I always made a wish on. *Luke*, I silently pleaded, *get home soon so we can be together again. I miss you.*

With my heart in a confused jumble, I climbed into the car and Sawyer closed the door behind me.

CHAPTER

four

"I hope you had fun tonight," Sawyer said as we stood outside my door.

"I did. Dinner was great, and that telescope was awesome. I think *I* might want to take astronomy now." I smiled up at him and then quickly looked away. My heart rate was accelerating again and confusing my judgment.

There had been other people in the astronomy tower, allowing me time to build up a wall of resistance. Now that we were alone again I felt that resistance crumbling.

"You should; it's pretty amazing." Sawyer dropped his voice a little and took a step forward. I had my back against the wall and he slowly put his hand to one side of me, leaning in even closer. "Eliza, I hope it's not too soon to ask, but what are you doing tomorrow night?"

"Oh. Um . . ."

His nearness was causing all of my thoughts to collide in confusion. It was hard to breathe! I had to do something. "We were actually planning on going dancing." I moved ever so slightly away from his arm.

His face fell a little. "Oh, really? That's cool." He looked at the floor and then back up at me with a slight grin. "So what are you doing Sunday after church?"

"Sawyer, I really like you, and I had a lot of fun tonight, but . . ." I focused on a crack in the pavement beneath my feet. "I'm just not sure if I'm ready to start like . . . dating, you know?"

He let out a sigh and leaned back on the railing across from me. "Yeah, I know—your missionary, right?" He smiled somewhat ruefully.

"Yes. He's coming home soon and I need to see what direction our relationship will take. It wouldn't be fair to you or to him if we started dating and I asked you to wait until I find out what happens."

"Well what if that's a chance I'm willing to take?" His eyes seemed to penetrate mine and I had to force myself to stay strong.

"That's really sweet of you, and I hope we can still be friends—but I don't think dating is a good idea for me right now."

Sawyer held up his hands in a gesture of surrender. "Okay, I won't bother you about it anymore. I know you just went out with me tonight as a favor." He slid his hands into his pockets and blew out a short, dejected sigh. "So we'll just be friends."

I laughed and lightly punched him in the arm. "You are so ridiculous! Laying on the guilt like that, you should be majoring in drama."

He grinned and then he held out his hand for a handshake.

"Friends?"

I shook my head and couldn't help but giggle as I shook his hand. "Yes. Friends."

He held on to my hand for a second longer and a devilish gleam rose in his eyes. "You know . . . my *friends* and I always give each other a hug."

I laughed again, but before I could say anything he pulled me into his arms. At first I felt stiff and resistant, but then I gave in and let him hug me. We stood there for a few seconds, with his arms wrapped around my waist and his face close to my neck. I felt a thousand tiny fireworks go off inside my body.

I hadn't realized how much I missed the feeling of being held like this; of the crazy excitement when a guy you liked looked at you in a certain way; of the explosion inside when he finally touched you.

"I've gotta go," I said abruptly as I tried to pull away from Sawyer, but his arms were still around me.

"Eliza, I really think . . ." he spoke quietly into my ear, but I cut him off.

"No, seriously. It's late and I need to go." I broke free from his arms and turned the doorknob. "Thanks again for the date. It was nice."

He gave me a small, wistful smile in return.

"It was my pleasure."

"Buen dia, compañero," Elder Martinez said.

"¡Ay! ¿Qué hora es?" Luke groaned as he rolled over and peered at his alarm clock.

"5:30. ¡No me diga que se olvidó!" Elder Martinez gestured to the running shoes he was lacing up. He smiled and continued in broken English, "We make a goal to exercise today, remember?"

Luke grunted and briefly considered turning over and falling back asleep, but one glance at his eager companion made him change his mind.

Elder Martinez possessed an almost manic amount of energy—but his enthusiasm for life was contagious. It was one of the things that made him a great missionary. Luke admired him, and as senior companion, he also wanted to set a good example for goal keeping.

Normally, he wouldn't have minded waking an hour early. He liked to get moving in the morning and was excited about their new commitment to exercise—but he had been dreaming about Eliza. He could still see her face in his mind. He'd often dreamed about her these past twenty-two months, but lately the dreams had become more vivid.

She had been calling out to him, her beautiful face twisted in fear and confusion. Luke was mere feet away from her, but she couldn't see or hear him. When he tried to move closer to her, it was as if an invisible wall was there, blocking the way.

Luke said his morning prayers and quickly started getting ready so Elder Martinez wouldn't have to wait for him. He tried to shake the dream from his thoughts, not wanting to read anything into it, but the nagging worry lodged itself in the back of his mind.

He thought about the last letter he'd received from Eliza. Everything had seemed normal. She'd told him that she loved him, which had to be a good sign because he knew she wouldn't lie. Especially about that.

He still couldn't believe what a miraculous blessing it was that she hadn't been snatched up yet. He prayed every day for at least the opportunity to see her again; to date her when he got home. Luke knew it was in the Lord's hands and he did his best to focus on the work. He loved being a missionary and had committed to give one hundred percent to the Lord as he served. His mission had been everything he had ever hoped it would be, and so much more. It was the hardest thing he'd ever done in his life. He'd loved every minute of it.

Now, as the countdown to return home was on, he resolved to make these last weeks the best yet. He would pray, seek, and work harder than ever before. When the time came to leave the mission, Luke would go home with no regrets. The only thing that threatened to break his concentration was anxiety over these dreams about Eliza.

As he poured bottled water onto his toothbrush, he smiled wryly to himself. That girl had caused him more trouble than she would ever know. Trying to keep from missing her, thinking of her, and wanting her for his own had been the biggest battle of Luke's mission. Learning the language had been nothing in comparison to trying to lock up his heart.

He rinsed out his mouth and placed both of his hands on the sink in determination. He would focus on the work and do his best to put Eliza from his mind. But if she was still available when he got home, she'd better watch out. As far as Luke was concerned, as long as Eliza wasn't married she was fair game, and nothing would stop him from trying to win her over. He wasn't sure why he sensed there would be any challenges—maybe it was the dreams making him think this way. One thing was sure though: no matter what the obstacle, he was ready to face it.

Elder Martinez knocked on the bathroom door. "You ready, Elder?"

Luke smiled at the progress Elder Martinez was making with his English. Now that Luke was fluent in Spanish, he was working to help his eager companion learn a second language as well.

"Yeah." He stood up from the sink and straightened his posture as he opened the door. "I'm ready."

"Try some clam chowder, it's only $5.99 for the container."

I was working at Sam's Club, handing out samples. Once I'd moved to school and gotten settled, I'd begun job hunting. When I saw the advertisement for this position it had seemed perfect: only a few hours a week, mostly on Saturdays. Of course I was stuck wearing a dorky apron again (I couldn't seem to get away from the dang aprons!), but I now had the lovely added accessory in the form of a hairnet. After that, the apron didn't seem so bad.

"Eliza, you're looking quite *stylin'* today," Drew said with a snicker as he and two of his friends sauntered up to my sample booth. Drew Anderson was perpetually up to no good, but somehow it made him all the more likeable.

I rolled my eyes and smiled. "Thanks, Drew. Here to get your lunch again, I see?"

He grinned and rubbed his stomach. "Of course! What's on the menu for today? Clam chowder?" He picked up the tiny white cup and spoon, and then turned to his roommates. "You guys want some?"

Ben and Paul stepped closer. Paul took one of the samples, but Ben scrunched up his nose. "No thanks, I'm not a seafood fan."

"Me neither . . . especially since *those who shall remain nameless*, left a rotten can of tuna in our bathroom." I gave them each a hard glare and they laughed. I frowned in disgust. "*Ugh*, I can still smell it!" (This earned more laughter). "So how did you guys get into our apartment yesterday, anyway?" I demanded. "You do realize that breaking and entering is illegal, right?"

Drew gave a final chuckle, then sighed and wiped at pretend tears. "I don't know what you're talking about," he said before changing the subject. "Did you have fun on your date last night? You missed some awesome episodes of our *Mystery Falls* marathon."

"Yeah, I had a good time. You guys will have to fill me in on what I missed."

Drew and his friends had gotten us hooked on a mystery series that seemed to contain never-ending episodes. But the shows were clean, and they offered an excuse for Drew and Lacey to hang out together. They were both still in denial of their mutual crushes, although Lacey told me that Drew had sat by her last night. They were like junior high kids—throwing spit wads at each other because they were afraid to admit their feelings.

"So who is this guy?" Ben asked, scuffing his shoe on the floor.

"Just a friend from my history class," I said, keeping my eyes trained on the chowder I was dishing out.

Bree had told me that Ben had been disappointed when I wasn't there last night. She suspected that he had a thing for me, but I didn't think so. Ben was quiet and a little shy, and he knew that I had a missionary.

"Well I hear you guys are goin' dancin' tonight, is that right?" Drew asked.

"Yeah, it should be fun. It's karaoke night, are you guys going to be there?"

"Absolutely! You ain't heard nothin' till you've heard me sing karaoke in front of a crowd. I'll even consider doing an autograph signing after the performance—*if* my fans cheer sufficiently loud enough, that is." Drew looked down his nose at me.

I laughed. "I'll be sure to prepare my friends for the incredible performance they are *privileged* to witness tonight."

He nodded sagely. "Yes. And one last thing—when you come tonight, *do* be sure to remove that hairnet . . . it embarrasses me."

I threw a plastic spoon at him.

❧

"If I ever smell clam chowder again, I think I'll vomit." I collapsed on the couch and rubbed my temples.

"Yeah, you better shower before we go out tonight. You smell like Fisherman's Wharf," Lacey chided as she sat down next to me.

"You can borrow that new shampoo I just bought, Liza. It's really good stuff," Charlotte said from her place at the kitchen table.

"Thanks, Char." I smiled at her before I stretched my legs and yawned. "Well, I guess I'll go and check the mail, although I don't know *why*." I frowned as I contemplated how long it had been since I'd heard from Luke.

"Oh, I wouldn't give up hope," Bree said as she stepped into the room. She stood behind the sofa with one arm behind her back. "You just never know when a letter might fall right. into. your. lap." She brought her arm around and dropped an envelope onto my knees.

I snatched it. "Oh my goodness!" I pressed the letter to my chest and rushed to my bedroom, beaming at Bree as I passed her. "Thank you!"

She grinned and nodded in a knowing way.

I sat down on my bed and opened the envelope with my index finger, thrilling at the sight of Luke's penmanship on the envelope. This was exactly what I needed! With all the confusion I'd experienced from my date last night, Luke's letter was coming at the perfect time.

I unfolded the paper and read, trying not to devour the words too fast.

Dear Eliza,

How have you been? I'm so sorry that my letters are not as frequent as they should be—the work has been keeping me super busy these days, but it's awesome! I wish you could have been there for our baptism this last week. Do you remember Jorge Cordova? Well he finally gained a testimony and agreed to be baptized—it was incredible! His wife was so excited, and now they're making the goal to be sealed in the temple. It's amazing to watch the light that comes into people's lives when they learn and accept the truths of the Gospel, and I am truly honored to have a small part in their conversion process.

I always knew that I wanted to serve a mission, but I never knew just how hard it would be—how much it would challenge me physically, emotionally and spiritually. Yet there is nothing that could possibly compare to it. I've grown in ways that I didn't know were possible and the rewards have far outweighed the challenges. The biggest challenge, of course, is not being with you.

Eliza, I think about you every day. I can't believe I'll get to see you in two short months! I eagerly look forward to that day, but I'm also grateful that I still have these two months that I get to serve the Lord full-time and do His work.

I was totally stoked to get your last letter! I've read it many times. How is school going? Did my mom tell you that she's already got me registered for fall classes? I get home a week before fall semester, so hopefully that will give me enough time to get organized and everything. It's gonna be weird to be back in school again, but I'm excited for it.

I'm thinking seriously of entering the engineering program. How do you feel about that? I've always been interested in that field, and I think it would provide a decent income. Have you decided on a major yet? I'm sure you're doing awesome in your classes, just like you did in high school. You are an amazing girl, and you do well at anything you put your mind to. Man, I can't wait to see you!

Well, again I apologize that I haven't been able to get more letters to you. It seems like I can't remember what it's like to have a regular mail system. But I want you to know, and never doubt, that I love you. You are the girl of my dreams, and I gave my heart to you long ago.

Sometimes I lie awake at night and look up at the stars, and I find that one special wishing star that you and I found together. Do you remember that? Anyway, whenever I see it, I wish for the same thing—that you'll still be there when I get home. Take care of yourself, Liza Lou, and know that even though we're thousands of miles apart, my heart is right there with you. Always.

Love,

Luke

P.S. I'll meet you in my dreams . . .

I smiled. Shortly after Luke had left, he'd written to me and we'd arranged to have "dream dates" until he got home. I did dream of him often, and after each dream it helped me to feel like we were still connected in some strange, cosmic way.

I sighed and kissed the letter. It was so good to hear from him again! There were times when it felt like he wasn't real anymore; that our time together had only been a wonderful figment of my imagination—but here was proof. Luke was alive, and he still loved me.

My heart felt warm and content and I couldn't keep the smile from my face. Luke was not only the man that I loved, but he was my best friend too. We'd only dated a few months before he'd left on his mission, but we'd grown through these letters in a way that I hadn't expected. We'd learned so much about each other and had formed a lasting bond.

I sighed and laid back on my bed, all thoughts of Sawyer and the confusion I'd felt last night fled from my mind. Luke would be home soon, and then I would never have to worry about dating, or boys, or the heartache that came with it, ever again.

CHAPTER

five

"Let's go ladies!" Bree said as we pulled into a parking spot at the dance club. It was a local place that hosted conservative clubbing: no drinking was allowed and they even had a dress code. It was where most of the Mormon crowd convened for dancing.

We'd had a fun time swapping clothes and getting ready beforehand. I had showered and finally managed to scrub the last of the chowder stench from my body, replacing it with a spritz of my favorite perfume.

Tonight was country dancing night. We were all dressed in our jeans and ready to line dance. Charlotte had even donned a pair of cute cowboy boots and a cowboy hat, her long blond hair flowing attractively beneath it. Altogether, I thought we looked pretty good as we walked into the club—a force to be reckoned with!

Loud music and laughter greeted us as we paid the cashier and walked in. The place was packed. There were three separate areas to the club: one for karaoke, one for pool, and the large dance hall.

"Let's check out the karaoke first," Lacey called over the din. We all nodded and Bree took my arm as we walked around the pool tables and toward the karaoke lounge. Several guys were crowding the tables and we heard a few catcalls as we walked by. Bree turned and winked at one of the guys who'd whistled, which made us all laugh as we kept walking.

We stepped inside the karaoke lounge just in time to hear some poor soul offer the final, off-key notes of a Rascal Flats song. It was painful, but the guy seemed to be enjoying himself so we clapped enthusiastically as he bowed and exited the stage.

"Hey look—there's Drew!" Lacey pointed as Drew took the stage. Ben, Paul and their other roommate, Spencer, took their places behind him. It was apparent that Drew was taking the lead mic, and the other guys would sing back-up.

"How's everybody doing tonight?" Drew called, drawing a raucous response from the gathered crowd. My roommates and I cheered loudly as we found seats on a jumbo-sized beanbag.

After the cheering died down, he continued, "Alright, well we've got a special song we'd like to sing for you lovely people tonight. It's an oldie, but a goodie, and we'd like to dedicate it to the girls sitting right over there from Birchwood Plaza, apartment number eight." Drew pointed over to where we were sitting, and the crowd roared with approval. We laughed and Bree offered a parade wave, earning more cheers.

The music started and I immediately recognized the tune to "You've Lost That Lovin' Feelin'". Drew gave an impressive performance, drawing the audience in with his strong voice and animated expressions. He handled the mic like a pro, and the back-ups did a great job too. After the final notes had been sung, Drew and his friends received a standing ovation and several requests for an encore. We all jumped up from the beanbag, clapping wildly. Lacey whistled as they bowed and then stepped off the stage.

We gave them all high fives as they came to sit down, faces beaming. "So what did you think?" Drew asked us, though he was looking mostly at Lacey.

"That was incredible!" Charlotte answered, and Lacey nodded in affirmation. The look of approval was obvious in her eyes and I was happy for her. She and Drew would make a good couple. If they ever got together.

Suddenly I missed Luke intensely. If he were here I would have someone to look at all dreamy-eyed the way Lacey was staring at Drew. I shook my head and scolded myself for thinking so selfishly.

Soon enough.

"What are you guys going to sing?" Ben asked as he came to sit down beside me. Our seating arrangement had become somewhat jumbled now that the guys were here. Lacey was now sitting by Drew, and all eight of us shared two of the giant beanbags. We were forced to sit pretty close to each other because the room was so full.

"I don't know, what do you guys think?" I asked as I turned to my friends.

"You better get on the list before it fills up," Paul advised.

"Liza, you pick the song. You can do the main vocal and we'll be your back-ups," Bree said.

"No way, we should all sing together," I protested.

My friends shook their heads and Lacey took things into her own hands. "I know which song to do," she said as she stood up. Before I could get a word in edge-wise she'd already made her way over to the karaoke jockey. She took the binder he offered and scanned down a list of songs, pointing to the one she wanted. She waded through the crowd back to us, a huge smile on her face. "Okay, we're set. This is going to be awesome!"

We waited through several more songs until it was our turn to go onstage. I felt a nervous twist in my stomach as I stepped up to the lead mic. How had my friends talked me into this? I'd made the Jubilee group in my senior year, and so had plenty of practice singing solos, but I was still nervous. At least I had my friends to back me up.

I turned around to smile at them, and realized that they weren't there. I scanned the crowd and saw that they had gotten up, making me think that they were following me, but then had sat back down. The traitors!

Music began playing and I didn't have any choice but to sing. The song was "When You Say Nothing at All," and I was grateful that Lacey had chosen a song that I knew well. Ballads were my strong suit, so I tried to ignore the sea of faces and lights and just sing. The crowd was responsive, and halfway through I mustered the courage to look out at the audience. I smiled at my friends, and then felt the smile falter as my gaze traveled to the back of the room.

Sawyer was standing there. He was watching me intently and when our eyes met his face broke into an enormous smile.

I almost dropped a note as I looked at him, and then I quickly moved my gaze to the screen and focused on the words. The final chorus was coming up so I took a deep breath and harnessed all of my vocal training for the last few lines. Finally the song was over, and I felt my cheeks flush as the room erupted with applause. I smiled and made a quick little curtsy before exiting the stage. I couldn't get out of that spotlight fast enough.

People were still cheering as I joined my friends. I noticed Sawyer cheering loudest of all. We made eye contact again and he grinned and started walking toward me.

"Liza that was mind blowing!" Drew exclaimed, bowing dramatically before me. "This isn't easy for me to admit, but I think your performance may have even rivaled my own."

Lacey punched him in the arm. "Dude, her performance blew yours right out of the park!" she chided and then stood to give me a hug. "I'm sorry we tricked you, Eliza. It was all my fault, but I knew you wouldn't get up there if we didn't force you into it."

She made big puppy-dog eyes, and her expression was so pathetic that I had to laugh. "I forgive you . . . it was actually pretty fun."

Bree and Charlotte gave me hugs too. Charlotte whispered in my ear, "He's standing right behind you, did you see him back there?"

I gave a subtle nod and then pulled away from her to face Sawyer. He was with another guy I didn't recognize.

"You've been holding out on me," he said. His eyes flashed with admiration. "I had no idea you had such an incredible voice."

"Thanks," I tried to stop the blush that was rising to my cheeks. My heart still hammered with adrenaline.

Sawyer stared at me for another second before continuing, "This is my roommate, Dustin."

Dustin nodded. "Nice to meet you. You did a great job up there." He wore a friendly smile and I liked him instantly.

"Thanks. It's nice to meet you too." I returned his smile and then looked at Sawyer. "I didn't expect to see you here tonight," I said, subconsciously toying with the hem of my shirt. His sudden appearance had caused that strange, tingling sensation in my stomach again.

"Yeah, well . . . we just thought it seemed like a good night for dancing." He shrugged, but Dustin gave him a smirk.

I tried not to be excited by the fact that he was here—or by that look he was giving me.

"Liza, do you want to come back up there with us? I signed us up to sing as a group this time."

I folded my arms and turned to Lacey with raised eyebrows.

"No, *seriously*. No tricks this time," she insisted.

"Thanks, but I think one performance is enough for me tonight. Good luck, you guys." I smiled at my friends as they made their way to the stage.

"Woo-hoo!" Drew yelled from his place on the bean bag.

I turned around and laughed at him, but caught Ben watching me. He didn't seem happy to see me talking to Sawyer. There was no time to worry about it though, because just then the music started. I got lost in cheering for my girls as they sang a rousing rendition of "Dancing Queen."

Bree and Lacey were totally comfortable in front of an audience, but I hadn't expected Charlotte to be willing to go up there. She was normally pretty shy, but she did a great job and the crowd ate it up.

Once the song was over, they walked quickly back to us on an adrenaline high. "Okay, now that we've all had a chance to sing, let's go dance!" Bree said.

"Sounds good to me," Drew agreed.

I turned to Sawyer and Dustin. "Are you guys coming?"

"You don't mind if we tag along?" He raised a questioning eyebrow. "I mean, you seem like you have enough *friends* here already." There was a teasing gleam in his eyes. The emphasis of his wording wasn't lost on me.

"Not at all—the more the merrier," I replied in an equally playful manner. I was fighting to keep my heartbeat steady.

Once we entered the dance hall we were instantly swallowed by the loud country music and strobe lights. I held on to Charlotte's hand—who held on to Bree—who was holding on to Lacey as she led us through the throng into a more open area. It seemed like the whole campus had turned out tonight. Once we found a decent spot and began dancing, we noticed that we'd lost both groups of guys we'd come in with.

"Should we go back and try to find them?" Charlotte half-shouted over the music.

"Don't worry, they'll find us," Bree answered. She was eyeing the guy she'd winked at near the pool table, and it looked like he was noticing.

One of our favorite line dancing songs came on and we all squealed as we got in formation. I laughed as Lacey yelled, "Yee-haw!" Her energy was infectious.

Once the song was over, I stood off to the side to catch my breath. A slow song came on. I turned in a circle, hoping to catch a glimpse of Sawyer, and almost smacked right into Ben.

"Hey, Eliza, do you wanna dance?" he asked.

I smiled at him, trying to collect my thoughts. "Sure."

He led me onto the dance floor and put his arms around my waist. "You know, you really do have an awesome voice," he said as we made the slow turn.

"Thanks, that's nice of you to say." I tried to keep my attention on Ben, but I knew I was looking over his shoulder for any sign of Sawyer.

"That guy you were talking to back there—is he the one you went out with last night?"

"Oh, um . . . yeah. His name's Sawyer. He's in my history class." I knew I was repeating the information, but as if summoned by Ben's question, I saw him. He was searching through the crowd. He saw me dancing with Ben and our eyes caught for a split second, then he turned back around and asked someone to dance.

I realized with a start that it was Monet.

I tried to fight down the wave of jealousy that rose within me to see him with his arms around her. Monet was one of those girls that guys gravitated towards. With her pretty features and friendly manner, she was constantly being asked out.

Why did I care? It wasn't like I had any claim on him. Not like I should *want* to have any claim on him.

I turned my attention back to Ben and we continued talking casually until the dance ended.

"Thanks." Ben looked at me for a few seconds as if he wanted to say more.

"Liza, over here!" Bree called as another fast song started up.

"Thanks, Ben." I smiled at him and then went to join my friends. We were dancing and laughing when I suddenly felt a hand on my arm.

"Wanna dance?" Sawyer asked as he looked down at me.

My heart skipped a beat. "Sure . . . but this is a fast song," I said in confusion.

He grinned. "I know."

He took me by the hand and led me over to where some of the dancers were doing complicated spins and lifts. Before I knew what was happening, Sawyer started spinning me around, twirling me across the dance floor with complete skill. All I had to do was hold on and let him lead me. It was exhilarating!

"Are you ready to try something a little more challenging?" He asked after we'd been dancing a few minutes, that uncanny sparkle bright in his blue eyes.

"I guess so . . . what kind of stuff are we talking about?" I was a bit breathless but having so much fun I didn't want to stop.

Sawyer pointed to a couple who were doing a lift. "Think you can handle something like that?"

My eyes widened, but I nodded. "Let's try it."

He gave me a few instructions, and then we were ready to go. I couldn't believe how easily he lifted me. I gasped in delight as my feet left the floor and he spun me around. This was incredible!

We continued dancing and I noticed my friends gathered on the edge of the circle. They were laughing and cheering us on. It felt like the song ended all too soon. Sawyer and I were completely breathless.

He put his hands on his knees to rest for a second and looked up at me. "Did you like that?"

"Totally *amazing*." I put a hand over my heart in an attempt to still the rapid beating. "Where did you learn to dance like that?"

He shrugged and stood up. "Last year one of my buddies convinced me to take a swing class with him so we could meet girls."

I laughed. "Did it work?"

"It worked for him—he's married now." Sawyer stepped a little closer to me and I suddenly noticed that a slow song had come on. "Can I have this dance?"

I smiled and nodded. He closed the distance between us and put his arms around me. I could smell his cologne. The heat of his body next to mine caused a warm ripple up my spine. We didn't speak, but he slowly held me closer as the song continued. My mind struggled in protest against the feelings building inside of me, but suddenly I was tired of fighting. All I wanted to do was be held—just like this—and enjoy the moment.

The song ended and Sawyer reluctantly pulled away. His eyes searched mine and neither of us spoke a word.

That dance had said it all.

CHAPTER

SIX

I tossed and turned in my sleep. I was dreaming that Luke was standing in a boat with his arms outstretched to me. I was on the dock, and every time I reached for him the boat moved farther away.

His expression was worried. "Eliza, you have to get in the boat. I'm losing you."

"I'm trying!" I cried, my arms outstretched. "I can't reach you where you are. You have to come back."

He didn't answer, but continued to stare at me sadly with his hand reaching out. I watched in horror as a gigantic whirlpool suddenly began to form in the sea behind him. His boat drifted dangerously close to it.

"Luke. No!" I tried to jump into the water but my feet wouldn't move. I stood in helpless anguish as his boat was swept into the whirlpool and he disappeared beneath the surface.

My arms continued to reach, but there was only an empty void.

I splashed cold water onto my face, willing my body to wake up. I wished I could wash away the dismal feeling my dream last night had caused. I shuddered as I pictured Luke's face as he'd been swept under the waves.

Just a dream, I reminded myself. It was only a dream. Yet, I'd never had a nightmare about Luke before and it left me with a dreadful weight of foreboding.

I glanced at the clock on the wall and groaned. We'd stayed out late last night and I couldn't resist hitting the snooze button when my alarm went off this morning. Nine o'clock church was going to be the death of me.

Lacey and Charlotte had already left. They'd tried to convince Bree and me to get out of bed by blasting their church music throughout the apartment as they got ready. However, my desire for sleep was stronger and I'd covered my head with my pillow, effectively drowning out their noise and any guilt they tried to toss my way.

Bree slept like a brick and didn't even require the pillow method to ignore the noise. Neither one of us had made it to Relief Society yet in the few weeks that we'd been in school. We usually got to church sometime during Sunday school, and I was grateful that Sacrament meeting was last. That was the important part anyway.

As I continued to get ready I justified away any guilt by deciding that next week I'd get to bed sooner on Saturday night. Never mind the fact that I'd been telling myself this for the past several weeks—*this* time I was serious.

"Sister Moore, I'm glad you could meet with me today," Bishop Clark said with a warm smile. He had asked me after Sacrament Meeting if there was a time we could meet. Now I sat in his office, nervously twisting the fabric of my skirt as I waited for him to continue. Was he going to say something about my lack of full attendance?

"I'd like to call you to be the compassionate service leader in Relief Society." He looked at me kindly and added, "Your name was submitted to me by Sister Stotter, and after praying over the matter, I felt a confirmation that this was the right thing to do. Will you accept this calling?"

I was completely caught off guard. I hadn't thought the Relief Society President in our ward even knew who I was, and she'd submitted my name for a calling?

The Bishop continued to smile at me as he waited patiently for my answer.

"Oh, um . . . sure," I said with an attempt to return his smile. I had no idea what this calling entailed.

His smile broadened. He had a cheerful, fatherly countenance. "Wonderful! You're going to enjoy working with Sister Stotter, and she'll help you with whatever questions you may have."

I nodded as I continued to fidget.

"As you know, our student ward is different from the family ward you left back home: you won't be taking meals to new mothers, or helping to coordinate a funeral, but there will still be many ways for you to serve. I know that if you'll be prayerful in your calling, the Lord will guide you to those sisters in need." Bishop Clark smiled at me again. "Thank you for accepting this calling, Sister Moore. If there's anything we as a bishopric can do to help you, please don't hesitate to ask."

I thanked him and, sensing that our meeting was over, stood up to leave.

He shook my hand and then opened the door. "Enjoy the rest of your Sabbath. We'll do the sustaining and setting apart next Sunday."

"How was church today, honey?" Mom asked over the phone.

"It was good," I said, hoping she wouldn't ask if I'd made it to the whole block.

I was lying on my bed with the phone propped against my ear. All three of my roommates were out in the kitchen so I had the room to myself.

"That's nice." I could hear her smile through the phone, apparently relieved that I'd been to church at all. I felt guilty and was about to confess that I hadn't made it to all three meetings when she changed the subject.

"Any letters from Luke lately?"

"Yeah, I got one yesterday. He seems to be doing really well . . . I can't believe he'll be home in two months." There was a note of uncertainty in my voice, which she caught onto immediately.

"Liza, is everything okay? You usually sound much more chipper after you've received a letter. It sounds to me like you're a little upset."

"No, I'm fine. It's just . . . I met someone the other day." I couldn't believe I'd spoken those words; especially to my mom. I was feeling confused and wanted her advice.

It was quiet on the other end of the line so I continued, "His name is Sawyer and he's in my history class. He's super cute and nice, and he took me out the other night . . . and I'm pretty sure he likes me. The trouble is, I sort of have feelings for him too, but I feel so guilty about it! I never thought I would be attracted to anyone but Luke, and he's coming home so soon, and I don't know what to do. I told Sawyer that I only wanted to be friends, but when I'm with him, that's not how I feel. Am I a terrible person?" My words seemed to gush out in one long sentence, spilling over the top of each other. I squeezed my eyes shut and pinched the bridge of my nose as I waited for her response.

"Sweetheart, you are *not* a terrible person," she said firmly. "I confess I am a little surprised by the situation—only because you and Luke have had such a powerful relationship—but that's not to say that you can't be attracted to someone else. When Luke left, he told you that he wanted you to continue dating. He didn't expect you to lock yourself away for two years. And you *have* been on several dates. Each time, you would come home and say that you'd had a good time, but that your date didn't measure up to Luke. This Sawyer must be pretty special if he's getting your attention."

I sighed. "I really don't know him that well, and I don't think that anyone could possibly compete with Luke . . . but why do I want to keep hanging out with him, then? It scares me."

"Honey, the only thing I can tell you is to be prayerful, and to follow your heart. You are a special girl and you know how to rely on the Lord. If you make good choices, He won't lead you astray. I'm sorry that this is so frustrating, but you'll make it through. I'm sure of it."

"Thanks, Mom." We talked for a few more minutes before she had to go. I'd detected a tiredness in her voice that normally wasn't there. Before hanging up I asked, "Mom, are you feeling okay? We've talked about me this whole time—how are *you* doing?"

There was a slight pause on the other line, but then she quickly assured me that she was fine. Not totally convinced, I was about to pry further when she said she had another call coming in and had to go. We exchanged quick "love you's" and then she was gone.

After ending the call I continued to lie on my bed, letting my mom's words sink in. This felt like a big deal—but not big enough to pray about. After all, I'd only met Sawyer two days ago. Maybe I was reading too much into the situation.

Maybe I was worrying over nothing.

CHAPTER

seven

I had my head bent down over my notebook in an attempt to focus on the notes I'd taken from the last lecture. I'd purposely come early to class to find a good seat—and (I admitted to myself) because I was excited to see Sawyer again. I'd half expected him to send me a text last night, but he never did. I leaned forward on my desk, resting my head on my fist while nervously tapping a pen with the other hand.

Would he choose to sit by me? Was he even coming to class today?

There was some shuffling at the end of the row as more people came into the room. I didn't dare to look up, until I sensed someone standing beside my desk.

"Hey there, *friend*. Mind if I sit here?" My heart skipped a beat as I heard Sawyer's voice.

I looked up at him and smiled. "Not at all—friend," I replied as he took the seat next to mine.

"Looks like your eager fan isn't too happy to see me sitting by you again," Sawyer said in a confidential tone. He made a slight gesture toward the door where Darren Fields was standing. He wore an unmistakable scowl as he looked at us.

I watched as he made his way up the stairs and then proceeded down our aisle. For one gut-wrenching moment I was afraid he was going to confront Sawyer, but then he stopped and took a seat two desks down.

Sawyer glanced at me and raised an eyebrow. "For a second there I thought he was gonna try and start something," he whispered.

"Me too," I whispered back.

"Good thing he stopped . . . I'm not sure I could've taken him." Sawyer kept a straight face, but his eyes were brimming with amusement. I tried not to laugh.

"Yeah, I'd hate to see you get humiliated like that in front of the whole class."

He playfully poked me in the ribs. "Easy now! You're not supposed to agree with me. A guy's pride can only take so much, you know."

A smile crept up at the corner of my mouth. "Yeah, but just look at him . . . I mean, *c'mon.*" I gestured with my eyes to where Darren sat. "You seriously think you would want to mess with that?"

Darren was short and skinny; a buck forty at the most.

Sawyer had played wide receiver on his high school football team.

"I'll tell you who's going down, and it ain't little Darren Fields," he teased as he looked at me. His eyes smoldered with a challenge.

My heart pounded as an electric charge seemed to pass between us. "You don't scare me one bit, Sawyer Murdock," I lied as I turned my gaze away from his. Actually he did scare me. A lot.

Professor Gunner began his lecture and I was thankful for the distraction. I took down meticulous notes in an attempt to ignore the ultra-awareness that Sawyer was sitting next to me. I didn't dare glance at him. Instead, I was determined to focus on the subject matter, convincing myself that I would get an A in this class and would have Sawyer to thank for it.

After the professor spoke for half an hour, he announced that he had a twenty-minute film to present. Suddenly the room was dark, and all attempts at ignoring Sawyer's presence evaporated. It felt like my senses were suddenly heightened a thousand times over.

The film began. After a few seconds he leaned and whispered in my ear, "Darren keeps looking over at us. I think he still doubts whether you and I are really dating."

"What makes you say that?" My throat suddenly felt dry.

He shrugged. "Just the vibe I get." He paused for a moment before lowering his voice even more, "I could make it look more convincing if you wanted me to."

I finally chanced a look at him, which was a mistake. His face was mere inches from mine and I could almost feel his breath on my cheek. His blue eyes held that attractive hint of mischief in them.

"O-okay . . . I guess," I said without thinking.

Sawyer gave a low chuckle. "Don't worry, I'm not about to bite you or anything. We'll just throw him off the track a little."

Suddenly I had a flashback, a memory of Luke teasing me with almost those exact same words the night of Prom—that he wouldn't bite me. The sight of his face in my mind made me stiffen for a second. *Luke*. What was I doing flirting with Sawyer? I'd promised my heart to Luke. I shouldn't have feelings for anyone else.

I was about to say something, when suddenly I felt Sawyer's arm around me. His fingers gently brushed against my arm, causing goose bumps to erupt over my entire body. I acted like I was absorbed in the film, but I found it difficult to breathe. After a few minutes he moved his hand up and began toying with my hair, gently twisting and untwisting it around his fingers.

I hazarded a quick glance over at Darren. By the angle of his posture, I knew he had noticed us.

"I think that's convincing enough. I'm pretty sure Darren won't bother me anymore," I whispered to Sawyer. Without looking at him I gently moved forward on my desk, a subtle hint that he didn't need to put on the act anymore.

I heard him release a short sigh. "Okay." He moved his hand away from my hair and didn't say anything else for the rest of the class.

"We have to strike now, while the iron's hot!" Lacey exclaimed.

"Lacey, you're impossible. Whatever evil plan you're cooking up in that scheming brain of yours—for all of our sakes—please drop it," Bree implored.

It was late Tuesday afternoon, and the four of us had agreed to meet after classes at our favorite ice cream parlor. I swiveled my spoon around in the Styrofoam cup, scooping up the last bite of caramel sauce.

"Oh come on, Bree, we can't let those guys have the last laugh. Where's the fun in that?" Lacey argued.

Charlotte and I exchanged glances and smiled. Lacey and Bree had been in semi-heated debate for the last fifteen minutes, but we both knew that Bree would eventually cave.

She sat back in her chair with a weary sigh. "Alright, Lacey, you win. One more prank—but only if you *promise* it's the last one." She shook her head as she waved her spoon at us. "And just for the record, I have a bad feeling about this."

Lacey slapped her hands together, ignoring Bree's dismal remark. "Good! Now we're all on the same page. So here's what I'm thinking . . ."

We waited under cover of darkness, armed with electrical tape, scissors, a bottle of PAM, a package of Oreos and a bucket of ping-pong balls.

"Okay, you guys, there they go," Lacey whispered. We were hiding behind some bushes outside of Drew's apartment building, watching for when he and his roommates would leave. We'd planned another *Mystery Falls* marathon at our place tonight, so we knew we wouldn't have much time to get back once they'd left. Bree had stayed behind as a decoy so she'd be able to offer an excuse as to why the rest of us weren't there yet.

We watched as Drew and his buddies piled into Paul's car and drove off. *So far so good!* We stifled a few giggles and my heart pounded with adrenaline as we quickly made our way to their apartment. Just as we'd suspected, they'd forgotten to lock the door.

We quietly stepped inside and closed the door behind us. Lacey made her way to the kitchen cupboards with the ping-pong balls, a fierce determination in her step.

Charlotte crept back to the bathrooms, bottle of PAM spray in hand.

I unraveled a good length of the black tape and snipped it off with the scissors. Then I carefully wound it around the sprayer near the faucet, the black tape blending perfectly with the plastic of the nozzle.

Next, I made my way over to where Lacey was performing her stunt. I handed the package of Oreos to her, which she strategically positioned on the shelf. We'd scraped out the frosting and replaced it with toothpaste. We had even eaten a few before scraping the others, just to give the appearance that everything was normal.

Lacey handed me the salt and pepper shakers. I untwisted them, leaving the tops just barely on so that the unsuspecting victim wouldn't notice anything unusual.

Finally, I went to work on the clocks, setting them forward an hour. Once I'd finished with those, I made my way back to the bedrooms to see what other clocks I could find. I heard Charlotte spraying the toilet seats with PAM and couldn't help but giggle.

These were some of the oldest pranks in the book, but I still wished I could see the looks on these guys' faces when it all went down. I hoped it would be

Drew who opened the kitchen cupboards first, to be greeted by an onslaught of ping-pong balls. He had it coming.

As I worked to change the clocks, Charlotte came in behind me. "You know what else would be funny?" she whispered. "If we short-sheeted their beds."

I grinned and nodded. "Yeah, let's hurry."

We folded their sheets up tightly in half, carefully replacing the covers and laughing as we pictured their reactions when they climbed into bed and couldn't stretch their legs.

Lacey joined us. "Okay, guys, I think we're done. Let's get back home before they get suspicious."

We were on an adrenaline high as we drove back to our place. Lacey laughed maniacally when Charlotte and I told her about the sheets, and then confessed to an added prank of her own: she had taken all of the cereal boxes and switched out the bags inside of them. Harmless, but it would get the point across.

I parked the car and we ran up the stairs, allowing the last of our levity to roll out before entering the apartment. We didn't want the guys to suspect that we'd been up to anything, so we had to play it cool.

I opened the door first, and then stopped short. Drew and his friends were spread out in the front room—but Sawyer was with them. I hadn't seen or heard from him since yesterday's class, and I definitely had not expected to see him sitting in my living room.

Bree got up from her perch at the kitchen table. "Hey, guys." She was trying to act casual, but her relief was obvious.

Drew had been talking to Sawyer when we walked in. They seemed to be getting along well enough, but there was definitely an undercurrent of tension in the room. I was willing to place my bets on Ben as the source. His unfriendly expression implied that he was not happy with Sawyer's presence.

"Liza, Sawyer dropped by to see you a few minutes ago. I knew that you'd be right back so I told him he could wait for you," Bree supplied, casting a quick wink for my sole benefit.

I turned to Sawyer as he stood up from the sofa. "It was nice of you to stop by—how's everything going?" I said somewhat awkwardly. The beginnings of a blush warmed my skin as I sensed the eyes of the others on us.

"I was just in the area and thought I'd swing by." Sawyer glanced around, his eyes resting momentarily on Ben. "But it looks like you guys already have something going on, so I'll take off." He waved at everyone and then made his way toward the door.

"Wait!" I blurted. Sawyer stopped and turned to me, a questioning look in his eyes. "We're just having another marathon of that show I was telling you about. Do you want to stay and watch it?" I couldn't believe I'd asked him to stay; especially when Ben was so obviously annoyed, but I couldn't help myself. I wanted him to be there.

"Sure. Sounds like fun."

I watched as the smile I'd come to admire slowly spread across his face.

"Perfect! I'll make some popcorn," Lacey said cheerfully. I could tell she was grateful to Sawyer; his presence had distracted Drew and his friends and helped to hold our cover. She was ever the opportunist, and I loved her for it.

CHAPTER

eight

These shows were scarier than I'd remembered. I sat on the couch next to Sawyer, and Drew and Lacey took up the other half. Everyone else had to fend for themselves on the floor. Our couch wasn't very big and we had to squeeze to fit two couples on it. I didn't mind one bit though, because each time the murderer appeared on the screen I would cover my eyes and cling to Sawyer's sleeve. He looked at me and chuckled, teasing me for being such a scaredy-cat. But I could tell he liked it.

Halfway through, he reached over and put his hand on my knee, palm up. I looked tentatively at his hand, and then at him. He gave me a half-smile and whispered, "I heard it was okay for friends to hold hands."

I smiled back cautiously, and then, ever so slowly, allowed my hand to find his. His skin was warm, and I instantly felt a sense of security as his fingers intertwined with mine. I leaned my head on his shoulder and allowed myself to enjoy the quiet thrill of the moment.

"Thanks for letting me hang out with you tonight," Sawyer said.

We were standing on my front porch. The marathon had ended a while ago, and Drew and his friends had already left. Ben had seemed somewhat dejected when he'd noticed Sawyer holding my hand. I felt bad, belatedly realizing that he must have liked me after all, but I didn't know what to say to him. I thought it was probably best to just let the situation work itself out.

"Thanks for staying—I had a great time."

Sawyer hadn't let go of my hand for the whole evening, and now he took my other hand in his, forcing me to look up at him.

"Eliza, we need to talk." His eyes held a measure of determination. "It's really nice to be your friend and everything—but I want to be more than that. I think you do too." His gaze penetrated mine and I couldn't seem to find any words.

When I didn't respond he continued, "I understand that you have a missionary, but I meant what I said the other night. I realize that you might choose to be with him when he gets home . . . I'm just asking for a chance to be with you until then. I know I might lose you in a couple of months, but that's a chance I'm willing to take if it means I get to be with you *now*."

I wrinkled my brow, uncomfortable with the direction this conversation was heading. "How can you really mean that? How could I ask you to wait? It just doesn't seem fair to you . . . or to Luke."

He gave a short laugh. "*Luke*, huh?"

I shot him a warning look. "See? I can't even say his name without you getting defensive."

Sawyer held his hands up in surrender. "You're right, I'm sorry. Luke is a great name—is his last name Skywalker?"

I pulled my hands away from him. "O-kay." I was dangerously close to crying and in no mood for his jokes. I turned and grabbed the doorknob, but he put his hand on mine, bringing me around to face him again.

"Eliza, I really *am* sorry. Please don't go in yet; not until we've figured this out." His eyes were sincere. "All I'm asking is that you give me a chance. There's something going on between us—you know there is. If Luke really cares about you, then he'd want you to be honest with yourself; to figure out what your true feelings are." He reached up and brushed a solitary tear from my eye, letting his hand rest on my shoulder as he took a step closer.

I involuntarily stepped away from him until my back was against the door. Sawyer leaned into me, his hand now gently cupping my face. "So what do you say—will you give me that chance?" He bent his head until his eyes were almost level with mine.

I felt a tingling sensation all along my back, and my breathing was uneven as his face moved slowly closer. I knew that I should pull away, that I should tell him to leave, but I didn't want to. Our eyes were still locked together, and I softly whispered, "Yes," seconds before he pressed his lips against mine.

His kiss was gentle, yet determined. Any resistance I'd felt was unsubstantial. After a few moments I relaxed and returned the kiss. I reached up and ran my fingers through the back of his hair. I felt him smile before his kiss intensified, causing me to lose my breath. Then, without warning, Luke's face suddenly came to my mind. The image was so clear it made me gasp and I pulled away from Sawyer.

"What's wrong?" he asked in concern.

"Nothing . . ." I put a hand to my forehead to try to make sense of what had just happened. "I have to go, I'm sorry."

"Eliza, wait."

"I'm so sorry." Without looking at Sawyer I opened the door and quickly closed it behind me.

I leaned against the door in a daze, waiting until I finally heard Sawyer's footsteps retreating down the hall. This was the second kiss I'd ever had in my life, and it had been amazing. Luke's kiss had been powerful; causing emotions within me that I could recall even now . . . but that had been so long ago. It was hard to remember *exactly* what it had felt like. I wasn't sure if it was possible to compare the two, but I knew that Sawyer's kiss was a close rival.

I stood there for a few minutes, taking in the events that had transpired within the last few hours. Everything was quiet and I guessed that my room-mates were all asleep. I slumped onto the sofa and finally allowed the tears to come.

Sawyer's kiss had been wonderful—magical even—but I couldn't help feeling like I'd betrayed Luke. Seeing his face so clearly for that brief moment had been deeply unsettling; almost like he was there. Like he knew what was happening.

I felt torment mercilessly rip my heart as I muffled my anguished sobs.

What was I going to do now?

Increase in Faith and Personal Righteousness

"Wherefore, ye must press forward with a steadfastness in Christ, having a perfect brightness of hope, and a love of God and of all men. Wherefore, if ye shall press forward, feasting upon the word of Christ, and endure to the end, behold, thus saith the Father: Ye shall have eternal life."

– 2 Nephi 31:20

CHAPTER

nine

E liza."

I sat up on the couch, realizing that I'd fallen asleep. It took me a moment to register that someone had said my name.

"Oh, my sweet child; how you've grown!"

I rubbed my eyes in disbelief, and then jumped up from the couch.

"Grandma?" She smiled and nodded as I threw myself into her arms. "You came back! I thought I'd never see you again!"

She laughed and stroked my hair as she embraced me. "It was a joyful surprise for me as well. It seemed that the time had come for me to return and pay you a visit."

I pulled back and gazed at her. She looked exactly the same as she had when she'd visited my dreams two years ago: the same flowing white dress, the same dimple in her cheek, and the same bright blue eyes that twinkled when she smiled.

My Great-grandmother, Eliza Porter, was someone I had come to respect and love deeply. She'd taught me many lessons that had changed my life in a profound way.

"I just can't believe it," I said as I hugged her again. "I've missed you so much! And I don't think I've ever needed advice more than I do now." I rubbed a hand across my eyes, which were still swollen from tears.

Grandma sighed and made a little tsk-tsk sound like a mother hen. "I've missed you too, sweetheart. I'm sorry things are difficult for you right now, but don't despair. Let's see if we can't brighten your outlook a bit. Are you ready for another one of my world-famous lessons?"

"Absolutely." I gave her a watery smile.

Only after my previous dreams with Grandma had ended did I realize just how significant they were. I'd seen glimpses from the lives of some of the most important women ever to walk the earth. I couldn't wait to see what Grandma had in store for me now. I needed all the help I could get.

"Alrighty then, here we go!"

I held on tightly to Grandma's hand as the walls of my apartment faded and the familiar blackness enveloped us. A huge smile played across my face. I'd missed these adventures!

The ground underfoot suddenly went soft.

Sand. I was standing in sand. The loud groaning of what sounded like camels filled my ears. Once my vision came into focus I noticed that it was dusk, but even in the dim light I saw that they were indeed camels—everywhere.

I jerked away as I felt something touch the back of my head. It was the nose of a camel. I'd reacted just in the nick of time. No sooner had I stepped away than the camel let out some kind of strange sneeze, shooting spit-like snot all over the ground. Dream or no dream, I didn't want any piece of that.

I moved through the herd of camels as I looked for Grandma, who had somehow disappeared.

"Grandma? Where are you?"

"Over here, Eliza. Follow the sound of my voice."

I broke through the furry maze and saw Grandma sitting on a . . . pile of stones?

"Come see this well." She patted the spot next to her.

Right . . . a well. That made more sense. I walked over and sat down beside her, peering curiously into the dark chasm for any sign of water. There was a rope tied to what I could only assume was a bucket at the bottom.

"Now isn't this cozy?" Grandma asked as she cheerfully bumped me in the shoulder.

"Careful!" I grabbed the stone beneath me. "One good bump might send me toppling into the fathomless depths below."

She laughed. "How poetic! And it's only appropriate; being in the desert tends to bring out a bit of the exotic in us all."

I smiled at Grandma's giddy mood and finally took a good look at my surroundings. We were in the desert, all right. This well seemed to be on the outskirts of a city. Beyond that, there was nothing but sand as far as the eye could see, interspersed with the occasional dried up bush. 'Exotic' wasn't exactly the word I would have used, but who was I to be the source of Grandma's disillusionment?

Suddenly I noticed a man standing a few yards off. He looked like he'd walked straight out of some Old Testament movie: with long, robe-like clothes and a turban wrapped around his head. He was walking around to all of the camels, tapping them with a stick to make them kneel down. He appeared overly intent in his task and I had the feeling that there were more than just camels on his mind.

"Okay, Grandma, who is that guy?"

"He is the oldest and most trusted servant of Father Abraham." She said matter-of-factly.

I looked at her with my mouth open. "You mean like Abraham from the *Bible*, Abraham?"

"The very one."

"Wow! So where is he?" I strained my eyes for any sign of another human being.

"I'm sorry to disappoint you, but Abraham is not the reason I brought you here. We came to see someone else—his daughter-in-law."

The man whom we'd been watching had finished his task with the camels and walked over to the well. He was mere feet away from where we sat and I marveled that he couldn't see us. He began to speak, and I was so startled that I nearly fell over backward. It took me a moment to realize that he wasn't talking to us. He was praying:

"O Lord God of my master Abraham, I pray thee, send me good speed this day, and shew kindness unto my master Abraham." He had been gazing heavenward, but now he gestured toward the well. "Behold, I stand here by the well of water; and the daughters of the men of the city come out to draw water. And let it come to pass, that the damsel to whom I shall say, 'Let down thy pitcher, I pray thee, that I may drink'; and she shall say, 'Drink, and I will give thy camels drink also,' let the same be she that thou hast appointed for thy servant Isaac; and thereby shall I know that thou hast shewed kindness unto my master."

He bowed his head as he ended the prayer. I was amazed by how humble this man was, and by how much he wanted to please Abraham. As far as he knew, there was no one around to witness his prayer, but his words had verified his sincerity and devotion.

As he continued speaking in hushed tones I could no longer hear, I looked up to see a young woman emerging from the city. She carried a pitcher on her shoulder and was making her way toward the well. I turned to Grandma with eyes wide, and she smiled and patted me on the knee, signaling for me to be patient and watch.

We moved away from the well as the girl approached, but I was still close enough to get a good look at her face. She was very pretty. Her head was covered with a shawl, but I could see her brown hair beneath. Her eyes contained soft warmth, and her countenance seemed to glow with the love of life.

Once she had filled her water jug, she placed it on her shoulder and began walking back toward the city. Abraham's servant had been standing by, watching, but now he rushed up to the girl. I couldn't hear what he was saying, but I could only guess that he was carrying out his part of the plan.

I waited intently for her reaction. She smiled at the man and quickly took the pitcher down from her shoulder, offering water to him. Once he had finished drinking, she dumped the rest of the pitcher out in a trough. She hurried back to the well and filled the pitcher again, and I gasped as I watched her bring the water to his camels.

"Grandma—she's the one! She's doing what the servant prayed she would do."

Grandma chuckled and nodded, but I kept my eyes glued to the servant to see what his reaction would be. As she moved about watering his camels, delight infused his entire face. He reached into the satchel tied about his waist and removed a golden bracelet and earrings, which he offered to her.

"What is that all about?" I asked as I turned to Grandma. "What's the jewelry for?"

"You can read this account in your scriptures; I'm afraid we only have time to discuss the reason why we came here: the girl. Do you know who she is?"

I wasn't exactly sure who Abraham's daughter-in-law was. I knew that his son was Isaac, but I couldn't remember who Isaac had married, so I made a guess. "Rachel?"

"No, Rachel was Isaac's daughter-in-law." Grandma made a little tsk-tsk sound, but she was smiling. "Abraham's daughter-in-law, Isaac's intended wife, was *Rebekah*."

"Rebekah," I repeated the name as I watched her. "She's beautiful."

"Yes, she is, and just as Isaac was promised that his posterity would be as the sands of the sea, so Rebekah was promised to be the mother of millions. She was a faithful daughter of God." Grandma turned to look at me. "This is the principle we're here to learn, Eliza. The first goal of the Relief Society is to Increase in Faith and Personal Righteousness."

"Relief Society?" My face fell. I'd hoped that Grandma was here to help me figure out what to do with my love life. I didn't want to be rude, but only one word came to my mind when I thought of Relief Society—Snoozeville.

Grandma was looking at me expectantly and I registered part of what she'd just said. "Hold on—did you say faith? You already taught me about that in your first visit."

"We did discuss it, yes. Do you think you've mastered the principle?" Her bright blue eyes were practically boring into my soul.

"No, but I'm trying," I said with more conviction than I felt. *Was* I trying? For the past few weeks I hadn't focused on much more than being on my own and having fun. It made me squirm to think how long it'd been since I'd read my scriptures . . . or stayed awake long enough to offer a meaningful prayer . . . or gone to all of my church meetings.

Grandma smiled at me and suddenly we were standing in a snow-filled forest. The snow came up to my knees and I shivered involuntarily. Everything was quiet and still, muffled by the fresh blanket of white all around us.

"Sheesh, talk about climate shock." I instantly hugged my arms about my waist. "Not lovin' the snow, Grandma—any chance we could go back to the desert?"

She laughed. "We'll only be here for a few minutes. Don't you just adore the peace that attends a snowy forest?"

"Yes. V-very nice." I clenched my jaw to stall the chattering.

"I'm sorry you're uncomfortable, dear. But as a matter of fact that's one of the reasons why I brought you to this place."

"To give me hypothermia?" I said wryly.

"No—to make a point." She smiled and clasped her hands together. "This mortal life that you're living is hard. The filth that surrounds you each day makes your spirit uncomfortable—though you may not even realize it. The longer you stand in the filth, the more numb your spirit becomes. The trick is to keep moving." She took a step and we began plowing through the deep snow, one slow foot in front of the other.

"The world would have you believe that you must feed your physical drives, at any cost. Satan wants your spirit to go numb; your body like an empty shell with no moral compass to direct it. Eliza, you know the things that you need to do to increase your faith and personal righteousness: sincere prayer, daily scripture study, attending your church meetings, fulfilling your callings, personal purity, etc. Those are the things that will keep you moving, and keep your spirit alive and well."

There was that guilty feeling again. It wasn't like I didn't have a good excuse for letting this stuff slide. Life was just so busy right now.

I frowned. "It feels like the list of things I should do is never-ending. How can I possibly keep up?"

"Does it sometimes seem like it would be easier to simply lie down and let yourself go numb, rather than trying to keep up with that list?" Grandma asked.

"Honestly? Yes." I let out a breath of exasperation, creating a puff of mist in the air. "There are so many things going on all the time. I'm not doing anything totally wrong in my life—but I don't know if I have the time to fit in all the good things I'm supposed to do." It felt wonderful to finally confess my feelings.

"That's just part of being human, sweetheart. The Savior himself said, 'The spirit is willing, but the flesh is weak.' That's why we need His atonement so desperately, to pick up the pieces and make us whole again when we fall short. But just lying down and giving up without a fight? That's Satan's greatest wish. The scriptures often use descriptions about the adversary 'lulling' into carnal security. He'd love nothing more than to have us gain an apathetic attitude toward our lives and the lives of others; to just drift off to sleep while the battle rages on."

She gave me a sidelong glance. "Your generation has had things pretty easy—in a physical sense. You enjoy comforts and freedoms your ancestors never even dreamed of; all with seemingly little-to-no cost or sacrifice on your part. Rather than spending your day toiling with heavy labor and arduous tasks, you have everything you could wish for practically at your fingertips. But, idleness is almost never a good thing. Alma counseled his son, Helaman: 'O my son, do not let us be slothful because of the easiness of the way.' What wise counsel that is."

Grandma stopped walking. "You mentioned hypothermia a moment ago. Have you ever heard someone explain what it's like to die from extreme exposure to the cold?"

I nodded. "Yeah, I've heard that you just sort of fall asleep and then you're gone."

"Exactly. When you stop moving in a spiritual sense—when you lie down and give up like you talked about before—your spirit becomes more and more numb. Unless you do something, you risk the chance of killing your spiritual awareness altogether."

I pondered this sobering thought as my legs began to feel stiff from the cold. Taking the initiative this time, I started moving again.

"Walking through this deep snow isn't easy, but it sure beats the deceptively 'easier' choice of lying down and giving up. Wouldn't you agree?"

I nodded and Grandma continued, "I love the scriptures that tell us to 'Awake' and to 'Arise'—those are words of action! As you study the scriptures, try to notice how many times those phrases are used. And don't forget the hymn 'Awake and Arise.' Some powerful lessons are taught in those verses."

She stopped and her face grew serious. "Eliza, this world is truly a battle zone. The Lord needs soldiers who are alert and ready to fight. But you don't have to fight alone." Grandma's eyes intensified. "Remember, as long as you choose the Lord's side of the line, you will never be left on your own."

I felt a warmth spread through me; a feeling I realized I hadn't experienced in quite a while. Grandma's visit was exactly what I needed to jumpstart my spiritual batteries. The time had come to move to action.

"I realize that it can be difficult to make the transition from Young Women to Relief Society; from adolescence to adulthood. When you're in Young Women, you're surrounded by friends your own age and you have weekly activities that keep you involved. You're all on the same page."

I nodded. She was voicing some of the exact thoughts that I'd had when I'd turned eighteen. It hadn't been easy for me to leave Young Women to go to Relief Society. Not that I didn't think I was ready—but I'd felt sort of lost somehow. With so many friends leaving on missions lately it had been a good excuse not to go to all of my meetings.

Grandma continued, "In Relief Society, suddenly it's up to *you* to make the decisions. You're there with a large group of women; women from all different walks of life. It's my hope that you'll gain a testimony of the importance of this magnificent Society. The Lord needs you to help build His Kingdom. No one else can take your place."

She gave me a warm smile as she searched my face. "You've had these dreams and other experiences to guide you, but powerful experiences are good for nothing if you don't keep moving. The fire of faith will die if you don't give it a constant supply of spiritual fuel."

I felt lighter as I made an internal commitment to act on Grandma's counsel. "I'll do my best. I promise." I sensed the dream was ending, and I didn't want to let her go.

She nodded and suddenly her face was somber. "One last thing, Eliza. You can't move forward and progress if you're not personally pure. Be wise."

I blushed. All I had done was hold Sawyer's hand and kiss him. What was she talking about?

I didn't have time to ask, because everything was growing dark. In the final moments before the dream ended I heard Grandma's voice softly echo again.

"Be wise."

CHAPTER

I can't believe you kissed him!" Bree squealed.

"*What?*" Charlotte stepped into the bathroom; her hazel eyes wide in amazement.

"I know. What was I thinking?" I said between brushes. It was the morning after I'd kissed Sawyer—the morning after my dream with Grandma.

We were in our typical stations at the vanity, getting ready for school. I rinsed the toothpaste out of my mouth and glanced at the mirror. I wasn't impressed with the reflection that stared back at me. After crying my eyes out, falling asleep on the couch, and waking after that intense dream, all I felt like doing was crawling into bed and staying there for the rest of the day.

"So . . . what? Are you guys officially dating now or something?" Bree squealed again.

Charlotte hesitated for a moment before asking the question I knew everyone was thinking, "What about Luke?"

I blew out a sigh and rubbed my eyes. "I don't know. I wish someone could tell me what to do. I'm so confused."

Bree put her hand on my shoulder. "Hey, don't worry, Liza. Things are going to work out. You'll see."

I turned and gave her a weak smile. "Thanks . . . I'm sure you're right."

"You guys have to see this!" Lacey said as she rushed into the bathroom. She held up her phone. "It's from Drew."

We all crowded around the screen and read his text. It contained one simple line: *You'd better watch your backs.*

"Man, I wish I could have seen it all go down," Lacey complained. "We should have hidden a camera or something." Her eyes glowed fiendishly as she nodded. "Next time."

"*What?*" Bree instantly objected. "Lacey, there is not going to be a next time. You promised this was the last prank and I'm holding you to it. I'm already freaked out about how they're going to retaliate." She turned toward Charlotte and me. "You guys heard her, right? This was the last prank."

We nodded.

"Yep. Sorry, Lacey, but you *did* promise. You and Drew just need to find another outlet—like admitting that you like each other," I teased.

"Hey, no fair ganging up like this! Cut me some slack; some of us aren't such fast movers when it comes to getting into a relationship," Lacey retorted. She seemed to realize what she'd said and her face crumpled. "Liza, I didn't mean for that to sound . . ."

"No, you're right. I *am* rushing into this. I mean, I only met Sawyer the other day . . ." I let my words trail off because I felt tears threatening. I grabbed a washcloth and started scrubbing my face so my roommates wouldn't be able to tell. As I held the soft fabric beneath the faucet I caught Charlotte and Bree giving Lacey an annoyed look and she shrugged.

Suddenly I remembered Grandma's words from last night. Maybe no one could tell me the answer I needed, but it couldn't hurt to try to ask for some guidance.

I finished getting ready for the day, and then I went into my room and shut the door. I only had ten minutes until I needed to leave for class, but I knew I had to make time for this.

I knelt by the bed and offered a heartfelt prayer; pouring out my feelings and asking for direction. When I was finished, I went over to my desk where I kept Grandma's music box. I opened it and pulled out my Young Women's medallion. I'd worn it for a few months after I'd received it, but then I'd fallen out of the habit and kept it in the box with the other dream tokens.

I clasped the necklace around my neck and tucked it under my shirt; close to my heart. Then I grabbed my scriptures and stuffed them into my backpack. I normally went to the library to study after class, but I determined that today I would start my studying off the right way.

"Do you have any plans for tonight?" Sawyer asked as he smiled down at me.

"None that I know of." My heart thrilled with the way his eyes studied mine. It was after history class, and we were standing in the hall together.

"Wanna make some?" He took my hand and stroked the backs of my knuckles with his thumb.

"Sure, what did you have in mind?" I'd said my prayer this morning, asking for guidance as far as dating Sawyer went, but so far all I felt were the familiar butterflies. I wondered briefly if I would be able to discern any impressions that came while he was with me. It was almost impossible to think clearly while he was near!

"My roommate and his girlfriend are going to a drive-in movie and he asked if we wanted to go."

"That sounds fun." I smiled shyly at him.

He grinned and it reached his eyes. "Cool. I'll pick you up at seven-thirty and we can grab a bite to eat beforehand."

"I'll be ready."

He pulled my hand up to his lips and kissed it, his gaze still holding mine. "I can't wait."

~~Dear Luke,~~

~~I'm not sure how to say this, but I felt like I needed to tell you that I met someone. Don't worry, it's nothing serious, and I'll still be here when you get back. We're just kind of dating in the meantime~~

~~Dear Luke,~~

~~I don't want you to take this the wrong way, but I also don't want you to be surprised when you get home and find out that I've been seeing someone. He knows that I love you and that I'm not committing to anything until you get home~~

Dear Luke,

I was so excited to get your last letter, it sounds like everything is going great! I'm proud of you for giving your whole heart to the work. I wish I could have been there for Jorge's baptism; I'm sure it was an amazing experience. I know you're going to enjoy these last two months—make them the best of your mission. Soon enough you'll be home and we can finally see each other again. We'll have so much to talk about; it's going to take a long time to get caught up. I don't mind if you don't.

I've been at school for a couple of weeks now, and it's been a blast! My roommates are super fun to hang

out with, and we all get along really well. I can't wait
for you to meet them. I've talked their ears off about
you, but they've been patient with me. You're going to
love it here; I can't wait to show you around campus.

I have a new calling as a Compassionate Service Leader.
I haven't done much so far; only taken some treats to a girl
who was homesick and given another girl a ride to her dentist
appointment. It's nothing compared to the service you are giving,
but it's helped get me more in the mind-set of serving others.
I hate to admit that I've been slacking in my spiritual growth
lately, so I'm putting more focus on that. You are growing
by spiritual leaps and bounds—I have to try to keep up.

It's crazy that this might be one of the last letters you
get from me, depending on how long it takes to reach you.
Just know that I love you and I think about you all the time.
Good luck with the work, and I'll see you in a few weeks!!

Love,

Eliza

P.S. I'll meet you in my dreams . . .

In the end I'd decided not to write Luke about Sawyer for two reasons:
One, I didn't want to distract him or ruin his last few weeks out in the field.
Two, I honestly didn't know where this thing with Sawyer was headed. Maybe
we would only date for a few weeks. Maybe it would be longer. But one thing I
was sure of—I would be there when Luke got home.

CHAPTER

eleven

H ave you ever eaten here before?" Sawyer asked as he glanced up at me
from his menu.

"No, but I've always wanted to. I've heard the food is really good." I was
still trying to hide my shock that Sawyer had brought me to one of the fanciest
restaurants in town.

"You're going to love it. My favorite dish is the salmon, but their steaks are
excellent too."

I tried not to raise my eyebrows. I'd been scanning the menu for any item
in the cheaper, ten-dollar range, but apparently Sawyer didn't mind spending
more. I'd never asked him about whether he was working, but I was suddenly
curious about his financial situation. Not many college kids could afford to take
their date to a fancy place like this. And he drove a brand-new, very expensive
car. His wardrobe wasn't bad either.

Sawyer's phone buzzed and he picked it up, quickly reading his text. A
frown creased his brow. "Looks like Kendall and Heather won't be able to make
it to the movie tonight," he said. "I guess she had some studying to do."

Sawyer's roommate, Kendall, and his girlfriend were supposed to meet up
with us after dinner, and I felt an odd tingle when I realized that we were on our
own now.

I thoughtfully placed my menu on the table. "That's too bad. So what do you want to do now?"

Sawyer raised his glass and took a sip of water before answering. "Well . . . we could still go if you want to." His azure eyes adopted an alluring spark. The expression was half-teasing, half-challenging.

My heart skipped a beat as I thought about being alone at the movies with Sawyer. At the moment I wanted nothing more than to be with him; to have him hold me and feel the warmth of his kiss again. However, I remembered Grandma's warning from my dream last night, and I knew that drive-ins were notorious for being a place to go and make out. When the other couple was going with us it had seemed fine . . . but now?

"What would we do without Kendall's truck there?" I questioned in an attempt at subtle escape.

Sawyer laughed. "I'm pretty sure they'll allow me to take my car in. Trucks aren't a requirement."

The waiter arrived and Sawyer ordered first, choosing a Porterhouse steak (the priciest item on the menu). I opted for a steak and shrimp combo. It was in a mid-price-range, and was what sounded the best to me. A win-win.

"So, I've never asked you this, but do you have a job right now?" I ran my finger around the tip of my water glass, carefully avoiding looking at him.

"No, not right now. I've had a few jobs here and there since I started school, but my parents thought it would be more beneficial if I just focused on my studies. My dad is a heart surgeon, and he knows how important it is to get accepted to a good medical school." Sawyer reached out and took my hand away from the glass, holding it tenderly as he stared at me across the table.

So that explained how he could afford all those nice things. A heart surgeon! I wondered what his house back home looked like and if his parents would like me. *Not that it mattered*, I reminded myself. I was never going to meet them.

"Do you have a job?" Sawyer's question brought me back to the present.

"Yes." I hoped he wouldn't pry further. It wasn't like I had the most glamorous job in the world, and I would *die* before letting him see me in that geriatric hairnet. As if in answer to my plea, the waiter came with our dinner salads. I made a big deal over how delicious it looked and dug right in, hoping he would do the same and let the "employment" subject drop.

"So where do you work?"

Blast!

"Oh, I just work part-time at Sam's Club." I pretended to be immensely interested in skewering an olive with my fork.

"That's cool." He smiled at me, raising an eyebrow. "And . . . ?"

"And, what?"

"What do you do there?" Sawyer could tell I was avoiding his question. He leaned forward eagerly.

"I . . . um . . . hand out samples." I squeezed my eyes shut and gave an embarrassed laugh.

He snorted, but tried to cover it up by taking another drink of water.

"What?" I crossed my arms, trying to look offended. "It's totally prestigious. I had to go through a rigorous interview process to beat out the other candidates. Putting food into those tiny paper cups—in *just* the right way—is much more difficult than you'd expect."

We stared at each other for a second, my expression daring. He tried to look serious as he nodded, but that only made it worse. We both laughed.

"Sounds like a good gig, and I'm sure it pays well," Sawyer kept up the teasing after our laughter died down.

"I don't like to brag—but I do all right." I smiled and winked confidentially.

His eyes turned thoughtful. "Seriously though, is this your only source of income, or are your parents helping you out?"

I was touched by the genuine look of concern on his face. "Well, I got pretty good grades in high school, so I was awarded a partial scholarship. That helps with tuition. I do my best to have a tight budget and stretch my income as far as I can. My parents help with the rest, but they're really big on independence. I used to complain about having to work and buy my own clothes and stuff, but now I realize it was good for me. My goal is to get awesome grades and raise my GPA so I'll qualify for a full-tuition scholarship." I looked at my near-empty salad plate, and then over at Sawyer's. He'd barely even touched his food.

"Not much of a salad fan, are you?" I asked, smiling.

"What?" He seemed lost in thought before glancing down at his plate. "Oh . . . no, I'm saving room for the good stuff." He patted his stomach and I laughed.

As the rest of our dinner was served, we continued to ask each other questions. I realized how very little I actually knew Sawyer—and I'd already kissed him! Sometime between the main course and dessert, his foot found mine under the table. He toyed with my shoe, and then my leg, causing an excited flip in my stomach.

If there was one thing I was sure about, it was that there was some incredible chemistry going on between the two of us. Up until this point, Luke had been the only other person to make me feel this way. I'd never dreamed that anyone else would enter the picture, causing such a massive attack of confusion in my heart.

The waiter brought the check and Sawyer slid his credit card into the leather folder. He'd barely even glanced at the bill, and again I was aware of the fact that he wasn't concerned about money. It was nice to be able to be treated to a dinner like this. I decided to enjoy the experience since it might not come around again anytime soon.

When we were ready to leave, Sawyer stood and pulled my chair out. He waited for me to go first before following me out to the car. It was almost 9:30

and night was falling fast. If we wanted to make it to the drive-in we would have to hurry.

"So what do you think? Still want to go?" Sawyer waited to start the ignition.

I subconsciously twisted the ruby ring on my finger, at war with myself. Did I want to go? Yes! Should we? I wasn't so sure.

I cleared my throat. "Well . . ." I looked over at Sawyer's face and my stomach jumped to my throat at the sight of his smile. His teeth and white polo shirt stood out in the darkness, and I could smell the enticing scent of his cologne.

He chuckled quietly. "Are you scared of me, Eliza?" He gave a crooked smile as he reached over and gently twisted a strand of my hair around his finger.

"No . . . why do you ask that?" Could he hear the rapid way my heart was beating?

"Cause you look a little nervous right now. We can do something else if you want to." Sawyer's eyebrows rose inquisitively. He wanted to go. I could tell he wanted to, but he wasn't going to force me into it.

I raised my chin slightly and met his gaze. "No, I want to. Let's go."

CHAPTER

Sawyer drove his car into the large parking lot of the drive-in. He found a space that had a good vantage point of the screen and turned off the ignition.

"Do you want to get any snacks before the movie starts?" he asked.

"No thanks, not after that ginormous dessert I just ate," I said with a laugh. I'd ordered a molten lava fudge cake, expecting Sawyer to share it with me, but he had refused. Instead he'd gotten a monster slice of apple pie, and we'd dared each other to finish them. I'd made a valiant effort, but hadn't been able to finish. Now I regretted trying; I was positively stuffed.

Sawyer nodded and laughed. "I know what you mean. Tell me if you change your mind, though." He reached into the glove box and retrieved a pack of gum. He pulled out a piece for himself and then offered some to me. I took it, trying not to read too much into the gesture.

We talked through the previews and fell silent once the opening credits began. This was an action movie about space aliens. It was PG-13, but I'd checked out the details online this afternoon and knew it was pretty clean. Just lots of aliens getting blown up.

How romantic.

After the movie had been going for a few minutes, Sawyer reached over and took my hand. He rubbed his thumb over my knuckles again, causing the hair on the back of my neck to stand up.

There was a suspenseful scene—one where you just knew an alien was about to come jumping out. I hunched down in my seat, with my free hand covering my mouth. When the alien finally appeared I screamed and buried my face in Sawyer's arm.

He laughed and pulled me closer. When I finally looked up, I saw that he was watching me. Our eyes met for a few seconds, and then we both slowly leaned in. His kiss was soft at first, allowing me time to relax, but as the minutes ticked by, the kiss grew more and more intense.

I had never experienced anything like this. I'd shared the kiss with Luke before he'd left, and that short kiss last night from Sawyer—but this kissing was entirely different. I was oblivious to the movie and anything else besides Sawyer. My pulse was quickening to an alarming rate and I began to feel a craving that was unfamiliar to me. The more he kissed me, the more that craving grew.

Sawyer's mouth left mine for a moment, and he began placing kisses along my jawline, and then my neck. It seemed like all rational thoughts had fled from my mind. I was vaguely aware that the first movie had ended, and the second one was beginning.

It wasn't until Sawyer reached his arms around me and pulled me over onto his lap that I finally jerked back to reality. I pulled away from him and shook my head, moving back over into my seat.

"What's the matter?" His breathing was unsteady.

"I don't think that's a good idea," I said, trying to regain control over my senses.

Sawyer nodded. "You're right."

We stared at each other for another moment and then he leaned in to kiss me again.

"Sawyer!" I protested as I pushed him away.

"You're right, I'm sorry," he apologized again, sitting back in his seat.

I reached for the chain at my throat and pulled up my Young Women's medallion. I rubbed my finger across the contours of the temple etched into the medal and remembered Grandma's words of warning last night. *This* is what she'd been talking about. I had no idea I could experience such powerful feelings of passion. I used to wonder how Jill could have had issues with chastity back in high school, but now I saw just how quickly things could get out of hand.

I pictured her sorrowful face the night she'd told me she'd made mistakes. I knew that I never wanted to take the path of heartache and regret that she had endured as a result. Not giving in to my desires was hard. *Really* hard. But disappointing myself, my parents, Grandma, and especially the Lord—that would be way worse. Not to mention what it would mean for Sawyer, his priesthood, and the temple covenants he'd already made.

I looked over at him as he watched the movie. Why did he have to be so dang good looking? He had a strong profile and I liked the way his light brown hair fell boyishly across his forehead.

There's nothing wrong with kissing . . . that's all you're doing. That's what every couple does; there's no reason to get all worked up about it. You're a good girl . . . you'll stop if things get out of hand.

My mouth began to water for want of Sawyer's kiss as these thoughts entered my mind. *Of course,* I thought. *This is harmless, and it feels so incredible.*

Sawyer turned and looked at me, the embers of restrained desire visible in his eyes. I reached for his face, pulling him close to me. We began kissing again, and my senses seemed to pick up exactly where they'd left off, only this time wanting more. In the back of my mind I felt a warning going off.

Nothing is wrong. This is a good thing. The thoughts persisted against the quiet warning. *How could something that feels this wonderful be bad?* Suddenly, I saw Rebekah's face in my mind; her beautiful, clear eyes and happy countenance.

I saw the faces of the women from my past dreams. Those were women of virtue, and I wanted to be like them.

I forcefully pulled myself away from Sawyer and sat back in my seat. I twisted the ring on my finger; the ring that Luke had given me.

"We need to go, Sawyer," I stated. "Now."

"Eliza, what's the matter?" he asked in confusion.

"We can talk when you drop me off at my apartment." I didn't want to allow another temptation to endanger my resolve.

"Okay." He waited for me to buckle my seatbelt, and then started the ignition. My hands shook slightly as we pulled out of the lot and made our way back to my apartment. It had been difficult to put a stop to things back there, but I felt a deep sense of peace and knew that I'd made the right choice. I hated to think of what might have happened if we'd stayed longer.

CHAPTER

Alright, are you going to tell me what's on your mind?" Sawyer asked as we stood outside my apartment.

"Sawyer, I really care about you, but I can't see you anymore . . . not like this. I think it's better if we just stay friends." I couldn't meet his eyes as I spoke to him. It was taking every ounce of resolution that I possessed to say those words, and I couldn't afford to let him see that.

"Is this about what happened at the movie? I'm sorry that I let things get so carried away. I shouldn't have kissed you like that." He tilted my face to look up at his and there was sincere regret in his eyes. "You were right about making us leave, but don't blow me off for making one mistake. Give me another chance and I promise to be a better gentleman."

I took a step away from him and he let his hand drop. I couldn't stay out here much longer. The more I was near him the harder this would be. "I'm sorry, but I just don't think that's a good idea. There's too much attraction between us and Luke gets home soon. This can only end with one or both of us getting hurt."

"So you admit that you're attracted to me?" His eyes lit up roguishly.

I blushed and turned to move to the door but he stopped me. "Look, I'm sorry for the way I acted tonight. I know there's no excuse, but I got so wrapped up in how beautiful you are and how much I love being around you. You're constantly on my mind." He raked a hand through his hair in frustration. "If it weren't for your missionary, would you be running away like this?"

I stopped and contemplated his question. If Luke *weren't* in the picture, would I be trying to end this relationship right now?

"No," I admitted.

An expression I couldn't define flitted across his face. He smiled gently. "Well then we already discussed this. I'm fully aware that he gets home in two months, and that you won't commit to anything or anyone until after he's home. I'm aware of the risk—but that doesn't stop me from wanting to be with you now. I won't put you in a compromising situation again. We can date in a group from now on. Heck—you can even tie my hands behind my back if you want to."

I giggled in spite of myself and he continued, "Just let me be with you. Let me be your 'stand-in' boyfriend until Luke gets home. Please."

I shook my head, staring at the ground. Why was this so hard? I should just walk through the door and end this, but as I stared into his eyes, pleading with me to give him another chance, I couldn't do it. I *wanted* to be with him right now. I wanted to erase the sad, longing look he wore.

Without saying anything, I stepped forward and put my arms around him. He let out a sigh as buried his face in my neck and held me tightly.

"You're impossible, you know that?" I whispered with a smile. It felt so nice to have him hold me, safe and warm in his arms. I didn't know if I was being selfish or just plain crazy letting him talk me into this, but I wasn't sure if I could have faced the alternative.

Like it or not, Sawyer Murdock was starting a game of tug-o-war with my heart. The problem was, I wasn't sure who was going to end up sitting in the mud once the game was over.

⟨✺

"What are you guys doing up still?" I asked in surprise as I closed the front door behind me.

All three of my roommates were at the kitchen table, eating a package of Chips Ahoy.

"We're just waiting up, making sure our little roomie made it back safely," Bree teased. It was one-thirty in the morning and we had classes tomorrow. I made a mental note to try not to schedule any classes before ten next semester.

I walked over and sat at the table, turning down the cookies they offered. I was fairly sure I wouldn't need to eat anything for the next week.

"So how was the date?" Lacey asked.

"It was . . . incredible," I said with a dreamy sigh.

"Aww!"

Their questions began tumbling out faster than I could answer them and we talked for another half an hour. I told them about my uncertainty and worries while they listened patiently.

"I just don't know what's going on here," I confessed. "I had everything all planned out. Luke would get home; we'd get married, and live happily ever after." I ticked the points off my fingers. "See? It was all going to work out perfectly. Meeting another guy was not. a part. of the plan." I felt like I might become hysterical.

"So why don't you just forget about Sawyer then?" Charlotte inquired as she nibbled on the edge of her cookie.

"I tried, but I can't seem to make myself do it." I told them about the conversation I'd just had with him. As I related his words I realized again how sweet he'd been to me.

We were silent for a few seconds, and then Bree spoke. "Eliza, we all know how much you love Luke, and he sounds like an amazing guy," she paused as though weighing her words carefully, "But maybe you need to consider that there might be someone else out there who would make you just as happy . . . maybe even happier."

I shook my head. "I don't think so. Luke is perfect. Just wait until you guys meet him. You'll see." Try as I might to deny it, Bree's words had penetrated me. Maybe she was right. I'd dreamed about marrying Luke for the past two years—even longer. Could it be possible that maybe that dream wouldn't come true, of my own choice?

"My older sister Valerie waited for a missionary. She totally thought they would get married, but when he got home he was completely different. Valerie was different too. She ended up marrying his best friend," Lacey stated matter-of-factly. Charlotte nudged her in the arm.

"What?" she demanded.

Charlotte just shook her head in disbelief.

"Lacey, you are hopeless!" Bree moaned, but she smiled as she said it.

We all laughed, but I felt a nagging worry as I thought about Lacey's story. One of my biggest fears had been that Luke would change so much on his mission that he would seem like a stranger to me when he got home. Or worse, that his feelings for me would be different. I never considered the possibility that *I* was the one who might change. I felt like I was turning into my own worst enemy.

"Who knows? Maybe you'll end up deciding to serve a mission and won't have to worry about making a choice," Lacey said.

We all nodded and fell silent. With the lowering of the age requirement for sister missionaries, serving a mission was something each of us had talked about. Charlotte was even getting ready to submit her papers.

I rubbed a hand across my eyes and stared at the table. My mind was too exhausted right now to think seriously about anything. Especially a life-altering decision.

As I said my prayers before bed, I recounted all of the things I could think of to be grateful for, and the list was long. Finally, I asked for help with my dating dilemma. I knew I wouldn't be able to get through these next few months alone. I needed the Spirit to guide my actions.

The light from a full moon spilled into our room, illuminating objects brighter than usual. As I finished my prayer, I lay back on my pillow and stared at the framed picture on my nightstand. It was a photo of Luke and me, taken just days before he'd left. He had his arm around my shoulders and we were both grinning. I envied the girl in the picture—she was so certain of her heart.

Although I still loved Luke and felt that my love for him would never, *could* never, waver . . . I just didn't know what to do with these feelings for Sawyer. It was hard to ignore the here-and-now, especially when I'd been lonely for so long.

I sighed and rolled over on my pillow. Choosing an eternal companion was the biggest decision I would ever make—the last thing I wanted to do was mess it up. For the next hour I continued to toss and turn. Finally, I said another silent prayer. I asked for clarity of mind and emotion, and that I would be able to make the right choice when the time came.

After finishing my prayer I thought about Sawyer and the many qualities I admired about him, but it was the memory of Luke's face that filled my mind before sleep finally claimed me.

fourteen

"Yo, Elder Matthews!"

Luke turned at the sound of his name, and then stifled a groan. It was Elder Benton, his companion from the MTC. He had endured two months with this guy back in Provo—but just barely.

From the very first day, Elder Benton had made it clear that he was only on a mission because his parents had promised to pay his college tuition if he served. He seemed to have a goal to see how many rules he could break without getting sent home.

In the beginning, Luke had thought of it as a challenge to try to help him find his testimony, but with no success. And from the rumors that circulated around the mission, it seemed that Elder Benton hadn't changed at all since those MTC days. Luke felt sorry for him, but he also tried to avoid his company at all costs and had considered it a blessing that he'd never been put in a companionship with him again.

Elder Benton swaggered up and put his arm around Luke's shoulders. "What's up, Elder Matthews? Long time no see."

"Yeah." Luke tried not to bristle as he moved out from under the arm. "What have you been up to these days?" He glanced around for his companion as a means for escape, but Elder Martinez was busy talking to a group of missionaries across the room. It was an area conference and everyone wanted to catch up with each other.

"Not much . . . just counting down the days till we're on that airplane headed back to the States—you know what I'm sayin'?"

Luke made a non-committal grunt as he continued to look around for an excuse to bail.

Elder Benton kept talking, oblivious to Luke's discomfort. "There's a word on the street I thought you might be interested to hear, bro." He took a step closer to Luke and lowered his voice in a confidential tone, "Apparently Hermana Chambers has a thing for you." He grinned and raised his eyebrows as he waited for Luke's reaction.

Luke blew out an irritated sigh and shook his head. "I doubt that. Hermana Chambers is a good missionary; she's totally focused." He gave Elder Benton a sharp look and then glanced away as he took a step back. "I'm sure it's just a rumor."

"No, dude! I heard it straight from her companion, Hermana Phillips. She's been crushing on you the entire mission and said she hopes your 'paths will cross' when she gets home. She's from Utah you know—you lucky son-of-a-gun!" Elder Benton bumped Luke in the shoulder and snickered.

Luke had to fight the urge to punch Elder Benton back. Hard. He considered himself a tolerant person, but he knew too much of Benton's character and his patience with him had worn thin. He had to get away before he lost his temper.

"Well, I guess I better go find Elder Martinez now . . ." he began to say when a female voice interrupted.

"Hola Eldéres, ¿comó están ustedes?" Hermana Chambers greeted as she approached with her companion.

Elder Benton grinned widely as he looked her over. "We're good." He put his elbow on Luke's shoulder and added, "As a matter of fact . . . we were just talking about you, weren't we Elder Matthews?"

Luke stiffened as Olivia Chambers cast a questioning glance his way. "Oh really?" She seemed guarded.

Benton tried to cover a smile with his fist, thoroughly amused by the awkwardness of the moment.

Luke was quick to fill the void. "Elder Benton brought up your name and I commented that you were a good missionary." He once again shrugged away from Elder Benton's elbow. The guy had a lot to learn about personal space. He caught Hermana Phillips giving her companion a quick, meaningful smile and decided that he needed to change the subject.

"So how's the work going in your area right now, sisters?"

Hermana Chambers was blushing and seemed just as eager to change the subject. "Really well. We have a few investigators that we're excited about. How about you? You leave in a few months, right?"

Luke nodded. "Yeah, it's coming up quick." There was a pause as everyone seemed to wait for him to make the next statement. It was common knowledge that Hermana Chambers would be finishing her mission and leaving the next week. "And you'll be home even sooner. How does it feel?"

"I have mixed emotions," she said with a shrug. "I'm going to miss this, a lot. It's been a life-changing experience." Her brown eyes were nostalgic for a moment.

Elder Benton suddenly donned a mischievous look and turned to Hermana Phillips. "Hermana, there's something I wanted to show you over—here." He gestured with his head to a group of missionaries standing nearby. Hermana Phillips immediately smiled as she picked up on the hint.

"Oh yeah . . . I was hoping you'd have time to show me that . . . thing." She winked at Hermana Chambers who was pleading with her eyes and subtly shaking her head. Hermana Phillips simply smiled back and walked with Elder Benton toward the other group.

"Yeah . . . I should go find Elder Martinez too," Luke said, trying to find a polite way out of the situation.

Hermana Chambers twisted the handle on her scripture bag and nodded. "There are some sisters I wanted to go say good-bye to as well." She scanned the large room of missionaries a moment before turning back to Luke. "Good luck on the rest of your mission, Elder Matthews. You've been an incredible missionary."

Luke smiled at her. "Thanks, and good luck to you too. I'm sure you've got great things ahead."

"Thanks." She paused a moment. "I hear you have a girl waiting for you back home, is that right?"

"Yeah, I do." Luke's eyes suddenly brightened and he reached for his inside suit pocket. "As a matter of fact, since you're going home so soon, would you mind doing me a favor?"

A slight frown puckered her brow, but she quickly replaced it with a smile and held out her hand. "You have a letter."

He grinned as he pulled out the envelope. "I'm guessing I'm not the first person who's asked?"

She took the letter from him, quickly glancing at the address. "I'm gonna have to bring an extra suitcase just to hold all of the mail, but I get it. I did the same thing."

Whenever a missionary was going back to the States, they were inevitably sent with stacks of letters to mail.

"Well I really appreciate it," Luke said with a smile.

She blushed and looked away. "I'm sure she'll be happy to get it."

"Let's hope so."

"Oh you don't have to worry about *that*." Hermana Chambers clapped a hand over her mouth, her face reddening more. "I-I mean, who doesn't like getting missionary mail?"

Luke nodded and looked away.

This hadn't been the first time he'd heard someone say that Hermana Chambers was interested in him, but he'd never believed it before. She was undoubtedly a beautiful girl and she distracted half the missionaries, even though she didn't realize it. She was a dedicated missionary and was serving for all the right reasons. She'd spoken less than five words to him the entire mission. Luke hadn't given the rumors a second thought, but by the strange way she was acting right now he began to wonder.

"Well, it was good to see you again, Hermana. Take care of yourself." He shook her hand and started to walk away.

"You too, Elder, and . . . maybe I'll find you on Facebook or something when you get home," she said.

Luke turned and gave her a half smile. "Yeah, good idea." He turned back around and tried to scout out Elder Martinez from the sea of black suits in the room.

He frowned as he realized that maybe there'd been some truth to the rumors after all. Hermana Chambers was great and he wished her all the best—but there was only one girl he wanted to see when he got home.

CHAPTER
fifteen

So what did you think of my little surprise this morning? Did you like it?" Sawyer asked.

We were walking hand-in-hand toward the library on campus. I stopped and beamed at him, suddenly stretching up on tiptoe to place a kiss on his cheek. "It was adorable! You're going to have to stop spoiling me like this. I can't keep up with you."

He smiled and tenderly traced his hand across my cheek. "Eliza, I don't do it because I expect something in return. Your being with me is all the thanks I need." He paused a moment and I caught an impish gleam in his eyes. "And don't worry, I'm keeping a tally of everything so you can pay me back someday— with interest."

I played along. "Good. I expect to receive an invoice soon. I like to pay my debts, you know."

Sawyer grabbed both of my hands and cocked his head to one side as he grinned at me. "I'm glad to hear that. In fact, I'll tell you how we can settle the account right now if you'd like." His voice dropped as his face inched closer to mine.

"Oh, I see . . . so that's how you operate," I teased. He leaned in to kiss me, but I darted playfully away. He laughed and caught hold of my hand again, lacing his fingers through mine as we walked through campus.

It had been over two weeks since Sawyer and I had had our talk on my balcony, and we'd been together every day since then. Sawyer had also begun leaving little surprises for me each day: flowers, candy, tickets to a concert. This morning I'd come into the living room to find a gigantic teddy bear propped on the couch; a single rose clutched in its furry paw.

My roommates seemed almost as excited as I was by each new gift. I secretly worried that Sawyer was winning them over before they had a chance to meet Luke. Part of me also wondered if this was typical dating behavior for Sawyer, or if he was trying extra hard to please me now that the countdown for Luke's return was on.

Even though I felt guilty accepting all of these gifts, I had to admit it was nice to be doted on. I couldn't afford to reciprocate with the kinds of things he was giving me, but I appreciated his thoughtfulness.

We reached the library and he held the door open for me. "Eliza, I've been thinking," he began slowly. I could tell by his tone that something was up, so I turned to face him with my full attention.

"Yes?" I had to smile at the cautious look on his face. It wasn't an expression Sawyer wore often.

"Well, you're going home this weekend—" he paused as if mustering courage, "and I'm really going to miss you."

My heart melted at the sincere look in his eyes. Truth be told, I was going to miss him too—more than I was willing to admit. It was the Fourth of July weekend and he'd invited me to the local fireworks and concert, but when I'd told my mom I might not make it home for our family get together she'd been enormously disappointed.

Feeling guilty, I'd told her I would be there and canceled my plans with Sawyer. It wasn't what I wanted, but when you only lived an hour away it wasn't easy to come up with an excuse to miss a major family event. Besides, I could tell that Mom was missing me and I didn't want to hurt her.

I gave Sawyer's hand a squeeze. "I know. I'm going to miss you too. I'm sorry I had to cancel like that."

He shook his head and looked at the ground for a second. "No, it's totally cool. I think it's awesome that your family has a traditional party—it's just," he glanced up at me through his lashes before continuing, "It's just that I'd really like to meet your family."

"Oh." His statement caught me completely off-guard. I hadn't considered inviting Sawyer home to meet my family, and for a moment I was at a loss for words.

"But, you know, I understand this is a family thing, so maybe another time," he rushed on, clearly embarrassed by my response.

I shook my head. "No, no . . . I didn't mean to sound like that. I think it would be great to have you meet them." I smiled, happy to see the uncomfortable look on his face quickly fading.

"You're sure? I don't want to pressure you into anything." He creased his brow.

"Yes, I'm sure. Besides, you haven't *lived* until you've experienced a Moore Family Fourth of July."

He chuckled and then continued talking as we made our way to the study section. I did my best to focus on his words, but I had an uneasy feeling in the pit of my stomach. *Was* I sure about bringing Sawyer home to meet my family? After all, we'd only been officially dating for a few weeks now. I liked Sawyer— a lot—but with Luke coming home so soon it was going to be interesting to see how this played out with my family. I wasn't sure if I was ready to go under the microscope with this new relationship. More importantly, I wasn't sure if Sawyer knew what he was getting himself into either.

"Sweetheart!" Mom flew at me before I was halfway through the front door. "Welcome home!" She had her arms around me so tightly it was almost difficult to breathe, but it felt good anyway. There's nothing like a hug from your mom.

"It's nice to be back," I managed to respond. This was the longest I'd ever been away from home, and it *was* nice to be back. I hadn't even realized I'd missed it until now.

"There's my girl!" Dad boomed as he entered the living room. Mom stepped aside so he could have his turn with a welcome. He scooped me up in one of his best daddy-bear hugs and I squealed as he spun me around like I was still in grade school.

Sawyer quietly came through the door and set our bags on the floor. He smiled as he watched the happy reunion. My mom immediately went over to him, offering her hand.

"Sawyer, it's so nice to meet you. Eliza's told me many wonderful things about you and we're thrilled to have you spend the weekend with us." She smiled warmly and I could almost see his muscles relax.

"Thank you, Mrs. Moore. It's really nice of you guys to let me stay here. Eliza's told me all about your Fourth of July traditions, and I'm honored that you're letting me be a part of it." He gave her one of his most charming smiles and it suddenly occurred to me how much he wanted my parents to like him. "I hope I won't be in the way, and please let me know if there's anything I can do to help."

Wow. Okay, he *really* wanted my parents to like him. I raised my eyebrows from behind my mom's back, but he pretended not to notice.

Dad had been watching the exchange, silently appraising Sawyer from head to toe. After a moment he stepped forward and offered an outstretched hand. Sawyer immediately accepted what I could tell was a bone-crushing hand-shake (one that Dad reserved solely for my boyfriends). He didn't flinch as he looked my father squarely in the eyes.

"So you're Sawyer Murdock, huh?" Dad asked in his most daunting tone.

"Yes, sir. It's a pleasure to meet you."

I wanted to cheer for Sawyer; he wasn't letting my dad get to him. He didn't even seem bothered that my dad was still gripping his hand.

"Well, son, it should be quite a weekend." Dad finally let go and seemed to acknowledge that Sawyer was not going to be intimidated.

I had prepared Sawyer for my dad's antics, and he was handling it like a pro.

"Why don't we all sit down and have a visit so we can get better acquaint-ed," Mom offered. She gestured to the nearby sitting area. "Sawyer, would you care for a glass of lemonade?"

"That would be great, thanks. Can I help you get it?" Sawyer was warming up quickly to my mom and I was sure he was anxious to escape my dad's pene-trating stare.

"Why, yes, actually that would be a big help. It's just right in here." I knew Mom was taking pity on him, and I gave her an appreciative smile before they disappeared into the kitchen.

"Alright, Dad—are we going to have to have another talk?" I whispered ur-gently once the others were out of earshot.

"About what, honey?" he asked with infuriating innocence. I knew he was baiting me.

"Dad, I'm eighteen years old—I'm in college now! This is the time in my life when I'm supposed to be dating, and I *know* that you know that. If you're going to scare every guy that comes to this house, I'm never going to bring any-one home for you to meet again. Is that what you want?"

Dad pretended to pick a piece of fluff off his slacks. He stared at the floor and then looked up at me. I was surprised by the hint of sadness in his eyes. "I'm sorry, sweetheart. You're absolutely right. You're not my little girl anymore." He sighed and smiled. "I'll try to remember that."

I reached over and put my hand on his knee. "I'll always be your little girl—even when I'm old and married, with a train of kids in tow. You don't have to worry about that."

He put his hand over mine and we smiled at each other as my mom and Sawyer entered with the lemonade.

"Here we are!" Mom said cheerfully as she handed a frosty glass to Dad. I accepted my drink from Sawyer, and then he sat down next to me on the sofa. Even though it was drawing into the evening, the air-conditioning was working full blast to battle the oppressive July heat.

"Where's Courtney?" I asked.

"Oh, she's out with some friends. She'll be home by dinnertime," Mom said. "Speaking of which, I hope you two brought your appetites with you because I've spent all afternoon preparing a welcome home feast."

There certainly *were* delicious smells emanating from the kitchen, but I noticed for the first time that she looked tired.

"That was really sweet of you, Mom, but you shouldn't have been slaving over the stove on a day like this. We would have been fine with something simple like pizza or sandwiches," I said in concern.

"Nonsense! You've been eating stuff like that for a month now. It's time you had a real, home-cooked dinner. Besides, this is a special occasion. It's not every day you bring a young man home to meet the family." She winked at Sawyer and I blushed.

"Well, Mrs. Moore, if that food tastes half as good as it smells, you might have a hard time getting rid of me after the weekend is over. A nice, home-cooked meal is something I haven't enjoyed in a long time." He grinned boyishly at her.

Mom beamed. "In that case, why don't we all go into the dining room and get started? Courtney should be home any minute. In the meantime we can enjoy some appetizers."

"Sounds good to me," I replied enthusiastically. Even though I felt bad that she'd been working so hard, I wanted her to know how much I appreciated her efforts. Sawyer stood and pulled me up with his free hand. We carried our glasses into the dining room, but he continued to hold my hand, giving it a squeeze before we sat down at the table. I smiled and gave him a sidelong wink.

It felt a little strange bringing a guy home for the first time in my adult life, but so far things were going much better than I'd hoped.

"No fair! I swear this game is rigged," Courtney complained as I set my final UNO card on the pile.

"Oh *please*, Court, you always say that when you lose," I teased, trying hard to keep the triumphant gloat I felt from showing on my face.

She huffed and folded her arms across her chest. "Well when *someone* in particular wins three-out-of-four games, it seems a little fishy to me."

Sawyer and my parents chuckled at Courtney's moping.

"Don't worry, honey. Eliza's winning streak is about to end—I taste victory this time!" Dad said as he eagerly rubbed his hands together.

I rolled my eyes. "Don't be too sure about that. You may have schooled us in dominoes, but UNO is *my* game."

Sawyer gathered up all of the cards. Even though it was his turn to shuffle, he offered the deck to Courtney. "Would you like to shuffle this time?"

She gave him a cool stare. "No thanks."

"Okay then . . . I'll deal." Sawyer smiled at her and began to shuffle the cards. He was being so nice to Courtney despite her rude behavior.

I, however, was horrified by the way she was acting. Ever since their first introduction at dinner tonight, Courtney had been less than civil with Sawyer. I'd expected this kind of conduct from my dad; I had *not* expected it from my sister.

I watched Sawyer as he expertly dealt the cards around the table. He'd been such a good sport tonight; surviving rounds of dominoes, Pitt, Pictionary, and now UNO. The Moore family could game night with the best of them, and Sawyer didn't miss a beat. I could tell that he was starting to get more comfortable now, which made me happy. He was beginning to show more of his relaxed, joking nature. He'd even made my dad laugh once, which was no small feat.

We played the game and Mom surprised us all by winning this round, coming from behind for a huge victory. The clock in the living room chimed and I was shocked by the hour. It was well past midnight.

"Good grief, we'd all better turn in if we're going to make it to the parade in the morning," Mom said. She stood and began to clear dessert plates from the table.

"Oh, sure—you just want to be the final victor of the evening," Dad teased as he helped clean up.

"Mom, can I see my phone for a second to check if anyone called while we were playing?" Courtney asked in her sweetest, most contriving tone. It was a rule that phones were confiscated during game night to avoid distractions from being with the family.

"Alright, but I don't know what good it will do you. It's too late to return any calls or texts tonight, and you know you need to hand it back once you're done," Mom reminded her.

My parents still enforced the "phone checking-in" rule they'd started a few years ago with me. However, now that I was graduated and out on my own, the rule didn't apply to me anymore (though I wouldn't have put it past my dad to try to take my phone if he could).

I watched Courtney as Sawyer and I cleared the games from the table. As

I'd always predicted, she was maturing into a very beautiful young woman. She was intently scanning through her messages and I wondered who she was hanging out with now—and which boys were chasing after her. Courtney's sixteenth birthday was just around the corner, and I knew my Dad was already gearing up with tactics to frighten her dates. Man, was he going to have his hands full! I almost felt sorry for him.

"Eliza, why don't you go get some fresh sheets and blankets to put on the couch in the family room? Sawyer, I hope you'll be comfortable. If you need anything, you just let us know, alright?"

"I'll be great. Thanks, Mrs. Moore," Sawyer replied with a smile.

"And remember, the floors in this house are very creaky. Anyone sneaking around at night is likely to be caught. Right, Courtney?" Dad asked.

"Da-*ad!*" Courtney and I protested at the same time. His inference about Sawyer and me sneaking around was so embarrassing! Then I realized what he'd said to Courtney.

I turned to her. "Wait—what? You were trying to sneak out?"

"Ugh! It happened like three weeks ago and I don't see why everyone has to know about it," Courtney grumbled. I let the subject drop, but Mom gave me a meaningful look.

Sawyer immediately picked up on the tension. "Hey, Eliza is there a place where I can change and brush my teeth?" he asked, diverting the topic.

"Yeah, it's just over by the family room." I smiled and led him toward the main-floor bathroom.

"Well, at least I think your mom likes me," he whispered once we were out of earshot.

I turned and gave him a hug. "Dad and Courtney will come around. Nobody could help liking you." I pulled back and smiled at him. Our eyes met and I could tell that Sawyer wanted to kiss me, but he didn't dare. We were alone in the hallway by the bathroom, but someone could come walking by without warning. My dad was in high-radar mode with a boy in the house.

He reluctantly pulled away and smiled at me before taking his bag into the bathroom. The smell of his cologne still hung on my clothes and I hummed to myself as I made my way to the linen closet. I couldn't believe my parents were letting my date sleep in our house, but it was hardly fair to make him drive two hours each day to be a part of the weekend activities.

I made up his bed on the couch in the family room. It wasn't a stay at the Ritz, but the sectional was comfy and I knew that Sawyer didn't mind camping out for two nights.

I'd just finished folding the down throw over the top when I felt strong arms wrap around my waist from behind. I turned and smiled up at Sawyer.

"Nice PJ's."

He was wearing a gray university T-shirt with flannel pajama bottoms.

"Thanks," he said, before leaning in to give me a kiss.

I kissed him back, but then quickly tried to pull away. "My parents," I began, but Sawyer pulled me back, capturing me in his arms.

"I just checked. They all went upstairs." He smiled roguishly before kissing me again. This time I gave in, kissing him the way I'd been wanting to all night. It felt like sheer heaven, and I didn't want the moment to end, but after a few minutes we heard footsteps down the hall. The floors really *were* squeaky.

We quickly separated and tried to act casual as my mom's face peered into the room. "All settled in, Sawyer?"

"Yes, this will be perfect. Thanks again, Mrs. Moore," he replied.

Mom smiled and turned to me. "Okay, sweetie, your father wants me to escort you to your room." She put her arm around me and then addressed Sawyer again, "We'll have breakfast at 8:30, and the parade starts at 10:00. Sleep well."

"Good night," Sawyer answered my mom, though his eyes were on me. I know we were both thinking the same thing; wishing we could have spent more time together. After that last kiss, though, I realized that it was probably better for both of us that my parents were there to keep an eye out.

Ever since my dream with Grandma and my talk with Sawyer a few weeks ago, we'd been extra careful to keep to a curfew and not be alone too often. But that still didn't make it easy.

Thoughts and temptations would creep up on me when we were together, and all the messages from the world shouted that it was okay to succumb to physical desire. Sometimes it felt like increasing in faith and personal righteousness and staying morally clean were uphill battles.

But I knew they were battles worth fighting.

CHAPTER

sixteen

W ell I don't know about the rest of you, but I think that was the best parade yet. That float with the rotating statue of liberty was amazing," Mom said.

I nodded and smiled. I loved how excited my mom got for parades. Her enthusiasm rivaled with that of a child—"ooo-ing" and "aww-ing" over each float like it was Christmas morning.

The parade was over and Mom, Dad, Courtney, Sawyer and I were milling through the crowds toward our car. It had been a lot of fun running into my friends from high school, but I'd noticed more than one curious glance in Sawyer's direction. A few people had asked discreetly about Luke, and each time it had made me blush.

I knew Luke's family always went to their cabin for the Fourth, so I hadn't worried about running into any of them this weekend. But I hadn't thought about all the other people who would speculate over seeing me out with another guy. I began to wonder if bringing Sawyer home this weekend had been a bad idea after all. The feelings of confusion and frustration were returning and I wasn't exactly sure how to deal with them.

"Eliza! Over here." I spun around to see Jill waving her arm as she tried to make her way through the crowd.

"Jill!" I squealed. We'd been texting each other back and forth over the past few days and I knew that she had planned on seeing the parade. I was curious to meet her new boyfriend, Aiden, and I knew she was equally curious about Sawyer. She'd nicknamed him the "dark horse" and I had to admit I was anxious to get my best friend's take on my new . . . boyfriend? . . . crush? . . . uh . . . *friend.*

Jill finally made her way over to me and we threw our arms around each other. "Hey gorgeous! It is so good to see you!" She laughed as she pulled away and looked at me.

"I know! And look at you, I love your hair!" I exclaimed as I grabbed a raven black strand. Jill and I had joked about how her hair would turn into a scary beauty school experiment, but she had stayed true to her classy style. When I'd last seen her, she'd worn her hair long and past her shoulders. Now it was cut in a shoulder-length bob, highlighting her beautiful Asian features.

We'd been so giddy to see each other that only now did I realize there was a guy standing behind her. Jill followed my gaze and turned to make an introduction. "Liza, this is Aiden Feldman. Aiden, this is my best friend Eliza Moore."

Aiden and I exchanged greetings, and then I turned to Sawyer and introduced him as well. Jill threw me a quick, loaded glance before striking up a friendly conversation with Sawyer. I knew this would be a subtle interrogation on her part and I would have loved nothing more than to eavesdrop, but this was also my chance to get to know Aiden.

I turned and began asking him the usual "get to know you" questions. Although his looks would probably be considered average, his congenial personality made him likable right from the start. I wasn't sure where their relationship was headed, but he was a great guy and I couldn't wait to give Jill my full approval.

"Eliza, I hate to interrupt but we need to get moving if we're going to be on time to the picnic," Mom said as she appeared at my side. She offered her greetings to Jill and introduced herself to Aiden, inviting them to join us for the picnic.

Jill politely declined. "Thanks Mrs. Moore, but we already have some stuff going on today." She smiled apologetically.

I hid a smirk. Jill had been to one of our Moore Family parties and she knew what a crazy shindig it was: every imaginable relation from my dad's side congregated for the event. And just like any family—our family tree had its nuts.

Entertaining? Yes. Fun if you weren't related? Not so much.

Each year there was a talent show, and I could almost see my uncle Ned's rendition of "Comin' to America" play across Jill's memory.

"Well, we'll have to catch up with you guys later," I said as I reached over to give Jill another hug.

"Definitely," she answered as she returned the embrace. Quietly whispering in my ear she added, "We have *a lot* to talk about." She pulled away and glanced sideways at Sawyer and then raised her eyebrows. I was practically bursting to talk to her, but that would have to wait.

I turned and Sawyer put his hand in mine as we walked back toward the car. Mom was already a few yards in front of us, in an obvious rush to get home to her potato salad.

"I can see why you and Jill are best friends. She's really cool," Sawyer said once we were alone.

"Yeah, I'm glad you got to meet her. Aiden's nice too," I added somewhat wistfully. I was happy for Jill, but something inside of me felt just the tiniest bit sad. Someday she would get married, and then things would never be the same. We would always be friends, of course—but things would change.

I'd never liked change, and I felt like the next few months would be packed full of them—changes that would affect the rest of my life. Holding Sawyer's hand seemed to illustrate that point as if in neon lights.

Whose hand would I be holding after Luke got home?

❧

"I'm pretty sure your uncle Ned has missed his calling in life. He should move to Vegas and start doing Neil Diamond impersonations," Sawyer said as he lay back on the blanket we shared.

It was now past dusk, and we were at a local park waiting for the city fireworks to start. This culminating event always drew a large crowd, but we'd come early and had managed to secure our own little patch of turf. We were surrounded by families with lawn chairs and picnic blankets, but no one that I recognized. Courtney was out with friends and my parents had decided to forego the crowds this time around.

I giggled, and then it turned into full-blown laughter as I recalled the afternoon's events. Uncle Ned had gone all-out this year, adding an unfortunate pair of tight leather pants and a rhinestone-studded shirt to his performance. It'd been like watching a train-wreck: incredibly horrific, yet you couldn't bring yourself to look away. His tone-deaf notes still reverberated around in my skull like a haunting echo.

"Yeah, that song has never been the same for me since Uncle Ned started performing it," I confessed, trying to sound sad but the laughter kept bubbling up.

Sawyer leaned up on his elbow and looked at me. "No, seriously. Do you think he'd consider letting me sign on as his agent? The man has really got something going for him."

He still hadn't cracked a smile, so I decided to join in his game. I pulled out my cell. "You know what? You're totally right. I have his number; I'll dial him and you can tell him all about your *big* plans." I pretended to search for his number and then acted like I was making the call. Sawyer grinned as he watched me, but his smile slowly faded and I could tell he was beginning to wonder if I was serious.

"Hey, Uncle Ned," I said in my best acting tone. Sawyer jumped up and grabbed the phone from me, but when he saw the blank screen he sighed in relief.

"You little rascal; you had me going for a second," he growled through a half-smile.

"Serves you right—and give me back my phone!" I grabbed for it but he held it out of reach.

"I think I'll hold on to this for a while, it might prove to be useful as—collateral." Sawyer's blue eyes ignited flirtatiously.

I folded my arms across my chest. "Oh yeah? Collateral for what, exactly?"

He leaned closer, but held the phone just far enough away to bait me. His eyes met mine and I began leaning in as well. We hadn't been alone in what felt like forever and I'd been waiting for his kiss all day. My heart sped up in anticipation, but just before our lips met, I heard a voice that made my heart stop.

"Eliza? Is-is that you?"

I turned slowly around and felt the blood draining from my face as I looked up at the ten year-old girl. It was Morgan Matthews—Luke's little sister—and she looked completely crushed.

"Morgan! Oh my goodness. Hi!" I stumbled to my feet and did my best to sound cheerful as I reached over and gave her a hug. She hugged me stiffly back and then looked away as she twisted the purple glow-in-the-dark necklace she wore. One of her little friends stood to the side, watching our exchange with complete disinterest.

"I thought you would be up at your family cabin. Did you guys not go this year?"

She shook her head.

"Oh . . . well I guess that makes sense since you're here. But . . . don't you always go?"

She shook her head again. I must have been wrong in thinking it was a tradition set in stone.

"Is the rest of your family around?" I tried not to look frantic as I searched the surrounding crowd.

"No, I came with Mandy's family." She gestured to her friend.

I felt my shoulders relax a little, but Morgan's tone had been flat. She was normally a chatterbox so I rushed on, talking about nothing in particular just to fill the void. I wished I could explain away the fact that I was out with another guy; wanting more than anything to erase the hurt and confused look on her face.

Since Luke had been gone, I'd been over to visit the Matthews' several times and his family now felt like an extension of my own. I knew that Morgan had even planned the dress she would wear when Luke and I got married. She was basically a little sister to me, and I hated myself for causing her any pain.

I stood there, rushing on about trivial topics to try to smooth over the awkward situation. Sawyer remained on the blanket, instinctively sensing to stay out of the way. Morgan still hadn't said much, just giving a short answer when I asked her questions and casting an occasional glance in Sawyer's direction. The whole situation was awful, and my nervous babbling was only making things worse.

I finally shut my mouth, and we stood there for a few uncomfortable seconds. Neither one of us making eye contact.

"Well, we gotta go now," Morgan said as her friend tugged her arm.

"Okay. It was good to see you, Morgan. Tell your family 'hello' for me, alright?" I said weakly. The last thing I wanted was for Morgan to tell her family about seeing me tonight—or more importantly—seeing who I was *with* tonight. But I knew that there was no point in trying to hide the truth now. I never should have tried to hide anything in the first place, but what was I supposed to do? Tell the Matthews that I was dating someone else who may-or-may-not-be a serious boyfriend, depending on how things went with Luke? Not likely.

I felt my heart sink into my stomach as I watched Morgan and her friend wander off through the crowd. Would Luke's family email him about this? Should I try to write a letter, or wait until he got home to explain things?

With his arrival only a couple of weeks away, it seemed that the only thing I could do now was to wait and talk to him in person.

I turned and somewhat shakily sat down on the blanket.

"Eliza, are you alright? Who was that girl you were talking to?" Sawyer asked, penetrating me with his eyes.

I dropped my gaze and began fiddling with the hem of the blanket. "That was Luke's little sister, Morgan." My voice felt tight and strained as I fought to keep the tears at bay. In these past few moments my emotions had taken a complete one-eighty. Seeing Morgan had forced me to realize that my actions were going to end up hurting someone. No matter what happened after Luke got home, one thing was absolutely certain—someone that I loved was going to get hurt. And it would be my fault.

"Ohhh . . . I see." He sympathetically rubbed the back of my hand with his thumb, but I'd caught the tiniest hint of satisfaction in his tone.

I narrowed my eyes at him. "Are you happy about this?"

Sawyer dropped my hand. "Why would I be happy about something that made you upset?"

"I don't know . . . maybe because now Luke's family will know I'm dating someone else." I was beginning to feel sick to my stomach.

The crowd erupted in cheers as the first firework exploded and filled the sky with fluorescent sparks. Sawyer and I were quiet for a moment as we watched the brilliant display. The sound of patriotic music blasted over the park speakers, but it was still easy to carry on a conversation.

"What makes you think his family will know that we're dating? They'll probably just assume you had a casual date tonight. They *do* know that you planned on dating other people while Luke was gone, right?" he asked, raising a cautious eyebrow.

"Yes, they know that I've been dating other people." I rolled my eyes in exasperation. "But this was different. We were practically making out when Morgan walked by." I covered my face with my hands.

"Eliza, we weren't even kissing!" Sawyer laughed. He made me feel like I was overreacting. Maybe I was.

I looked up at him and shrugged. "I know, but I could tell from Morgan's expression that she sensed there was something between us. I just feel like I'm messing everything up. I shouldn't have agreed to be with you so close to when Luke is getting home. It was selfish of me and it isn't fair to anyone." I looked away as the tears finally began spilling down my cheeks.

"Eliza." Sawyer took my chin in his hand and turned me to face him. Another firework detonated, bathing his face with golden light. "You're being too hard on yourself. Maybe Morgan won't say anything to her family about this. She probably won't give it a second thought. Most kids don't get too involved with their siblings' dating life."

I was about to say something contrary to this, but Sawyer hurried on, "Besides, even if his family did find out that you were 'practically' kissing another guy at the park, what's the worst that could happen? Luke will be home in what? Thirty-eight days? And then you can explain to him that I was a passing fling . . . just a guy to hang out with until he got home." He dropped his hand and looked away.

I felt my heart break inside. I'd had no idea that he was actually counting down the days until Luke got home. And his words about being just a 'fling' made me want to cry even harder.

"Sawyer." I grabbed his hand and gently pulled on it until his eyes met mine. I could tell he was trying to mask the sadness behind them, and I couldn't help myself. I pulled him toward me and kissed him, trying to will the hurt away. He returned my kiss and I was thankful for the cover of darkness. I hoped that the people around us would be distracted enough by the fireworks that they wouldn't notice.

Neil Diamond's "Comin' to America" began to play and Sawyer and I pulled apart. He pressed his forehead against mine and we laughed. It was a much-needed break to the tension that had been hanging thickly between us.

After a few moments, I pulled back and looked him squarely in the eyes. "Sawyer, you know you're not just a passing fling to me, don't you? Our relationship is . . . um . . . uncertain, and confusing to say the least—but I hope you know me better than to think I'm just using you to pass the time."

"How *do* you feel about me, Eliza?" Sawyer asked quietly. There was a sudden earnestness in his expression as his eyes searched mine.

I looked up at the sky and pretended to study the glittering red and orange lights above me. I had always loved fireworks, and never grew tired of watching them.

Luke and I had come to this park two years ago to watch the fireworks. He had forgone going to the cabin with his family so that we could be together. The memory caused a pain in my chest; making it difficult to breathe.

Luke was my first love. I missed him so much it hurt, and I couldn't wait to see him again.

Yet, I *did* have feelings for Sawyer and hated the thought of losing him when Luke got home. My heart was being torn in two.

"I wish you wouldn't ask me that," I answered softly. The music was building to a crescendo as the finale began, but I knew that he had heard me.

"*Why?*" Sawyer's face drew closer to mine as he whispered urgently, "What is it that you're afraid of, Eliza? I know we didn't mean to let our feelings go this far—at least *you* didn't—but sometimes things happen that are beyond our control. I think we met when we did for a reason."

The music continued to swell, as if choreographed by Sawyer's intensity. I looked down at the ground, uncomfortable by the direction this conversation was taking. Everything was happening too fast. I wanted time to think, to be alone with my thoughts and splintered heart.

Sawyer took both of my hands in his and forced me to look at him. "You and I are perfect for each other. We were *meant* to be together." He paused and then spoke with the final bursts of flame in the sky.

"I love you, Eliza."

Everything went dark. The crowd erupted in cheers and applause as Sawyer and I stared at each other. The air between us was charged with the words he had just spoken; heavy with the question of whether or not I could utter the same phrase.

His eyes continued to search mine, and it pained me to see the hopeful longing in them slowly give way to disappointment. I wished that I could say the words that he wanted to hear, but I knew it wouldn't be fair. I wasn't sure of my feelings. I wasn't sure of anything in that moment.

"I'm sorry," I finally whispered. It seemed a pathetic thing to say, but it was all I could offer. I dropped my gaze and stared at the blanket as the crowds began their mass exodus from the park.

Sawyer blew out a breath and gave a short, ironic laugh. "Eliza, you have nothing to be sorry about." He stood and began gathering up our stuff.

I stood as well; feeling only too eager to get out of there. I wished I could leave this conversation behind us too, but the words had been spoken. Sawyer had told me that he loved me, and that simple statement had changed everything. I could no longer pretend that our relationship was just casual. Things were getting serious—too serious.

As we walked hand-in-hand back to the car I realized there was only one possible solution to this mess I was causing.

It was time to end things with Sawyer.

CHAPTER

Neither of us spoke on the drive back to my house. There just didn't seem to be words to fill the empty space his declaration had caused. We were lost in our own thoughts, and the silence was uncomfortable.

When we reached the house I couldn't stand the tension anymore. "So, do you want to watch a movie or something?" It was a meager attempt at smoothing things over. We both knew I was avoiding the real topic at hand.

"No thanks. I'm pretty tired. I think I'll just go to bed if that's all right." He offered a brief smile but avoided looking at me.

I knew that I'd hurt him, but I also knew that there was only one possible solution to the problem. My stomach felt like it had turned to lead as I considered what I had to do. I would have preferred to just get the conversation over with right then and there, but he was staying at our house. It wasn't like I could break up with him and then expect him to leave so late at night, or sleep comfortably on our sofa after officially breaking his heart. And mine.

The conversation would have to wait until our drive home the next day. I felt my throat tighten at the pain of emotional separation that was already coming between us.

"Okay. Do you need anything before I go upstairs?" I had to get out of there quick—before I looked at his handsome, hurt face again and caved on my resolution to end this.

"Nope. I'm good. See you in the morning."

He was still avoiding eye contact. He wasn't going to kiss me, or even give me a hug good night. I didn't blame him, but now the pain was so intense that I couldn't stand it. I nodded and quickly turned, heading for the safety of my room.

I was almost to my door when I heard a muffled sound coming from the direction of my parents' room. It had sounded like my mom. Crying.

Suddenly forgetting about my own heartache, I crept down the hall to where my parents' door was open a crack. The light was on and I peeked inside, curious as to why they weren't already asleep.

What I saw made me start: my mom's face was buried in my dad's shoulder and he was gently stroking her back. I hated to see my mom cry. The sound of her muffled sobs tore through my heart.

"Everything's going to be fine, honey," my dad was saying as he continued to console her. "I'm sure there's nothing to worry about; you'll see."

I couldn't hear her reply, but she took a deep breath and I could tell her tears were subsiding. I wanted to go in and ask what the problem was, but something about the situation made me feel like I was intruding. They obviously thought I was still out with Sawyer and I knew that Courtney wasn't home yet. Whatever the issue was, it was something they meant to keep between themselves.

I backed away from the door and crept silently to my room. Without turning on the light I made my way to my bed. I felt distraught and alone. I needed help.

I don't know how long I prayed, but it was long enough to make my legs start to feel numb and tingly. I cried silent tears as I pleaded for answers. I even waited for several minutes after the prayer, hoping for an answer in the ensuing silence—but nothing came.

Apparently I was on my own to think this through. I couldn't see any way around it. I had to break up with Sawyer until I figured out which direction I needed to take.

I sighed and went into the bathroom to blow my nose and wash my face. I didn't bother looking in the mirror. I wasn't feeling so hot about myself in that moment and knew that I probably looked as rotten as I felt.

I wondered if Sawyer was downstairs feeling as terrible as I was. I was half-tempted to tiptoe down there and throw my arms around him. I wanted to turn back the clock to before he'd said he loved me and go on as before—pretending to myself that things weren't serious between us; lying to my heart that there wouldn't be any consequences for enjoying his company as much as I did. But no matter how much I'd tried to fool myself, deep down I knew the truth: my feelings for him were more than just casual.

Feeling exhausted I climbed into bed, dreading what the next day would bring.

Strengthen Families and Homes

"The family is central to the Creator's plan for the eternal destiny of His children."

– The Family: A Proclamation to the World

CHAPTER

eighteen

As soon as I entered the dream, I knew Grandma would be there. I could sense her presence almost before I was fully asleep.

She stood near a river of water; her white hair and simple dress swaying in the soft breeze. The first rays of morning sun gently bathed the green plants and foliage around her. We seemed to be in a tropical climate. I could hear several birds and what sounded like monkeys chattering in the trees that lined the other side of the river.

I smiled at Grandma as I approached her, but she was focused on something hidden from my view. She looked up and gestured for me to come forward while keeping a finger to her lips.

I followed the signal and stood beside her so I could see what had caught her attention.

There, in a clearing beyond the tall bushes, knelt a family in prayer. They had dark hair and wore mainly animal skins for clothing.

Something sparked a memory in my mind. I'd seen people like this before—in the dream I'd had about Abish two years ago. The way this family looked and dressed was very similar to the way King Lamoni and his people had appeared.

I wanted to ask Grandma if I was right, but when I met her eyes she gestured for me to remain quiet and pointed at the family again.

I gave her a curious look before following her gaze. There was a father and mother, a girl who looked to be fifteen or so, and a boy I guessed to be around my age.

I studied the face of each family member, and suddenly realized there was something significant going on. The father was the one offering the prayer. Although I couldn't hear or understand his words, his expression was pleading. His brows were knit in concentration as tears streamed silently down his face.

The daughter was also wiping tears away. She shook in an effort to control her emotion and my heart immediately went out to her.

The other two members of the family puzzled me. The teenage boy looked completely at peace. There was a certain dignity about his expression; a determination that instantly evoked admiration. I'd never seen that look on anyone so young before. I stared at him for several seconds before pulling my gaze away to look at his mother.

What I saw in this woman surprised me the most. While the father and daughter were visibly upset, *she* seemed more at peace than anyone else. She was the embodiment of strength, nobility, and beauty as she knelt, surrounded by her family members. Her face and countenance seemed almost immersed in light. It was an incredible sight and an overpowering feeling of reverence filled the quiet space.

I couldn't figure out what was going on. I began to feel impatient for Grandma to say something, but she seemed content to just watch.

After a few moments the father ended the prayer and the family stood. Everyone's focus immediately turned to the young man. The girl threw her arms around her brother and began to cry openly as he hugged her back. His expression was sympathetic, but unwavering.

The mother allowed her daughter to continue crying a few moments before she touched her arm. The girl pulled away and offered her brother a watery smile in an effort to regain composure. He smiled back at her and said something that made her laugh. I could tell they were close and it was touching that he was trying to console her.

The father stepped forward and embraced his son. I saw the look of pride and suppressed agony that quickly crossed over the man's face as he held him. The hug was brief, but there was no doubt of the love that existed there.

There was a loud noise from the distance that made me jump. It had sounded almost like a battle horn.

"Grandma, what was that?"

She winked at me. "Just watch. The most important part is coming up." She pressed her fingers to her lips once again, and we turned our attention back to the family.

It seemed that everyone was in a flurry of activity as they made sure the young man had what he needed: food wrapped in cloth and an animal skin tied up like a blanket roll.

The father stepped forward then, holding a spear in his hands. He stared at the weapon for several seconds. Finally, he looked up at his son and passed the spear to him.

Something significant passed between them in that exchange. Something symbolic. I felt chills cover my arms.

Now I knew what I was seeing.

The boy turned and looked at his mother. He was no longer a young man—he was a warrior. I saw the briefest look of doubt cross his features as he looked to her, but she only smiled. She walked over and embraced him. When she pulled away there was moisture in her eyes but she was still smiling.

The young man smiled back at her and nodded as he squared his shoulders. In his eyes I could see a faith that was unshakable; the faith that his mother had placed there.

The family followed him as he began to make his way through the thicket, and Grandma motioned that we should fall in behind. In a few minutes we were past the undergrowth and on the edge of what appeared to be the center of an ancient city. But it wasn't the buildings that made me stare.

What I saw caused me to stop dead in my tracks: Over two thousand young men were congregating here. They were so young—some of them younger than me—yet they were warriors in every sense of the word. They were strong and noble and each had a light in his eyes that spoke of perfect faith. They were a royal army.

The story of the two thousand Stripling Warriors had always been one of my favorites. The fact that they were young and yet so strong and faithful had resonated with me each time I read the account. But to stand here, and actually see the event unfolding was something I knew I'd never forget.

A man whom I knew must be Helaman was on horseback in the center of the gathering crowd. Another man was on horseback next to him, holding the horn I'd heard earlier. He raised it to his lips and blew again, causing the same piercing battle call to echo throughout the city.

The sound caused a fresh wave of chills over my body. It was a call to arms. It was the sound of war.

I watched as Helaman began to organize the young men. From the scriptures I knew that he loved these boys like his own sons. I wished I could tell him not to worry; that not a single one of these boys would be lost.

I studied the face of each young man that passed and saw that none of them looked nervous or scared. They didn't need someone to tell them that they would be protected. They knew they would be. They had perfect faith.

I looked around and noticed the families bidding farewell. Each woman I saw held the same look of love, courage and absolute faith that I'd witnessed in the mother earlier. I couldn't believe these women weren't crying—not a single one! I'd seen more tears shed over a missionary leaving than I did here (and

I had to admit, I'd shed more than my fair share when Luke had left), but that was only two years. These boys were going off to war. Their families didn't know when or *if* they would return.

I studied the mothers again. These women who had raised and loved and taught their sons, who probably felt the sacrifice the most, were steadfast and immovable.

I felt warmth in my chest as I remembered the scripture that these young men did not fear death and had perfect faith, because their *mothers* had taught them.

⌒∾

"Well, Eliza, what did you think of that?" Grandma asked.

All at once we were sitting at my kitchen table back home.

"Wait!" I protested. "Do we have to leave already? That was one of the coolest things I've ever seen! I want to go back." I rubbed my eyes in an effort to recapture the image.

Grandma chuckled. "I thought you would like that, which is why I chose to remain silent. I wanted to allow you to soak in as much of the experience as possible."

"Thanks." I slouched in disappointment when I realized we weren't going back. Too bad these dreams didn't come with a rewind button.

"And I gather that you knew which story we were witnessing." It was statement rather than a question.

"The two thousand Sons of Helaman, of course," I said with just a hint of gloat.

"Correct. And why do you think I chose that account? What stood out to you?"

I was eager to recount the things I'd just seen. There was plenty to comment on, but when I reached the part about the mothers, Grandma stopped me.

"*That*, my dear, is exactly the thing I had hoped you would notice. Those mothers were the reason why I showed you this event. The Ammonites were some of the greatest people to ever walk the earth, and a large part of that can be attributed to the faith of their women."

"Yeah. I mean, you read about it, but until you've actually seen those women—wow!" I shook my head in wonder.

"Precisely. What better way to illustrate the second aim of Relief Society? Of 'Strengthening Families and Homes,' which is the reason I'm here tonight." Her blue eyes twinkled.

I glanced around for a moment. "And is there a reason why we're sitting at the kitchen table? Cause I gotta say, Grandma—not your best trick. You usually take me somewhere interesting in these dreams," I teased.

"Goodness me!" She placed a hand to her chest while trying to hide her amusement. "I can see that I've spoiled you far too much. You know there's a reason for everything I do." Grandma cast me a reproachful look before continuing.

"As I was saying before I was *interrupted*," she cleared her throat and I smiled, "I am here to help you to learn about the important, no—*imperative* need to strengthen the home and family."

Grandma's voice became serious and I felt as if her eyes were suddenly piercing into my soul. "Eliza, you're at a place in your life where you have many roads to choose, and choices to make that will shape your future. One of those choices will be the most crucial decision of your life: choosing an eternal companion."

My eyes widened. "Oh, Grandma—you know my situation with Luke and Sawyer? Have you come to tell me what to do? I've been praying and studying and trying to find the answer but nothing has come. I was planning on breaking up with Sawyer tomorrow and the thought just kills me . . . but I can't see any way around it. Everything is a mess. I'm so glad you're here to help!" I knew my voice was edging near hysterics but I was too desperate to care. Grandma would tell me what to do. She'd make everything better.

She listened to my torrential plea with an expression of concern. "Sweetheart, I would give anything in the world to take the hurt and confusion away from you, but I'm afraid it doesn't work that way."

My head dropped. For one brief moment I'd believed there would be an easy solution to my problems.

"I can't tell you what to do, or which choices to make in your life. That would be interfering with your agency and opportunities for growth. And I *certainly* wouldn't rob you of the wonderful privilege of choosing the man you will marry. That's something for you and your heart to decide, with the Lord's guidance."

She looked at me with sympathy. "Although it may seem like He's not listening, I promise that He hears you. You'll receive an answer when the time is right. As I said before, choosing your eternal companion is the biggest decision you'll ever make, and the Lord cares about that. You just have to trust Him and try to be patient."

I sighed and nodded my head. I knew Grandma was right, but it wasn't what I wanted to hear. I wanted answers *now*, before feelings were more deeply involved and the potential for hurt was greater. I wanted to rip the band-aid off, not suffer the agony of one small tug at a time.

Grandma smiled at me with soft eyes. "Eliza, you know the qualities you seek in a companion, and I know that you're not willing to settle for anyone who doesn't meet up to that standard. Remember your list?"

My head shot up. "How did you know about that?"

She smiled. "I know a lot of things, remember?"

The "list" she referred to was something I'd written in junior high and kept in my journal ever since. It was a compilation of qualities I wanted in a husband, beginning with the most important and moving on down.

"I think that list is right on track, but if I can offer some advice . . ."

I perked up and waited for her to continue. I would seize any morsel she was willing to toss on the subject.

"I would advise you to find someone who loves you the way you are, yet makes you want to be a better person. Someone who will be your friend as well as your sweetheart. Find a man who will treat you with love and respect, who understands that a successful relationship involves compromise and a great deal of selflessness."

She gazed at me. "There is no such person as 'Mr. Flawless.' We each have our weaknesses, but look for someone who has those qualities, and you can't go wrong."

"Okay." I felt deflated. Couldn't she have dropped me a little bone? Like, "Pick Sawyer," or, "Go team Luke!" Was that too much to ask?

"Choosing your companion and getting married is the season you're in right now. Naturally it will be occupying most of your thoughts, but tonight I'd like to focus on another subject. One that certainly applies to you as it will pertain to the largest portion of your life."

As much as I didn't want to move away from the topic of marriage, Grandma's words had me curious.

"I'm talking about what happens *after* you're married: becoming a mother and raising your family."

"Oh." I tried not to sound disappointed, but didn't I already hear enough about this in Relief Society? Motherhood seemed so far away. I would worry about that when it happened.

Grandma sensed my lack of interest and her face grew serious. "Eliza, I know you feel that this doesn't apply to you yet, but what you don't realize is that the time to prepare is *now*. Motherhood is the greatest calling you'll ever receive on this earth, and the need for noble and strong women has never been greater. We are at war." She spoke with force and I felt a slow chill rise up my back.

"Never in the history of the earth has Satan waged such a fierce attack on the family. As the time for the Savior's return draws closer, the adversary is doing his utmost to destroy this most fundamental unit of society. And sadly, he is doing a good job of it."

"The Lord is calling on His special forces—the righteous women of the world—to guard and protect their families. Your husband and children will be faced with the dark and evil influences surrounding them at work and at school. It's up to *you* to make your home a refuge. You must be fierce and unwavering, just as those Ammonite women were. They were constant in teaching and raising their children in the way of truth, so that when they were called to battle, those boys were ready for it. The mothers weren't afraid, because they knew they had done everything they could to prepare and empower their sons."

I was stunned into silence by the intensity of Grandma's words. Something deep inside felt pierced by the truth of what she was saying. I would be raising my children in a spiritually corrosive world. I had to prepare them for the battles they would face each day. The thought was overwhelming.

As if reading my thoughts, she continued, "You won't be alone in this task. The Lord will be on your side and will guide you daily with the things you'll need to do to help each individual in your family. The catch is—*you* have to be doing the things that will allow Him to guide you. And you know what those things are."

I nodded. "Primary answers, right?"

"Right." She smiled. "I have the greatest confidence in you. You've already been making changes to increase in faith and understanding. It's a constant process, but remember that it's those small, daily steps of prayer, scripture study, and serving others that will make the biggest difference in the end."

Grandma looked away from me and gestured around the room. "And don't forget the power of spending time together: sharing meals, establishing traditions, and family home evenings are a great way to do that. Limit the extracurricular and other unimportant things that can get in the way of spending time with family. In the end, those things aren't important. Simplicity is the key."

Her words reminded me of something. "Speaking of keys, Grandma—I noticed you didn't show me a dream token last time. Was there one?"

She shook her head. "Now that you're an adult you must learn to find the meaning of these dreams without a token to remind you. Life is full of teaching moments if you learn how to recognize them." She winked at me.

"While there are leaders and friends in the ward to help you, things will be different than they were when you were a teenager. There won't always be someone to carry you along; now you must find your own faith and gain your own personal understanding of the teachings and experiences that are presented to you."

I nodded. "That makes sense."

"And one last thing, Eliza . . ." There was an unusual intensity in Grandma's eyes that made me feel uneasy. "Don't forget about your family now. They're going to need your help more than ever in these next few months."

"What are you talking about?" My thoughts instantly went to my mom. The question hung in the air as Grandma's kind face faded from view and everything went dark.

CHAPTER

nineteen

"How did you sleep last night?" Sawyer asked.

We were on our way to church Sunday morning. I couldn't seem to get away from nine o'clock church no matter where I was. The early morning rush hadn't allowed time for conversation and this was the first time Sawyer had spoken to me.

"I slept . . . pretty well, I guess. How about you? Was the couch okay?" I tried to gauge his feelings. He didn't seem to be as upset as he'd been last night, and I wished he didn't look so handsome in his white shirt and pale blue tie. It was distracting me from the unavoidable task ahead.

"The couch was fine, but I tossed and turned all night because I couldn't stop thinking." He glanced at me. "Eliza, I'm so sorry about the way I acted last night. I was a total idiot, reacting the way I did. I never should have tried to push you into feeling or saying something you weren't ready for. I know I totally freaked you out, and I'm sorry. Can you forgive me?" His blue eyes were filled with remorse.

My heart felt like something had just jabbed it. "Of course I forgive you! I was worried you were mad at *me*. I feel like I'm the one who needs to apologize." These weren't the words I should be saying right now, but I wouldn't have him blaming himself. I was the one who'd decided to date him until Luke came home, and I was the one responsible for any pain involved.

He grinned in relief and reached over to take my hand, pulling it up to his lips for a kiss. "I was miserable last night. I almost texted you to come down and talk, but I didn't want to risk the wrath of your dad."

I laughed. "Yeah, that's not a pretty sight. Trust me."

We arrived at the church and Sawyer walked around to get my door. I questioned whether it had been wise to bring him to my home ward. Gossip and speculation would really be buzzing now! But it didn't matter. Sawyer was a friend. I hoped that after my conversation with him later he would still consider me one.

∼

I was in my room packing my bag when Courtney popped her head in. "Mind if I come in?"

I turned and smiled. "Nope. I'm just finishing up."

She entered the room and plopped herself on my bed. "You should have heard the way my friends at church were talking about Sawyer. They all think he's totally hot." She rolled her eyes.

I was grateful for this chance to talk. I knew Courtney didn't like Sawyer and I wanted to know why. "Court, what is it about Sawyer that bugs you?" I asked.

She looked up at me quickly and then darted her eyes away. "He doesn't bug me."

"Whatever! You've been totally rude to him this whole time. You've never acted this way with my dates before. What's going on?"

She picked a feather out of the down comforter on my bed. "I haven't been rude to him."

"*Court,*" I warned.

"Fine, I don't like him alright? So sue me." She blew the feather away and crossed her arms.

"But, why?" I asked again. "I'm not mad at you or anything, I just want to know why you don't like him."

Her eyes finally met mine and she shrugged. "He's not right for you, Liza. You and Luke are like total soul mates and I don't know why you're throwing that away. He gets home so soon and you're going to ruin everything."

Her words stung. "I know. I've totally made a mess of things . . . but don't worry. Sawyer is just a friend, nothing more."

She raised her eyebrows. "Uh, I saw you guys making out in the family room Friday night and you brought him home to meet *mom* and *dad*. I'd say you're a little more than just friends."

I cringed and tossed a pillow at her. "You little sneak, were you spying on us?"

"No! I'd left my iPod in by the couch and went to get it, but I changed my mind after seeing you two glued together. So gross."

I laughed at her repulsed expression. "Okay, well you have a point about the friend thing. I guess what I meant was, we'll only be friends," I paused, "*after* today." My heart felt a sharp pang as I glanced up at the clock. Sawyer was probably already packed and waiting for me downstairs. There was no more putting this off.

"Ohh, I see." Courtney looked at me and smiled in a knowing way. "Well I'm glad. Good luck with that."

"Thanks." I couldn't muster a smile in return. I didn't see anything to be happy about in the situation. "Sorry I can't chat with you longer. I want to hear how your summer's going and everything. Any boys I need to know about?"

She gave a secretive smirk. "Maybe. I'll tell you about it later though."

I raised my eyebrows, but didn't press her. I knew she'd tell me about her boy issues when she was ready. If I pried too much she would only back away. "Okay. Promise me you'll be smart though. Remember, you're not sixteen yet."

She rolled her eyes. "Don't worry, mom and dad only tell me that like every-other-second."

"I'm sure they do, but it's because they love you." I smiled as I reached over to give her a hug. "See you soon, okay?"

"Okay." she smiled back at me. "Maybe I can even come up and stay with you for a few days?" she asked hopefully.

"I don't think mom and dad would go for that, but maybe. We'll see."

I turned and started for the door when Courtney's voice stopped me. "Liza, I hope you know I do think Sawyer's a nice guy, and I admit he is pretty hot," she added wryly. "But he's not Luke."

I considered her words for a moment and then nodded with a small wave before leaving the room. Not Luke. Of course he wasn't; no one was like Luke. I just had to keep repeating that to myself so I could find the words I needed to end things with Sawyer.

I walked down the hall to my parents' room. Ever since my dream last night I'd wanted to talk to my mom. When I reached her room I saw that it was empty. Undoubtedly she was downstairs keeping Sawyer company as he waited for me to finish packing.

I was right. I entered the living room to find Sawyer talking with my mom. He had removed his tie, but was still wearing his slacks and white shirt with the sleeves rolled up. My heart jumped a little as he looked at me and smiled.

This would be so much easier if he was unattractive.

"Ready to go?" he asked.

"Yeah, um . . . would you mind taking my bag out to the car? I just want to say good bye to my mom."

She gave me an apologetic smile. "Sorry Dad couldn't be here to see you off. He had some meetings he couldn't miss."

"It's okay, I already said goodbye to him at church."

Sawyer picked up my bag and extended his hand to my mom. "It was so nice of you to let me stay here this weekend, Mrs. Moore. Thanks for your hospitality."

Mom ignored his hand and reached over to give him a hug. "You're welcome here anytime, Sawyer. It was a pleasure to have you."

He hugged her back with his free arm and smiled at me over her shoulder.

When she pulled away he turned to me and said, "I'll just wait for you in the car, okay?"

"Kay, I'll be right there."

Mom leaned in to hug me next. "Thank you so much for spending the weekend with us, honey."

"It was fun. I'm glad we came," I said as I returned the hug.

Once the door closed behind Sawyer, she pulled away from me and whispered, "He's a fine young man, Liza. I can see why you like him."

"Yeah." I looked away, not wanting to talk about my relationship with Sawyer at the moment. "So, Mom . . . can you tell me something?"

"Sure, what is it?" She smiled at me warmly and I saw a fleeting resemblance to Grandma.

I looked her straight in the eyes. "Is everything okay? With you, I mean?"

A guarded look crossed her face before she wiped it away with a smile. "Of course; why do you ask?"

I wasn't going to beat around the bush anymore. I placed a hand on my hip and raised an eyebrow. "I saw you crying last night. What's going on?"

She frowned. "I'm sorry you had to see that, honey, but I promise everything is fine. I just haven't been feeling . . . quite myself these past few weeks. Your father wants me to have some tests done to make sure that everything is . . . normal, but I really don't think that's necessary. With a little more rest I'm sure it will blow over."

As soon as mom had said the word "tests" I knew we were both thinking the same thing: Both my Grandma and my aunt had died of breast cancer.

"Well I agree with Dad. You need to go in and make sure nothing is wrong." I tried to keep the strain from my voice, but I felt a nagging in the pit of my stomach.

"Don't worry, honey. I've been getting my routine mammogram for years and nothing has ever looked suspicious. I'm sure everything's fine."

"Just promise me you'll get a check-up, okay? I'm sure it's nothing too, I just . . . want to make sure."

She sighed. "All right, I promise. Now go on out there before poor Sawyer melts in the heat. I'll call you soon."

"Okay. Love you." I gave her one last smile before heading out the door.

"Love you, too!" she called.

Sawyer was waiting in the car with the air conditioner on. He smiled at me through the windshield and I took a deep breath.

Here goes nothing.

CHAPTER

twenty

The drive back to school took an hour, and for the first thirty minutes we
made small talk about the weekend. He had been holding my hand, rub-
bing his thumb across the backs of my knuckles as we talked.

I felt sick to my stomach and almost decided to put the conversation off
until tomorrow . . . or over the phone . . . or maybe just a text like a kid in junior high would do. I couldn't seem to get up the nerve to say the words. A lay-
er of sweat began to form on my upper lip.

"So is your family always like that?" Sawyer asked, distracting me from
my thoughts.

"Like what?"

"You know . . . giving each other hugs, having 'family game night', re-
unions and stuff?"

"Yeah, I guess so. Why?" I gave him a puzzled look.

"Wow, that's . . . wow." He shook his head.

"What? Doesn't your family do stuff like that?" We weren't perfect, but I
considered my family pretty normal.

"No."

I stared at him, realizing again that I knew little about Sawyer's back-
ground.

"I thought maybe they were just putting on an act to impress me, but you're serious that it's always like that?" He glanced away from the road to look at me.

"Yep. We're a pretty touchy-feely group. I have mostly my mom to thank for that. She's big on 'togetherness.'" I smiled as I thought of how she always insisted we do things as a family, even when Courtney and I were ready to tear each other's hair out.

Sawyer looked thoughtful as his eyes focused on the freeway. I wanted to ask him more about his family, but he changed the subject. "So what do you want to do tonight?"

Here it was: my opening.

"I was thinking I could make you dinner. Believe it or not, I make a pretty mean fettuccini." He smiled and looked over at me, but misinterpreted the uncomfortable expression on my face. "That is . . . unless you're sick of me?"

I quickly shook my head. "No, it's not that at all, Sawyer. It's just . . ." the words seemed frozen on my tongue. I was mute! I reached over and turned the air conditioner up a notch. Why was it suddenly so hot?

"It's just what?" he asked, his voice growing soft.

I was going to vomit, right here all over his leather interior. I knew I shouldn't have started to say something.

"It's just that you don't think we should see each other anymore, is that it?" he continued quietly; his eyes never leaving the freeway.

It was silent for a full minute before I squeaked out a timid, "Yes."

Sawyer remained silent. His jaw was set as he flashed his blinker to change lanes.

After a few moments of the agonizing quiet, I finally found the nerve to speak. "How did you know that's what I was going to say?"

He gave a short laugh. "Oh I don't know—maybe because we've only known each other for a month and in that time you've already tried to end things with me twice—no, *three* times. It was a lucky guess."

"Sawyer, I'm so sorry. You are one of the most incredible guys I've ever known and it's not what I want, but after last night . . ."

"Did you just hear yourself, Eliza? You said it's not what you want. So why are you doing this?"

I stopped short. "I did?"

"Yes, you did."

"Well I didn't mean . . ."

"Look, I know what you're going to say. We've been down this road before. I know the turmoil you've been feeling and seeing Luke's little sister last night was probably the last straw. It hasn't been fair of me to do this to you, and I'm sorry."

I was silent as he changed lanes again. He wasn't going to fight me this time. Maybe he wanted to be the one to break up with me to save face. That was fine with me; it would help me feel like less of a jerk. But now that things were officially ending between us, the hurt began seeping into my chest. I hated this.

"I did a lot of thinking last night." Sawyer looked over at me and gave a half-hearted smile. "I sort of expected this conversation to happen today, even though I hoped it wouldn't. You've put up with me for long enough already, and I don't have any right to ask—but I'm hoping you'll do me one last favor."

"What's that?" At that moment I would have done almost anything to erase the sadness behind his eyes.

"Go on one more date with me before you break things off."

"Sawyer, I really don't think that's a good idea."

"Please, Eliza. Just one date—that's all I ask." His blue eyes were pleading now.

I shut my eyes and turned away. "I know I sound heartless, but I just can't do that." I felt a lump forming in my throat, making it hard to say the words.

"I promise not to call or text you or sit by you in class anymore. Just give me that date."

I dug my fingernails into my palms. "I can't do it because my heart can't take it, Sawyer! Don't you get that? It was hard enough for me to find the courage to have this conversation. You were right; I *don't* want to break up with you. I don't want to stop seeing you every day. I don't want to end things between us, because I . . . I care about you."

My frustration had built into anger. He was forcing me to say things I wanted left unsaid. It wasn't doing any good to confess my feelings, and it would be even worse to drag the pain out longer. This band-aid needed to be ripped off. Now. I couldn't stand to prolong it.

Sawyer was completely silent as he pulled into the parking lot of my apartment complex.

My breathing came faster than usual as the adrenaline from my tirade took over. All I wanted was to get out of this car and never look back. I wanted to close the door and leave all of my feelings for Sawyer and the hurt I was causing him behind me like a bad dream.

He put the car in park and turned off the ignition. "Let me help you with your bag."

"Thanks." I struggled to make my voice level.

He came around and opened my door before getting my small duffel out of the trunk. I gave him a weak smile and reached for the bag, but he held it back.

"I got it."

We walked up the stairs toward my apartment. Neither one of us said a word; our footsteps the only sound as they echoed through the hallway.

I wished Sawyer would say something. The air around me seemed heavy and uncomfortable with his silence.

We reached the door and he set my bag down. Before I knew what was happening, he took my face in both of his hands and kissed me.

This kiss was different from the others. It tasted like sadness. He pulled away, his breathing unsteady as he looked at the ground. "You win, Eliza. It's over. I won't bother you anymore."

My mouth dropped open, but I didn't have time to respond. He had already turned and started walking down the hall. I watched his retreating figure. He never once looked back. His broad shoulders were set in determination and he raked a hand through his hair before getting into his car.

I watched Monet do a double take in the parking lot when she saw him drive by.

It was over. Just like that.

I couldn't believe he had finally let me break up with him. I couldn't believe I'd been stupid enough to break up with him. My heart felt like it had been pummeled and then steam-rolled flat.

The tears I'd been keeping in check came in a rush as I picked up my bag and stepped into the apartment.

I was relieved to find that no one was home. This way I could have a good, long cry without having to hide in the bathroom. When had I become such a bawl baby? I couldn't seem to help it.

I flung myself on my bed, releasing the pent up sobs in my chest. It seemed like the tears would never stop.

If only I had a letter from Luke, I knew I would feel better. It had been weeks since his last letter, and I just needed to hear from him. To feel that connection again and know that he still loved me.

My crying had finally subsided into hiccups when I heard the apartment door open, followed by the lively conversation of my roommates. A quick glance in the mirror at my red eyes and streaked makeup told me that I needed to do something, quick. Otherwise I'd face a full-blown interrogation and I wasn't up to that right now.

I darted down the hall and into the bathroom. A nice long shower would make me feel better and hopefully wipe away the evidence of my sob-fest. I allowed the hot water to run over my face, imagining that it was rinsing my heartache as well as my tears down the drain. The imagery made me feel better, and after about fifteen minutes I felt somewhat human again.

I stepped out of the shower and reached for my towel, vigorously scrubbing my face to remove any telltale makeup streaks that may have been left behind. As I dried I noticed the sweet, fruity scent of Charlotte's shampoo I'd borrowed. I had to get some of that stuff the next time I was at a salon; it really did make my hair feel silkier.

I continued to dry off the rest of my body as my thoughts trailed back to Sawyer. I was so distracted that it took me a full five seconds to realize that both of my arms and one leg were streaked green; *neon* green.

I screamed and jumped around, trying to find the source of the stain.

My roommates came running and banged on the door.

"Eliza, are you okay? What's going on?" Bree called.

I quickly wrapped the towel around myself and realized my mistake a moment too late: A shower of powdery substance fell from the towel and around my feet. It instantly turned green as it made contact with the water on my skin. That fruity smell wasn't Charlotte's shampoo—it was Kool-Aid.

"Oh my heck, you guys!" I yelled. Realizing that the worst damage had already been done, I furiously wrapped the towel tighter and opened the door.

All three of my roommates screamed and backed away. I caught a reflection of my bright green face in the mirror, and that coupled with their horrified expressions finally made me crack.

I tried to stay angry, but I couldn't help myself. I snorted, and then burst into laughter.

Charlotte and Lacey continued to stare, but Bree was already giggling.

"Eliza, what did you do? What *is* that stuff?" Lacey demanded. She was looking at me like I was some kind of bottled science experiment.

"It's Kool-Aid—and I'll give you one guess who put it on my towel," I said between fits of laughter. I had no idea why I was laughing when I should be furious. Maybe I really was cracking up. At the moment, crazy seemed a nice alternative to miserable. It felt good to release the tension I'd been holding in all day.

Charlotte began to laugh with me, but as soon as I'd mentioned the prank, Bree's smile faded. Lacey looked downright menacing.

"I'll kill 'em," she said as she went to investigate the other towels. Sure enough, each one had been generously sprinkled with what looked like invisible Kool-Aid. I had been the lucky winner to shower first.

"I hope you're satisfied, Lacey," Bree fumed. "Look at poor Eliza! What if her skin stays like that for weeks?"

I choked. "Don't say that! It's going to wash off . . . isn't it?" I wasn't comforted by the quick, worried glances they gave each other. "Oh man, you guys—someone say this stuff is going to wash off." I felt a nervous pinch in my chest as I stared at my face in the mirror. Finals were coming up and I couldn't afford to miss class, but there was no *way* I was going out in public like this. It looked like I was trying out for the cast of *Wicked*.

"I'll Google it," Bree said quickly.

"Good idea." Lacey nodded. "In the meantime, Eliza, I think maybe you should try taking another shower. I'll find you a clean towel."

I could tell she was feeling guilty about the situation.

Charlotte gave me a sympathetic smile. "You can use my shampoo if you want to; as much as you need."

"Thanks, I just used some, but I don't think I'll need to wash my hair again." Fortunately I hadn't dried off my hair before I discovered the prank. At least one part of my body wasn't ghoulish.

A loud knock sounded at the front door and I stepped further into the bathroom. "If it's for me, I'm not home," I whispered.

Charlotte nodded and disappeared into the front room. I listened at the door, straining to hear. Maybe Sawyer had come back.

I was disappointed to hear a girl's voice, and then mad at myself for being disappointed. *It's done, get over it.* My head got the point, but my heart wasn't convinced.

I was about to close the door and commence shower number two, when Charlotte came back and whispered, "There's a girl here who said she has something for you. I told her you were busy and offered to take whatever it is, but she said she wanted to deliver it in person and would wait. What do you want me to do?"

I frowned. "What does she look like?"

"She's really pretty; looks like she's about our age. Do you want me to go ask her name?"

Jill! A smile spread across my face. She had texted this morning to say she wanted to talk and she must have driven here to surprise me.

"No, it's fine, I know who it is." I clutched the towel and ran down the hall for my bedroom. Jill would think my green skin was hilarious and would probably give us some great ideas for a comeback. I threw my robe on, thankful that it was washable, and hurried back down the hall. When I reached the living room, I stopped short. The girl waiting for me visibly started.

"Oh my!" She stepped back in fear. "I-I'm sorry, I just wasn't expecting . . . are you okay?"

My face flushed a deep red, and I briefly wondered what a blush looked like on green skin. Probably a nasty, mottled brown like when you mix green and red paint together.

I had never seen this girl before, but Charlotte had been right—she was *very* pretty, which made me feel all the more embarrassed to be standing there like a slimy toad.

"I'm looking for Eliza Moore, are you . . . ? Is she here?" She tried not to stare with her wide brown eyes, but she was losing the battle.

"I'm Eliza. Sorry about this," I gestured at myself in general. "It's a long story, but I thought you were someone else so I came out of hiding." I gave her an apologetic smile. "My friend said you have something for me?" I had no idea who this girl was or why she couldn't have spared me this humiliation by giving whatever she had to Charlotte.

My roommates tried to act casual as they made their way to the kitchen, but I knew they were coming in to eavesdrop.

The girl smiled back at me, and I saw something like satisfaction in her eyes. Now that she was over the initial shock she seemed almost happy to know that I was the person she was looking for. "It's nice to meet you, Eliza. My name is Olivia Chambers." She reached out and shook my hand.

This was starting to get weird. No one besides old people shook your hand when they introduced themselves . . . and why was she looking at me like that?

"I served with Elder Matthews and I got home just a few weeks ago. He asked me to mail this letter, but I was in the area and thought I'd just bring it in person."

Old people and missionaries. *Missionaries* shook hands like that. My brain tried to process that this beautiful girl had seen Luke just a few weeks ago; had talked to him and probably smiled at him with those pretty brown eyes.

"Thanks . . . that's really nice of you." My fingers felt numb as I reached out to take the letter. "So you served a mission with Luke? How well did you know him?" Realizing I didn't want to hear the answer to that question, I quickly corrected myself, "I mean . . . how is he? Is he excited to come home?"

"Oh everyone *loved* Elder Matthews." There was an eager sparkle in her eyes. "He's practically legend for being such an amazing missionary. You should be really proud of him."

I hated the condescending way she said that. I hated the fact that this girl had seen Luke and knew things about him that I didn't. I hated that she'd been holding on to that letter for who knew how long, and I hated that she was here in my living room looking all gorgeous while I stood in a robe with wet hair and a green face. It was as if my skin had taken on an outward manifestation of the way that I felt: insane jealousy!

"I *am* proud of him, and thanks so much for stopping by to bring me the letter." I began walking toward the door to hint that I was ready for her to leave. "He was so thoughtful to want to get it to me right away; especially since we'll be seeing each other so soon." I couldn't help but throw a little barb in. I hoped she caught my meaning that Luke was already spoken for.

"Yes, he definitely is thoughtful," she stated as if she knew. I thought she was probably baiting me, but by the way she'd said it I began to doubt.

"Take care of yourself, Eliza. It was nice to finally meet you in person." She looked me up and down and then flashed a quick smile before turning to leave, her dark hair shining in the porch light.

"Holy Smokes . . . for a second there I thought she was going to take a picture of you with her phone," Lacey said as I closed the door and locked it.

All three of my roommates stared at me as they waited for my reaction. I was still clutching Luke's letter, causing green fingermarks to appear on the envelope.

Another minute passed; the only sound the ticking of the clock on the kitchen wall. I finally turned to Bree. "Did you find out how to get rid of Kool-Aid stains?"

She relaxed into a grin. "Yes! You just use toothpaste like soap and it should come off."

I nodded. "Good. Now somebody get me some toothpaste."

⤸

Thirty minutes later I was sitting on my bed reading through Luke's letter. My skin was red and tingling and I smelled like a giant peppermint stick, but I'd managed to remove every last trace of the Kool-Aid.

I hadn't spoken to my roommates because I still didn't feel up to telling them about my breakup with Sawyer—or about the gorgeous returned sister missionary who was on friendly terms with Luke.

After my shower I'd emerged from the bathroom and heard their whispers in the living room come to an abrupt halt. I knew they were all itching to talk to me about this unexpected development, but they would respect my space until I was ready.

My fingers trembled slightly as I opened the envelope and pulled out Luke's letter.

All during my shower I'd imagined the worst: that he had fallen for this girl and was writing to tell me things were over. But if that was the case, surely he wouldn't be so cruel as to send her as messenger?

I'd noticed that she'd said he had asked her to mail the letter for him, yet she'd chosen to deliver it in person. Probably so she could get a good look at me, the little weasel!

I cringed as I pictured her frightened face when I'd walked in the room. It would be funny if it weren't so depressing. If only I could have entered looking stunning, and made her feel like she couldn't compete. That triumphant look in her eyes was all I needed to know that she felt she'd already won.

Darn that Drew! I had been on Bree's side and was all for stopping the pranks, but now I wanted revenge and I wanted it bad. Someone had to pay for this.

I sighed as I finally unfolded the paper in my hands. If it was bad news, I may as well get it over with.

Eliza,

Today I found out one of the missionaries from
the States is going home soon and I was totally stoked
because that means I can get a letter to you.

It sounds like school is going really well. I'm proud of you
for accepting that calling. Don't think that those small acts
of service don't matter. Sometimes it's the little things that
make the most difference in a person's life. It's awesome that
you're working to strengthen your spirituality. We all have our
ups and downs—it's just human nature—but I'm impressed that
you're aware and doing your best. You're an amazing girl, Liza.

I've been thinking about you more than ever these past
few days. For some reason, I've been having weird dreams
and they've kind of been freaking me out. I hope you're okay;
you've been in my prayers just in case (actually you've
always been in my prayers, but I still hope you're okay).

Man, I can't wait to see you! It seems like an eternity
since we've been together, but then again, I almost feel
like we've never really been separated. I guess that's
because I left a part of me with you and I feel like I've
had a part of you with me these past two years.

I know I go on and on about how much you mean to me, but
don't worry, I'm still focusing on the work here. I feel like I'm
in the last push to find and teach as many people as I can. I
think I've even run poor Elder Martinez ragged, and believe
me, that's no small accomplishment. The guy has more energy
than should be humanly possible! But he's a good sport and
he knows how much these last few weeks mean to me.

It's crazy because now I'm fluent in the language, and have finally grasped the vision of this incredible work we're doing. I'm not afraid to talk to anyone, and I feel a closeness to the Spirit like I've never felt before. I can suddenly see things so clearly. Almost like looking at the world around me from a completely focused perspective, and I realize how blurry that perspective was before.

I've been guided to find people and to say things that I know are independent of my own thoughts. This gospel is amazing, and I want everyone to know it! I want everyone to feel the joy that I feel and I want to build the Lord's kingdom in whatever capacity that I can.

There is so much opposition and adversity out there. This world we live in is a mess; but I don't want to sit down and do nothing about it—I want to fight! Our souls are precious and I don't want Satan to have the victory of gaining even one of these special children of God. I feel so blessed to be in this position, and to dedicate all that I have to this work while there's still time left. And I want to do everything I can to keep fighting when I return home.

Do you know what the best part is, though? I know that you'll help me to do just that. You've always made me want to be a better person, Liza. You have so much faith and I can't wait until the day when we can serve a mission together (I hope!). So take care of yourself, because you've got my heart and if anything happened to you my heart would have no desire to keep beating.

I love you, beautiful girl. See you in a few weeks!

Love,

Luke

I pressed the letter to my chest and smiled through my tears. Luke still loved me. He was one of the most incredible guys on the planet and he loved *me*.

I was so anxious to see him again I could hardly stand it. I felt like receiving this letter had been a sign. (Ha-ha, Sister Chambers!) Unbeknownst to her, she'd given me the very answer I'd needed tonight: reassurance that I'd done the right thing in ending my relationship with Sawyer.

Now I could move forward feeling absolutely no pain at his loss.

I smiled and kissed Luke's letter before placing it in the secret box under my bed.

I could hear my roommates in the kitchen talking and laughing as usual. That was a good sign; it meant they'd moved on from worrying about me. I would talk to them tomorrow after class and tell them about my break-up. Right now all I wanted to do was climb into bed and crash.

After my scripture study and prayers I couldn't resist. I picked up my cell phone and looked to see if I'd missed a call or text from Sawyer. My phone hadn't been on silent, but I wanted to check . . . just in case.

My hurt stung when I saw the empty screen. I told it to behave. There was no reason why I should expect to hear from him. Dating 101: A guy usually didn't try to contact a girl after she'd dumped him.

I hopped into bed and shut my eyes, forcing my brain to think about Luke and his sweet letter. I just wished I could plug my heart into my brain and force it to be logical. Sawyer was an incredible guy and I had . . . l-liked . . . him, but he wasn't right for me.

I had absolutely no reason to be broken-hearted. No reason at all.

CHAPTER

twenty-one

The next morning I arrived to history class early, once again pretending to myself that it wasn't because of Sawyer; it *wasn't* because I missed him and it wasn't because I wanted to see if he would sit by me today.

I had even put Luke's letter in my backpack as a reminder that I had no reason to feel broken-hearted.

I looked up just as Sawyer walked into the classroom and our eyes met. My face flushed and I quickly looked away, but I was all-too aware that he was walking up the stairs toward my row. I'd intentionally sat next to an empty desk in case he decided to sit next to me. I tried to steady my pulse as I imagined what I would say to him. He would be turning down the row any moment.

I realized I was holding my breath, so I slowly blew it out. When I couldn't take the suspense any longer, I finally hazarded another look. He reached my row, but didn't stop. He was making eye contact and waving at someone a few rows behind me. I glanced back and saw a guy return the wave and gesture to an empty seat beside him. Sawyer nodded and made his way down that row, without a single glance in my direction.

It felt like someone had kicked me in the stomach. Things were officially over now. Sawyer was moving on with his life and I had been nothing more than a tiny bump on the path. He probably hadn't lain awake last night, wondering if he should call me. In fact, by the look Monet had given him yesterday, I was sure he already had a string of dates lined up for the week.

Well good for him.

I opened my binder and reviewed my notes as I waited for class to start. I noticed Darren Fields come into class and felt his gaze resting on me, but I didn't care. I almost hoped he would come and sit by me just to see how Sawyer would react.

Stop it, Liza! I scolded myself. *Now you're just being childish.*

I straightened my shoulders and resumed studying my notes. Finals were around the corner and I was grateful to have a reason to immerse myself in the material.

Darren didn't sit by me, but I could sense that he was looking from Sawyer to me and back again all throughout class. Professor Gunner droned on and on. Once the hour was finally over I grabbed my bag and left as quickly as possible.

Monet: *Hey, I'm just gonna grab a snack and then I'll be over to get you, ok?*
Me: *Sounds good.*

Monet was my visiting teaching partner and this was the first time we were going out to do visits. The girls we were assigned to visit, Jodi and Sarah, both lived in our complex. I didn't know either of them very well, but I was eager for a distraction.

It had been three days since my breakup with Sawyer. Three days of sheer torture. I hated seeing him in class while both of us tried to pretend the other didn't exist. At least, *I* was pretending. He hadn't so much as blinked an eye in my direction. What hurt even more was that he seemed happy. Not that I wanted him to suffer and be miserable like I was—ah, who was I kidding? That's exactly what I wanted.

I knew it was selfish to feel that way, especially when I had been the one to break things off, but I had missed him like crazy these past few days and it was eating me alive that he didn't seem to feel the same way.

A knock sounded a moment before Monet walked in. "Eliza, are you ready?"

"Yeah." I stood from my spot at the kitchen table. "That was a fast snack."

She shrugged. "A granola bar. I just needed something to hold me over until dinner, you know?"

Actually I didn't know. I hadn't had much of an appetite these past few days, but I nodded anyway. We walked out of the apartment and down the hall together.

"We're going to visit Jodi first, and then Sarah right after. Do you have the lesson?"

I nodded and held up my phone. It was handy to have the Church materials app. I'd read the Visiting Teaching message between classes today.

"Awesome." She paused for a few moments. "So—I haven't seen Sawyer around much lately. Is he out of town or something?"

My gut wrenched at the mention of his name. I stared at the pavement as we continued walking. "No, he hasn't been gone. We . . . broke up."

"Really?" Monet's head snapped around to look at me. "When did this happen?"

"A few days ago . . . it's still kind of a touchy subject." I felt my hackles rise. She was trying hard to hide it, but her eagerness was almost palpable.

"I'm sorry. Breakups are the worst." She gave me a sympathetic smile, but it didn't hide the excited glimmer in her eyes. "Let me know if you ever need a shoulder to cry on, okay?"

"Thanks." I avoided looking at her as I knocked on the door to Jodi's apartment; a little harder than I meant to. I needed something to take my thoughts off of the negative track they were on with Monet.

After a few moments, the door opened and a girl our age peeked out from the crack.

"Hi, Jodi!" Monet said cheerfully. "I'm Monet and this is Eliza. Is it okay if we come in for a minute?"

Jodi stared at us for another long second before nodding and opening the door wider. I cast Monet a quick, curious glance before following her into the apartment.

"Wow, your place is so nice and clean," Monet remarked, trying to find the positive. The apartment *was* clean . . . spotless even.

Our apartment and those of the other girls I'd gotten to know all had pictures, posters, and other random décor attributed to college life. We hadn't wasted any time making our surroundings our own. Jodi's apartment was completely bare . . . not a picture or rug to be found. It felt empty and sterile.

Jodi folded her arms across her chest and wordlessly sat on an armchair. I shifted my weight and looked at Monet.

"Is it okay if we sit down?" she asked Jodi with a questioning smile.

"Sure."

I let out a tiny breath of relief and sank into the couch beside Monet. The negative feelings I'd had quickly evaporated into gratitude that she was handling the awkward situation so well.

"So, thanks for taking time to let us stop by. Are the rest of your roommates around?" Monet asked.

"I only have one roommate and she's at work right now," Jodi replied.

"That's cool, so you each get your own room?" Monet was working hard to make conversation.

Jodi nodded. She still had her arms folded in an "I'm-only-putting-up-with-this-for-a-few-minutes-so-make-it-quick" way. I wondered that she'd agreed to let us come at all; her overall vibe was not a welcoming one.

It took only a few of Monet's friendly questions to discern that Jodi and her roommate did not get along. Judging by Jodi's behavior my heart went out to the poor girl that shared the apartment, but to be fair, I only had half of the story.

After a few more minutes of Monet's failed attempts at getting Jodi to warm up to us, she finally turned and gave me a pointed look. "Well, Eliza, we don't want to take too much of Jodi's time. Why don't you go ahead and read the message?"

"Okay." I fumbled to unlock my screen and retrieve the article, reading through the brief message as quickly as possible. It was on the importance of family. My palms got sweaty as I noticed Jodi's mouth pull from a frown into a downright grimace. Had I offended her? I nervously shared a few of my own thoughts and a brief testimony of the importance of family; drawing heavily from my recent dream with Grandma. After closing, I cleared my throat and was about to stand when Monet spoke up.

"Jodi, I forgot to ask where you're from. Do you have family close by?"

The question seemed to catch her off guard, and there was the tiniest bit of sadness beneath the annoyance. Several moments of silence followed and I instinctively tightened my stomach muscles at the awkwardness of it.

Finally, Jodi gave a faint answer. "I'm from Iowa. That's where my mom and younger brothers live. My parents got divorced a few months ago. My dad cheated on my mom and now he lives in Boston with his girlfriend."

I was wrong about there not being anything in this apartment. There must have been a clock in the kitchen, because I could hear it ticking as Monet and I sat in stunned silence. The icy wall that had separated us from Jodi now opened up a crack and I saw a tiny glimpse of her pain. My heart ached for her. I couldn't imagine what she must have been dealing with, and I'd just thrown salt in the wound by giving her a lesson all about family.

An apology was on my lips, when Jodi began to cry. Monet went over and put an arm around her, allowing her to release the pain. I spotted a box of tissues in the kitchen and went to get some. It was the only thing I could think to do. In the few seconds it took to grab them, I said a silent prayer asking for guidance.

A warm feeling flowed through me. As I handed Jodi the tissues and she gave a small smile, that feeling grew. Monet and I sat back down on the couch as Jodi started talking.

The ice was melting.

That night when I said my prayers, it was with sincere gratitude. The rest of our visit with Jodi had gone much better than I could have imagined. We weren't able to solve her problems or take away the pain and hurt she was enduring—but we'd been there. She had talked, and we had listened. A small bond had formed between the three of us, and now she knew we would be there for her whenever she needed us. It had been such a small thing, doing that visit. But it mattered.

Our visit with Sarah had been short and sweet. She had a bubbly personality and was in her third year of school. We'd gotten to know her, shared our message, and made a new friend in the process.

The month's message on family had made me remember Grandma's dream. In a way, it seemed like the girls in my ward and visiting teachers were the "stand-in" family I had here at school. Even more for someone like Jodi, who didn't have family close.

I climbed into bed and felt my heart squeeze painfully.

Dang.

I knew where the pain was coming from. It haunted me endlessly—what if I'd agreed to go on that one last date with Sawyer? What would he have planned?

I pictured Monet's eager expression again before quickly erasing the image. I refused to be angry toward her. She was an amazing person, and someone that I admired.

During those visits I'd been distracted enough that I hadn't thought of Sawyer. Maybe that was the key. Maybe if I could stay busy enough I wouldn't feel the pain anymore. I could be happy and go on like nothing ever happened—the way he did.

⌒⧓

I could feel Darren's eyes on me all throughout history class. He'd been watching me more and more these past few days. I tried to block it out, just like I tried to block out the *lack* of staring I got from Sawyer. I officially hated this class now.

As soon as Professor Gunner ended his lecture, I hurried to gather my things. I hadn't made it five steps through the door when Darren accosted me.

"Hey, Eliza, how's it going?" he asked as he stepped in my way.

"Fine, thanks." I quickly moved to get around him but he mirrored the movement, effectively blocking my path.

This guy wasn't just annoying—he was starting to creep me out.

"I noticed you weren't sitting by your boyfriend again today. You two get in a fight or something?" he lowered his voice and I bristled by his proximity.

"No, we didn't get in a fight. Not that it's any of your business," I snapped. I'd had enough. I spun on my heel so he couldn't keep me hedged in anymore.

"Hold on a second." He reached out and grabbed my arm, but before I could react I felt his grip suddenly break free.

"What do you think you're doing?" Sawyer growled.

I turned and saw that he had Darren by the collar.

"Dude, chill out." Darren held up his hands. "I was just talking to her."

People around us started to take notice. Sawyer dropped his collar and took a step toward him. "That's not what it looked like to me. Just keep your hands to yourself, alright?" His face was menacing.

"Okay. No problem." Darren shrugged his shoulders and didn't look back as he walked through a crowd of students and disappeared.

Sawyer turned to look at me; his blue eyes on fire. "You okay, Eliza?"

"Yes . . . thanks," was all I could manage.

He nodded and then turned and walked away. As I watched him go, I felt my heart breaking all over again. I couldn't stand it anymore.

"Sawyer!"

He stopped at the sound of my voice and turned around. I caught the pain in his eyes before he had time to mask it.

"Yeah?"

I rushed up to him. "I've changed my mind. I want to go on that date . . . if you still want to take me."

Something in his expression seemed to release. He gathered me into a tight hug. "Yes, I want to." He hugged me for several seconds before letting go. I felt the pieces of my heart that had splintered slowly fuse back together.

When he pulled away his eyes were dancing. "Man, these past few days totally sucked."

"I know." I arched my brow. "But you seemed like you weren't bothered at all. I thought you were mad, the way you were ignoring me like that."

"I was. I almost dropped history class because I didn't want to see you anymore. You've really messed with my heart, you know that?" He was smiling as he spoke the words.

"I know—I'm sorry. I feel like my heart is all messed up too." I frowned as I considered what a pathetic weakling I was. I should have just let Sawyer go, but I couldn't handle the pain. I was too selfish and wanted the healing power of his smile and his touch. I couldn't seem to let him go, no matter how much my brain told me I should.

Sawyer noticed the change in my expression and he took my hand, quickly changing the subject. "So you're willing to go on that date, huh? Does that mean

I can sit by you in class again too?" he asked. "I don't think Darren will bug you anymore, but it wouldn't hurt to have a bodyguard around just in case."

I laughed. "Yes, that might come in handy—but I'm not sure I could afford one."

"We'll figure something out," he said as he glanced sideways at me.

I loved that he was flirting with me again. My head told me that I should feel guilty about that, but I told it to hush up. I was tired of thinking.

"So when is this monumental date supposed to take place?" I asked as I continued to smile up at him.

He grinned mischievously. "Just keep this weekend open."

I raised an eyebrow. "O-okay . . . my weekend *is* open, except I have to work Saturday."

Sawyer shook his head. "That won't fly. You have to clear the entire weekend."

I laughed. "I can't do that, I already had to trade to take last Saturday off. How long is this date going to be anyway? Why can't you tell me a specific time?"

He held up a hand. "No more questions. Just get Saturday off; even if it means you have to quit your job."

"Quit my job to go on a date?"

"Yeah. Why not?"

I put a hand on my hip. "Because then I *definitely* couldn't afford to hire a bodyguard."

He smiled. "I told you we would work something out. If you have to quit I'll help you find another job—although I can't promise it will be as prestigious."

I poked him in the ribs. "Hey! We can't all be aspiring heart surgeons."

"Just promise me you'll get work off, okay?"

I sighed and finally relented. "Okay."

His face relaxed and he grinned as he dropped my hand. "Good. Well I gotta run, but I'll see you in class tomorrow."

"Okay." I was surprised and disappointed that he was leaving. Apparently he really was just going to see me in class and we would have that final date and nothing else. I had thought that maybe we were getting back together, but I realized it was better this way.

"What?" he asked as he looked in my eyes. He hadn't walked away yet.

"Nothing." I forced a smile as I waited for him to leave.

He stared at me a moment longer before he leaned closer and whispered, "Yes there is." He pulled me against him and kissed me right there in the middle of the hall. I was sure people were looking at us, but I didn't care. I wrapped my arms around his neck and returned the kiss. It was brief, but it was exactly what I'd wanted.

He pulled back and pressed his forehead against mine before he turned and walked away.

I was sure I'd completely lost my mind, but as I watched him leave with an eager stride, I couldn't help but smile.

"Has anyone seen my red shirt?"

My roommates were in the living room watching TV when I rushed in.

"You know—the one I bought when we went to the mall last week?"

They all gave me blank stares.

"Sorry, Liza, I haven't seen it," Bree said while the others shook their heads.

"Ugh, this is so frustrating! Where could it be?" It was Thursday afternoon and Sawyer would be there any minute to pick me up for our big date. I'd specifically bought that shirt because Sawyer had told me I looked good in red. I didn't want to change my wardrobe plan last minute.

"Maybe it got left in the laundry room?" Charlotte said as she glanced at the other two.

"No, I already looked there."

I didn't know why everyone was acting so weird. I loved my friends and thought I could trust them to tell me if they borrowed my clothes. Maybe some-one had borrowed it and ruined it and didn't want to confess to the crime.

I glanced at my watch. "Sawyer will be here any second. I guess I'll just have to wear something else."

"What about your short-sleeved navy cardi?" Lacey suggested. "I love that on you. It really brings out the color in your eyes."

Bree and Charlotte were nodding vigorously.

"Yeah, wear that one! It'll be perfect," Bree said.

"I guess I'll have to." I was still surprised that no one had offered to help me find the red shirt; the one I *really* wanted to wear, but oh well.

I hurried back into my room and threw the cardi over my fitted white shirt, but when I went to find my favorite pair of jeans, they weren't on the shelf with my other pants.

I gasped and began rummaging through my closet. Several of my shirts, pants, and even some of my shoes were missing.

"Guys, come here!" I yelled.

All three girls came running into the room.

"What's wrong?" Charlotte asked.

"A bunch of my clothes are missing." I looked at each of them separately. "And I know *exactly* what's going on."

Bree started. "You do?"

"Yes—isn't it obvious? Drew. He must have snuck in and taken our clothes sometime during the *Mystery Falls* marathon last night."

Lacey's mouth dropped open in dumbfounded silence. I knew she'd be fu-rious when she realized I was right.

"Go check your closets. I'm sure they got a bunch of your clothes too; un-less they've decided to make me the primary target," I grumbled. "I can't believe those jerks! We didn't even retaliate from the Kool-Aid prank and they're still pulling stuff." I looked forlornly at my closet. "Of course they *would* take all of my favorite outfits."

I turned and wagged a finger at Lacey. "I don't care what promise you made—we are going to get back at these guys! Wait up for me tonight and we'll make some plans."

She had recovered from her look of shock and nodded somberly. Bree and Charlotte were doing their best to look angry too, but I got the distinct impression that they were trying not to laugh. How could they be so heartless? Just because I was the one who was getting the brunt of the pranking didn't mean they couldn't sympathize.

"Well aren't you guys going to make sure your clothes aren't missing?" I demanded as they continued to stand in the doorway.

"Yeah . . . of course." The corner of Bree's mouth twitched as she moved to her closet.

She wouldn't look so amused when she found *her* favorite pair of jeans missing.

A knock sounded at the front door.

"That's probably Sawyer." I took one final glance in the mirror before grabbing my purse. "When you hang out with the guys tonight, try to find a way to get our clothes back, okay?" I called over my shoulder.

"Okay," Lacey said, but I heard Charlotte stifle a giggle.

What was going on? Those guys needed to start getting more sleep; they were totally loopy today.

I opened the door and a huge smile spread over my face. Sawyer was standing there, looking more handsome than ever. I didn't know if it was the delighted expression he wore when he saw me, the way his clothes fit him perfectly, or the smell of his cologne that made me want to reach out and kiss him. Everything about him at that moment seemed perfect.

"Hi." His blue eyes gleamed with excitement. "You ready to go?"

"Yep." I smiled and closed the door, trying to keep the bounce out of my step as he took my hand and we walked down the hall. "Are you ready to tell me what we're doing tonight?" I asked.

"You'll see soon enough." He drew my hand up to his lips and kissed it. "But I guarantee you'll be surprised."

CHAPTER

twenty-two

He was right. I was surprised when we drove to Salt Lake City, and even *more* surprised when he turned west and began following signs to the airport.

"Okay, what's going on?" I laughed. "I know you're not taking me on an airplane—are we picking someone up?"

Sawyer grinned. "I told you to wait and see. Haven't you ever heard that patience is a virtue?" he teased.

"Sawyer Murdock if you don't tell me where we're going I swear I'm going to call my parents and tell them I've been abducted." I tried to sound threatening. Virtue or no, I'd been patient long enough.

"Go right ahead," he said, reaching for his phone. "Here, I'll dial the number for you."

I snatched the phone away from him. "You're not supposed to do that while you're driving."

He laughed. "You're pretty feisty when you're impatient, but somehow it only makes you cuter. Why is that?"

I grumbled and folded my arms across my chest. He was impossible. I watched out the window and tried to hide my surprise as we pulled into the long-term parking lot.

He wasn't seriously going to take me on a trip somewhere . . . was he? My parents would completely freak out. *I* would freak out. There was no way the two of us could go on a trip somewhere alone without it being inappropriate—unless we were . . . we were . . .

"What's going on? Where are you taking me?" I asked in sudden alarm. Visions of Las Vegas and a tacky chapel wedding suddenly filled my mind.

Sawyer pulled into a parking spot and turned off the car. He looked over at me and there was an amused expression in his eyes as he sighed. "Okay, okay. I thought it would be a fun surprise, but you look terrified. Eliza, don't you trust me at all?"

"I did, but that was before you asked me on a date and then unexpectedly drove to an international airport." I looked at him questioningly. "This is just another one of your jokes, right? Like slaughtering chickens?"

He slowly shook his head back and forth. "I'm flying you out to California to meet my family."

"Yeah right." I laughed but it quickly died in my throat. He wasn't smiling. "You're *serious?*"

"Are you mad at me?" He looked unhappy with my reaction.

"I'm not mad, I'm just—shocked." I shook my head. "And my dad is going to kill you and probably me if he finds out."

"Don't worry about that, he already knows."

"Okay, now I *know* you're joking," I said. "My dad would never go for this in a million years."

"Seriously, I called your parents and asked their permission before I booked the tickets. At least, I called and talked to your mom. I have to confess I'm still a little scared of your dad."

I laughed and he smiled as he got out of the car. Under normal circumstances I would have allowed him to get my door, but I was too impatient. I hopped out and said, "So we're going for the weekend? What am I supposed to do about clothes and stuff?"

He grinned and popped the trunk. I walked around to look inside and my eyes widened. "You packed my bag?"

"Actually your roommates did. They were in on this too."

Realization dawned and I quickly unzipped the main compartment. My new red shirt was right on top, along with my favorite jeans, some shoes, and a few of my favorite outfits. They'd also packed my makeup, toiletry bag and hair stuff. It was all here.

I put a hand to the side of my face and laughed. "You should have heard the way I was going off before you got to our apartment. No wonder they were trying not to laugh—I totally accused Drew and his friends of stealing my clothes."

"Really? I wish I could have heard that. Your roommates were awesome about keeping everything a secret. I hope I never get on their bad side 'cause they are some seriously sneaky girls."

"Yes they are." I grinned as I tried to still the butterflies that were erupting in my stomach. I couldn't believe this was actually happening.

"So when did you book the tickets?" I asked as I re-zipped the bag.

He waited for me to finish and then lifted our luggage out of the trunk.

"After you agreed to go out with me again I didn't waste any time getting things arranged."

"Those tickets must have been expensive. I'll pay you back." I reached for my bag but he shook his head and placed it on top of his suitcase.

"You're not going to pay me anything. My parents have like a gazillion SkyMiles and they both really want to meet you." He lifted the handle and began walking as he rolled our bags behind him.

I stood there dumbfounded for a moment. I couldn't believe I was actually going to do this. I couldn't believe my parents were cool with it, and I couldn't believe I was going to meet Sawyer's family. All of a sudden I was really scared.

Sawyer stopped and looked over his shoulder. When he saw that I wasn't following he came back and took my hand. "Come on, Eliza. You don't want us to miss the flight, do you?" His eyes held so much excitement that I couldn't help but smile. I just needed to look at this as an adventure. Besides, I'd never been to Sacramento before.

I gave his hand a squeeze and swallowed.

"I'm coming."

⤬

As we waited to check in for our flight I sent my mom a text:

Me: *So I'm on my way to CA!!! U knew about this??*

Mom: *Yes! I hoped it would be a fun experience for you. I called Sawyer's mom & she's anxious for your visit. She said she'd keep an eye on both of you, which is the only reason your father relented. ;)*

Me: *I'm so nervous! What if they don't like me?*

Mom: *Just relax and have fun. Sawyer told me everything he has planned. You're going to love it!*

Me: *Can u give me any hints??*

Mom: *No! But call me every day with updates ok?*

Me: *Whose side are u on, anyway? :)*

Mom: *Sorry sweetheart, but I'm not going to spoil the surprise for you.*

Me: *Bah! Ok, I'll be sure to call w/ updates. Did you make an appt. w/ the dr. yet?*

Mom: *Yes, I go in for a check-up next week. I'm feeling fine, don't worry about me.*

Me: *Well, take it easy. Thanks for letting me do this . . . I guess.*

Mom: *You're welcome. :) Have a safe flight and don't forget to call. Love you!*

Me: *Love you too!*

We still had a few minutes so I sent a group text to my roommates.

Me: *I can't believe you guys!!! I'm never going to trust you about anything again! ;)*

They replied back with hilarious responses which Sawyer and I laughed over until it was time to board the plane.

I knew we were only taking a trip to a different state to meet his family. We would be on an airplane surrounded by tons of people and then his sister would pick us up at the airport. In reality we weren't going to be alone for one second, but something about getting on this plane with Sawyer felt momentous. Possibly for the first time in my life I felt like a real adult; one who could make her own decisions and go on exciting weekend trips. The feeling was completely liberating!

A flight attendant looked at our ticket stubs and directed us to our seats. When she stopped in the third row of first class I thought my eyes were going to drop out of my head.

First class? There had to be some mistake. First class was something a girl like me could only dream about. I'd been on two other flights in my life, each time shuffling past the first class passengers with barely suppressed awe. The sheer size of the seats and the fact that they had their own lavatory was nothing short of impressive.

And here I was, about to sit with all the muckety-mucks in their suits and designer clothes. I was afraid someone would stand up and call me out for the imposter that I was.

I turned and raised my eyebrows at Sawyer. "Is this where we're sitting?" I asked out of the corner of my mouth.

He grinned. "Yep. Go ahead and sit down. I'll put your bag in the overhead."

"Would you like anything to drink?" the young flight attendant asked as her eyes travelled over Sawyer in approval.

"I'll have a ginger ale," Sawyer said as he put our bags in the bin and sat back down.

"And for you, Miss?"

"I'll have the same, thanks." I tried to contain my smile as I was swallowed into the large seat. I felt as giddy as a kid at Disneyland and suddenly wished we had a longer flight.

I turned and saw that Sawyer was watching me in amusement. "This is the first time you've flown first class, isn't it?"

I bit my lip. "Is it that obvious?"

"No, I just love how excited you are." He reached over and took my hand, his eyes dancing with pleasure. "I'm so glad you didn't fight me on this, Eliza. I know it was a lot to take in and I'm glad you weren't mad."

"*Mad?* How could I be? This is the most thoughtful thing anyone's done for me."

The flight attendant brought our drinks and flashed Sawyer a big smile, but he didn't seem to notice. I grimaced slightly and waited for her to leave before I continued, "Sawyer, I'm amazed that you went to all of this trouble for *me.* Especially after everything I've put you through. And it might take me a while to do it, but I'll earn the money to pay your parents back for my ticket."

"Eliza, will you stop worrying about the ticket? I told you, they have more SkyMiles than they know what to do with. They would be offended if you tried to pay them back; trust me." He winked and then took a sip of his drink.

"Okay . . . if you say so." I couldn't tell him how nervous I was to meet his parents. What if I was a disappointment? What if they just plain didn't like me and I spent the weekend completely uncomfortable in their house?

I stared out the oval window and watched the sun set slowly over the tarmac. Soon Luke would be looking out of an airplane window like this one, wearing his suit and missionary nametag. What would he think if he knew I was on my way to meet the family of a guy I'd only known a little over a month? A guy I had kissed and who had told me he loved me. A guy I couldn't seem to break up with.

I felt confusion swell in my heart and I said a silent prayer, once again asking for guidance. Why wasn't I receiving a direct answer about this? Had I received one and just didn't recognize it? I'd told myself that Luke's letter had been the answer, but deep down I knew I had only been trying to convince myself. I hadn't felt an answer in my heart one way or the other.

I only knew that Sawyer was someone I cared deeply for, and when I wasn't with him, I ached. I glanced over and admired his profile as he checked his phone before turning it off. It was so sweet that he'd planned this surprise weekend, and I was completely flattered that he wanted me to meet his family.

I looped my arms through his and gave him a squeeze before putting my head on his shoulder.

"What was that for?" he asked as he nuzzled his face into my hair.

"Just because you're awesome," I replied. I lifted my head slightly until my face was mere inches from his. "And because I feel lucky to know you."

His blue eyes narrowed and his face inched closer to mine as the lights in the cabin dimmed for takeoff. "I'm the one feeling lucky right about now," he whispered. He pressed his lips to mine and kissed me as the airplane accelerated and lifted off the ground.

CHAPTER

twenty-three

It was after ten when we landed in Sacramento. The flight had passed far too quickly as Sawyer and I talked and joked about which items we would buy from the in-flight catalog.

The airport was small and we didn't have to wait for checked bags. In what seemed like a matter of minutes, we were waiting at the curb for his sister to pick us up.

I'd already known a lot about Sawyer's family from the things he'd told me on previous dates. He was the oldest of three kids: himself and two younger sisters. The one picking us up, Rachel, was twenty-two and living at home while she went to a local University. Anna, the youngest, had just graduated from high school (which meant she was my age). She was coming out to Utah to go to college in a few weeks.

Sawyer had assured me that everyone would love me, but I felt sick to my stomach as he waved at the sporty red Mercedes that was pulling up to the curb.

"There she is." He smiled as the car parked. A gorgeous blonde emerged from the driver's seat. "Hey, Rachel," he said.

"Hey." She smiled at him before turning and looking me over from head to foot.

"Pop the trunk okay?" Sawyer wheeled our bags to the back of the car.

"'Kay." She pushed a button on her key fob and then checked her cell phone. I got the distinct impression that she was bored.

After tossing our bags in and closing the trunk, Sawyer went over to her side of the car. He gave her a quick hug, which she returned with one arm while she continued to look at her phone.

He pulled back and introduced us, which was slightly awkward because I was still standing on the other side of the car. "Rachel, this is Eliza."

She glanced up from her phone and offered the same disinterested, "Hey," that she'd given Sawyer a minute ago.

I attempted a friendly smile and was about to say it was nice to meet her, when the car behind us honked its horn.

"Geeze, what's that about?" She flipped her head around to glare at the car. "It's not like they're boxed in or anything." She opened the door and got in the driver's seat, seemingly unaware that I'd been about to say something to her.

Sawyer watched the exchange and gave me an apologetic shrug, before walking back over to get my door. "Do you want to sit up front?" he asked.

"No thanks," I said without hesitation.

He winked and opened the back door for me. The car behind us honked again.

"Seriously?" Rachel angled the rearview mirror to look at the car.

"Okay, all set," Sawyer said as he sat down in the passenger seat and buckled his seatbelt.

Rachel responded by pushing down on the accelerator. The car lurched ahead, causing me to slam back into my seat. I hurried to get my seatbelt on and then gripped the door handle. Maybe I wouldn't have to worry about meeting Sawyer's parents after all. Maybe 'Road Rage Rachel' would finish me off before I even got there.

We drove for about twenty minutes, passing city buildings and small neighborhoods dimly lit by streetlights. I was content to look out the window while Sawyer and Rachel carried on a conversation.

I overheard that she had recently broken up with a guy she'd been on-and-off with for a few years, but she insisted that this time it was final. I couldn't help but flinch as I realized that that was exactly how I'd been with Sawyer: on-and-off—except we'd only been dating for weeks, not years.

Rachel did the bulk of the talking while Sawyer offered an occasional mumble of interest. She reminded me of Chelsea Andrews from high school—completely gorgeous and self-absorbed. The type of girl who made me feel frumpy and out of place, even when I was at my best. But I had misjudged Chelsea, so it was possible I wasn't giving Rachel a fair shot.

I stared at the back of her perfectly styled blonde head and noticed the way her bracelets jangled as she turned the steering wheel. She was totally chic. Guys with pretty sisters usually sought out girls who were at least as pretty. How had Sawyer been attracted to me? It wasn't that I thought I was ugly, but I definitely wasn't about to feature on the cover of Vogue.

I tugged at the hem of my shirt. I used to feel like this was one of my cuter outfits, but suddenly it seemed a little dated and juvenile; which was just how I was feeling.

"Well here it is—home sweet home!" Sawyer turned and looked at me with a smile.

I'd been so distracted in my thoughts that I'd lost track of our surroundings. My eyes widened as I watched a wrought iron gate slowly open in front of us. Beyond the gate was a house so gigantic that "mansion" didn't even begin to describe it. *Estate* was more like it.

There were canned lights all over the house and grounds, illuminating every enormous square inch.

"Wow." I didn't know what else to say. "This is your house?" For a minute

I wondered if maybe this was a country club and the house was hidden somewhere behind it.

"Yep. Wait till you see inside."

I could tell Sawyer was proud of his parents' house and he had a right to be, but something about the way he'd said that bothered me. Almost like he was showing off.

"I'm heading over to Crystal's house so I'm just gonna drop you guys here," Rachel said as she pulled through the circle drive that led to the front door.

"Okay. Thanks again for picking us up, Rach," Sawyer said as he got out of the car.

She nodded and then popped the trunk, impatiently tapping her manicured fingernails on the steering wheel.

"Yeah, thanks. It was really nice to meet you," I said in a final attempt to befriend her.

She glanced back as if she'd forgotten I was there and gave me the tiniest imaginable smile. "No problem," she said without eye contact. She turned back around and pressed the button to turn on the radio.

So much for that.

Feeling like a complete idiot, I climbed out of the door Sawyer was holding open for me.

I glanced up . . . and up . . . and up, at the house before me and sighed. I felt like little orphan Annie on her way to see Daddy Warbucks—but if Rachel had been any indication, I seriously doubted there was going to be any singing or dancing inside.

Sawyer opened the front door and gestured for me to go in. I tried to keep my jaw in place as I stepped through the door. The entry hall had cathedral-height ceilings and a grand, curved stairway, which led up to the second floor.

An intricate water feature stood at the base of the stairs, and the tinkling of the water was the only sound to be heard.

Sawyer stepped in behind me and closed the door just as a woman called from a room down the hall.

"Is that you, Sawyer?" asked the high, ringing voice.

"Yeah, we're here, Mom," Sawyer replied as he took my hand and led me toward the room.

I took a deep breath as I tried to steady my nerves. *Fake it till you make it, Liza,* I chanted to myself as I pasted on a big smile. I felt like an ant in this palatial space, and was completely out of my element.

Sawyer led me into the library where a petite woman was sitting in a recliner, reading a fitness magazine. She had to have been in her fifties, but she could have passed for early forties—or younger. Her face was flawless and smooth, with nary a wrinkle to be seen anywhere.

"Well, hello!" She smiled at Sawyer, revealing perfectly white teeth, and set her magazine aside. She opened her arms to give Sawyer a hug without getting up from her chair.

He grinned. "Hey, Mom."

I knew this must be his mother, but she was so different from what I'd pictured that it took my mind a few moments to process the fact.

"How was your flight?" she asked him as he pulled away.

"Just great, thanks." He stood and then reached for my hand and drew me in front of him. "Mom, *this* is Eliza. Eliza, this is my mom, Evelyn."

The woman gave me a bland smile before offering a tiny hand. "It's so nice to finally meet you, dear. We're glad you could come and stay with us." Her gaze swept quickly over me in just the same way her daughter had. I felt like she'd summed me up in a total of two seconds, but her expression didn't reveal what that conclusion was.

I took her cold hand, and by the weak way it was offered wasn't quite sure if I was meant to squeeze it or shake it. I ended up doing something sort of in between and returned her smile. "I can't thank you enough for letting me come here this weekend, and for flying me out here—it was too generous."

She released my hand and waved in a dismissive manner. "It was nothing at all. Sawyer seemed quite determined to have you visit. We're just glad you could come and stay with us."

Hadn't she already said that? I felt acutely uncomfortable by the way she'd implied this was Sawyer's doing, rather than her own wish. I wondered if that entrance gate was still open, and if not, how high the fence was.

"Honey, Eliza looks tired. Why don't you show her up to one of the guest rooms?" She picked up her magazine again. "You just let Sawyer know if you need anything, all right?" She glanced at me over the top of the page she was reading.

"I will . . . thanks again." I was only too happy to get away from this awkward situation. She was clearly done with introductions and wanting to get back to her magazine. I pulled gently on Sawyer's hand but he didn't budge.

"Where's Dad?" he asked with a frown. "Has he already gone to bed?"

She met his eyes and something passed between them. His frown deepened and he shook his head.

"He wanted to wait up for you, sweetheart, but he has a surgery early in the morning and needed his rest."

"Yeah . . . I know." Sawyer looked exactly like a hurt puppy and I gave his hand a sympathetic squeeze. He gave me a half smile before turning back to his mom. "Well where's Anna? I wanted her to meet Eliza."

"Out with friends." She covered a yawn.

Sawyer turned to me with an apologetic smile. "I guess you'll just have to meet the rest of the family tomorrow. Come on, I'll show you to your room."

We walked back into the entryway where Sawyer collected our bags. I followed him up the long staircase, gaping at each piece of artwork we passed. Upon reaching the landing, he stopped and turned to me.

"So which direction?" he asked. There were hallways going both directions from where we stood. It was no surprise that his mom had said guest *rooms*, plural. With only four occupants in the house there had to be at least a dozen bedrooms left over.

"I don't know; this is your house. Put me wherever you want . . . wherever I'll be least in the way," I quickly added.

There was a roguish gleam in his eyes. "Okay." I followed him as he turned to the left and we passed several rooms before he stopped at a door. "How about this one?"

I peeked curiously inside before stepping in. There were trophies and sports memorabilia lining a shelf on the wall, as well as some pictures. I walked up to get a closer look at the smiling Sawyer in his high school football jersey. I quickly spun around. "This is your room?"

He had his head leaning on the doorpost as he watched me. "Yeah. This is where I want you to sleep."

"Sawyer!" I gasped.

He grinned wickedly before holding up his hands. "I meant that I would take one of the guest rooms, of course."

"Oh." My face flushed with embarrassment and I quickly changed the subject. "So this was your room growing up, huh?" I looked at the luxury king-sized bed and huge flat screen on the wall. "Tough childhood."

He laughed. "Yeah, it was pretty rough." He was still watching me intently. "You don't mind sleeping in here then?"

I shrugged. "I don't mind if you don't, although I feel bad kicking you out of your own room."

He shook his head and the rakish look returned as he walked over and pulled me in his arms. "I like the thought of you sleeping in here."

A tiny thrill ran up my spine at the smoldering look in his eyes right before he kissed me. Something about being here alone with Sawyer made the kiss seem more intense, and I felt a dizzy sense of euphoria as he continued to press his lips against mine.

After a few minutes, I began to feel that same, intense craving that I'd felt when we were at the drive-in. I couldn't seem to get my fill of Sawyer's kiss: the more he kissed me, the more I wanted. He slowly moved us backward until the back of my knees hit the bed, and then he gently pushed me back onto the bed.

Whoa!

A warning went off like a siren in my head and I broke out from under Sawyer's grasp, quickly standing up and away from the bed.

"What's the matter, Eliza?" He turned and I saw that same look of pent-up fire in his eyes that I'd seen before.

"You know what." I struggled to regulate my breathing and to put up a wall against the thoughts in my mind tempting me to stop resisting. I put my hand to my chest, feeling for the pendant beneath my shirt. "You need to get out of here. Right *now*."

"I'm sorry." He sat on the bed and reached for both of my hands, pulling me closer to him again. The air around us was still charged with desire.

I shook my head and broke free from his grip. "I mean it, Sawyer. Get lost or I'm going to . . . to . . . call for a taxi."

He chuckled and raised an eyebrow. "A taxi? Heaven forbid."

I put my hands on my hips. "Well I'll do something . . . I'll . . . I'll scream! Your mom will come running and I'll tell her you're trying to seduce me."

His eyes danced in amusement and he stood, lowering his voice as he took me in his arms again. "*Trying*, huh? I thought I was succeeding."

The craving was rising within me again at that look in his eyes and the feel of his arms around me. I had to do something or I knew I would cave. "All right—you asked for it . . . " I shut my eyes and was about to open my mouth to scream, when Sawyer quickly clamped his hand over it.

"Okay, you win, you little rascal. I'll leave." He gave me one more quick kiss on the mouth before I could stop him, and then he pulled away and continued, "But only because we have a big day tomorrow and I want you to get your rest."

I scowled, fighting to ignore how much I'd enjoyed the kiss as I pushed away from him. He laughed again and winked at me before he finally picked up his suitcase and left.

I quickly closed the door behind him and locked it, which earned another chuckle from down the hall. I couldn't be too careful with that scoundrel; that much was certain!

I shook my head in disbelief when I remembered my mom's text telling me that Sawyer's mom would keep an eye on us. *Ha!* I doubted she would do more than bat an eyelash my way for the rest of my stay here. And as for Sawyer himself . . . I realized it was going to be up to me, and me alone to guard my virtue.

I unpacked my bag into Sawyer's empty dresser and then went into the ensuite bathroom to get ready for bed. It was late, well past midnight, but I read my scriptures on my phone before saying my prayers and turning off the light. I was going to need all the help I could get to stay strong this weekend.

CHAPTER

Twenty-four

"I cannot believe what an incredible day this has been!" I sighed in delight. It was evening and a gentle breeze blew a strand of hair across my cheek as I breathed in the ocean air. We were dining at a small, hilltop café that overlooked the Golden Gate Bridge.

Sawyer smiled as he reached over and brushed the hair away from my cheek, leaving his hand to rest on my face. "Did you really like it?" he asked with a sincere question in his eyes.

"Oh, Sawyer—this has honestly been one of the best days of my life. I didn't know that days like this could exist!" I couldn't keep the smile from my face.

Sawyer had knocked on my door early this morning and informed me that he was taking me to San Francisco. I had been shocked and giddy all at once. We'd eaten a quick breakfast and left the house before anyone else was awake, which was fine with me. After meeting Rachel and his mom I wasn't sure I wanted to meet the rest of the family, although I was a little surprised his dad wasn't up. Hadn't his mom said he had an early surgery? When I asked Sawyer about it he shrugged and said that "early" to his dad meant anything before eight am.

The drive to San Francisco had been longer than I'd expected, but I'd loved watching the scenery. When I commented casually on the length of the drive, Sawyer had laughed and told me I should experience it during traffic.

It was my first visit to the city and he made sure it was a good one. He'd taken me to Fisherman's Wharf, on a tour of Alcatraz, a trolley ride, bought me a pound of chocolate at Ghirardelli Square, and shown me dozens of other sights before bringing me to this quaint, expensive café in Sausalito.

I leaned back in my chair after taking the last bite of my dessert and sighed. "This day was perfect—does it really have to end?"

"Only when we want it to." Sawyer smiled as he took my hand and drew it to his lips while keeping his eyes locked on mine.

I didn't know how he could look at me when there was such a beautiful view around us. It was that fleeting time of dusk, when the sky is soft and infused with whips of color. I loved the vibrancy of the big city and I loved being so near the ocean. It was a dramatic change from life back home and the contrast was intoxicating.

I turned to Sawyer and smiled. "I wish that were true; I wish I could stretch out time as long as I wanted it . . . but only on days like this. For finals, I'd like to shorten it to a non-existent blip."

He laughed. "I would do that for you if I could." He leaned toward me and lowered his voice, suddenly becoming serious. "I would do anything for you, Eliza."

"Would you?" Our eyes met and neither of us spoke for several seconds, the spell only breaking when the waiter brought the check. Sawyer handed him his credit card. When the waiter walked away he returned his attention to me, putting his hands on his knees. "So what do you want to do next? The night is young and I'm completely at your service."

I looked out at the steady stream of traffic heading away from the city. "Shouldn't we be heading back soon? I mean, it took us two hours to get here . . . and that was without traffic."

"Do you want to go back right now?" he asked.

"Not really, but . . ."

"Well then let's stay. We can always get a hotel if we need to."

"Sawyer." I gave him a withering look.

"What? We can get two rooms."

"No."

"But I don't see the problem with . . ."

"No!" As much as I didn't want to go back to his huge, cold house and his less-than-friendly family members, there was no way I was staying in a hotel with him. That was pushing things too far—no matter how many rooms we got.

Sawyer sat back in his seat and gave me a look that was half admiration, half frustration. "You're a good girl, Eliza. That's one of the things I love about you—you help to keep us on the straight and narrow."

My heart quickened. He hadn't used the "L" word since the night of the fireworks. Even though he'd said it in a different way this time, it still made me blush.

He wasn't finished. "But you need to realize you're an adult now. This is your life, and you can make your own decisions. If we stay here tonight in separate rooms it's no big deal. You'll just lock the door anyway," he teased.

I straightened my back and met his gaze. "You know what, Sawyer? You're absolutely right. I *am* an adult now. And as an adult, I know that if I choose to spend the night in a hotel with you—separate rooms or no—there will be consequences. Even if the consequence is only my guilty conscience. So I *choose* to ask you to take me back to your house instead."

He laughed and nodded his head. "Fair enough."

I looked away to hide the turmoil inside of me. What was going on? Why did I feel like I was always the one who had to be the "good girl"? Didn't we have the same beliefs? Wasn't he a returned missionary? I shouldn't have to constantly make a case on things like this.

We both stood and I took one last glance at the breathtaking sights below. The city lights were turning on; sizzling to life with the enticements of everything the nightlife had to offer. It would have been fun to stay longer and explore everything there was to see. I wanted to drink it all in until I was full to overflowing, but I was starting to get tired. It didn't take a rocket scientist to figure out that: tired, plus hormones, plus Sawyer and I alone in a hotel equaled trouble.

I had never been in traffic like this before. I couldn't believe the never-ending line-up of cars ahead of us wasn't caused by construction or an accident. It was simply the result of too many people living in an overcrowded area. Crazy.

A beeping noise in my purse alerted me to the fact that my cell phone was dying. "Uh oh," I said as I reached down for the phone. "I hope my roommates packed a charger in my bag, 'cause I don't have one in my purse." I saw that I'd missed a call from my mom. "I totally forgot I was supposed to call her today," I mumbled. I knew she'd worry if she didn't hear from me.

"Use mine," Sawyer offered as he handed me his phone.

I looked at the clock and realized with the time change my mom was probably already in bed, so I sent her a quick text.

Me: *Had an awesome day in SF! Can't wait to fill you in on details but my phone's dead. Call Sawyer's cell if u need to reach me.*

Mom: *Thx for the msg, I was worried. Hope you're having a great time! I'll try to call tomorrow.*

Me: *Ok, love you!*

Mom: *Love you too.*

I smiled as I finished reading her text. I appreciated my mom more than ever; especially after meeting Sawyer's mother. It made my last dream with Grandma hit home as I realized what a huge impact a mother could have on her home and family.

His mom was almost the complete opposite of what I thought a mother should be: warm, loving and involved in her children's lives. Maybe I'd just caught her at a bad time, but from what I'd gathered, I felt extremely sorry for Sawyer. His parents had provided him with everything he could ever ask for—everything except for what he needed most.

Love.

It was Saturday morning and Sawyer and I were eating cereal by ourselves in the kitchen. We sat on barstools at the granite island that could easily have seated twenty people.

His mom had come in briefly; all dressed in her designer workout clothes, to announce she was heading to the gym and that we should help ourselves to whatever we could find in the pantry. I was pretty sure she didn't notice that we already *had* helped ourselves; hence the cereal bowls in front of us.

When Sawyer asked her when his dad would be coming down, she announced that he'd had a tee time with some of his colleagues and had left early this morning.

Secretly I began to wonder if Mr. Murdock did, in fact, exist. I also wondered if everyone in his family was LDS, or if Sawyer was a convert. He'd never said anything that made me think otherwise, but there were no religiously themed pictures anywhere. Not even pictures of their family—just expensive décor and art pieces. And I certainly didn't get a spiritual vibe from his mom or sister. I would have to try to find a smooth way of asking Sawyer about it later. Not that it mattered, but I was curious.

We had just finished our breakfast when a younger carbon copy of Rachel came groggily into the kitchen.

"Hey, Anna!" Sawyer said as he hopped off the barstool and went over to give her a hug.

"Hey, bro," she said with a sleepy smile. She looked at me over his shoulder. "Who's this?"

Sawyer turned. "This is Eliza, I'm sure you've heard she was staying with us."

She gave him a blank stare.

"Didn't Mom or Rachel tell you?"

Again the stare.

Sawyer rushed on, "Well anyway, Eliza, this is my baby sister Anna."

He was making such an effort to make his family like me. I felt so sorry for him that I almost wanted to cry.

I smiled at Anna and said, "It's nice to meet you. I hear you're coming out to Utah for school in a few weeks, is that right?"

She gave me the same quick once-over I'd received from her mom and sister. It was almost like they'd been trained . . . or cloned.

"Yeah, I am," a pause, "You look like you're about my age. Are you and Sawyer . . . dating?" She raised an eyebrow, as if she couldn't comprehend what I was doing here in her kitchen.

I blushed.

"Well, it was good to see you, sis. We've gotta run but I'm sure we'll catch you later," Sawyer interjected. He was clearly embarrassed by her behavior and neither of us knew how I would respond to her "dating" question.

He quickly led me down a series of halls and out to the garage. There was a large selection of vehicles to choose from. Yesterday he'd driven a sporty SUV, but today he went over to a BMW convertible and opened the passenger-side door.

"Why don't we take this one? It's a nice day and we can put the top down if you want."

I smiled, determined to make him feel better after the unpleasant encounter in the kitchen. "That would be awesome! I've actually never ridden in a convertible before."

He grinned and kissed me on the cheek as I climbed into the car. "You're amazing, you know that?"

I laughed. "Why? Because I've never ridden in a convertible?"

He shook his head. "No, because you appreciate the simplest things."

"What's not to appreciate?" I asked as I gestured around me. "This is one of the fanciest cars I've ever ridden in, and who knows if I'll ever have the chance to ride in a convertible again. It's just so cool!"

It seemed impossible that anyone could *not* enjoy a fun ride in a fancy car, but then I thought about the perpetually bored expressions his sisters wore. I guessed if you'd been spoiled with nice things all of your life, eventually you'd just take it for granted. I wondered if anything ever excited them, or if they ever stopped to express gratitude for the amazingly abundant life they had.

"Well it's just one more thing I love about you," Sawyer said before starting up the ignition.

There was that word again. It seemed like it was starting to creep up into his conversations more often and I felt a nervous stirring in my stomach. I was trying not to think too much about our complicated relationship and just go with the flow, but it was constantly nagging in the back of my mind. I knew that Sawyer was more to me than just a friend—much more. But how much more, I wasn't sure.

I dug my feet into the warm sand and sighed as I listened to the waves crashing along the shore. It had been another adventure-filled day, and now I was enjoying sitting here on the beach with Sawyer.

We had eaten lunch in Old Town Sacramento and browsed the little shops there, before driving to this small, secluded beach. Sawyer grabbed a blanket that he had stashed in the trunk and we sat and talked as we looked out over the water.

"What time is our flight back tomorrow?" I asked as I traced my finger lazily in the sand.

"Why? Are you ready to go home already?" Sawyer teased.

"No, I'm just curious . . . will we be going to church with your family?" Here was my chance to get a little more info.

"We can. Our flight doesn't leave until two and my parents' ward starts at nine so we could go to Sacrament meeting if you want."

"I'd like that. It would even be cool to go to the whole block." I surprised myself with this suggestion, but found that I really meant it.

"Sure, we've got time." Sawyer smiled at me with that same look of admiration I'd seen before.

There was something else I wanted to know. "Sawyer . . . I hope you won't mind my asking, and I don't want this to come across the wrong way, but . . ." I wasn't sure how to phrase the question.

He was lying on the blanket with his arms folded under his head. "Yes?"

"Well . . . why is it that you wanted to bring me out here to meet your family? I mean, don't get me wrong—I've had the best time ever, but it seems like they don't really . . . care that I'm here."

I stared at my hands and blushed, embarrassed to have said something we both knew was true but had avoided acknowledging. Maybe if I'd been more beautiful or stylish his family would have liked me better.

Sawyer continued to stare at me, but remained silent. His mood was difficult to decipher and I felt awkward by the silence so I pressed on.

"I just want to know why you were set on 'one more date'. Why did you bring me out here? Why not just take me on a date back home?" I was probably annoying him with my persistence, but I had to know.

Sawyer sat up and put his elbows on his knees, staring out at the sea for a moment. His jaw was working and suddenly he seemed nervous.

Had I made him upset? The way he was acting seemed so strange. It was silent for another minute before he finally spoke.

"I wanted to bring you out here, because I wanted my family to meet you before . . . " he paused and seemed to change subjects, "I wanted to you to see what my life back home was like. I wanted you to know that you had options and to see all of the things you could have if you were married to a heart surgeon."

Did he just say what I think he said?

Sawyer suddenly moved around until he was kneeling in front of me. He drew something out of his pocket and I pulled my knees up to my chest and hugged them, pressing them into my chin.

Sawyer's blue eyes met mine and he spoke slowly, "Eliza Moore, you are the girl of my dreams and the person I want to spend the rest of eternity with . . . will you marry me?"

My eyes widened in shock and I gasped as I looked from his questioning gaze, to the ring box in his hand, and back again.

Could this seriously be happening? A thousand thoughts ran through my mind as I stared into those eyes that I'd come to know so well.

A few seconds passed and he cleared his throat, making me realize that I still hadn't answered.

This was one of the most pivotal moments in my life; the moment when someone was asking me to be his wife. I'd imagined what this moment would feel like, but I'd never expected it to be like this.

I saw the shadow of uncertainty cross his face as he realized what was happening. He knew me well enough to understand the truth—that I didn't know how to answer his question.

"Sawyer, are you serious?" I finally managed to breathe.

He opened the ring box and revealed an enormous diamond solitaire ring. "Is this serious enough?"

I gasped again as I looked at the ring; my mind working at a furious pace to try to believe what I was actually seeing. Everything had happened so suddenly; I was still trying to recover from the shock.

"When did you buy that?" I stalled.

"Eliza that's not important, answer my question please."

"You answer mine first; I want to know how long you've had that ring and where you got the money for it."

He sighed. "I used the credit card my dad gave me—but I plan to pay him back, and I bought it on Wednesday, after you told me you'd go on this date."

"What?" If I'd been shocked before, that was nothing compared to the way I was feeling now. "You went out and bought a ring after I told you I would go out with you? You were *that* confident that I would agree to marry you after you brought me out here to wine and dine me for a few days—is that it?" I stood up and began pacing back and forth. This whole situation was so bizarre. I'd only known him for a month and a half!

Sawyer shut the ring box and stood up, taking me by the arm. "Hold on—it wasn't like that." I gave him an incredulous look. "Okay, maybe it was a *little* like that, but you're twisting it all around. I didn't expect that you would immediately say yes, and I didn't bring you out here to try to buy your love. You know me better than that, Eliza. Will you look at me, please?"

I stood still and reluctantly looked into his eyes.

"I brought you out here because I wanted my family to meet you before I proposed. I realize we've known each other for less than two months and I know this seems crazy. Under normal circumstances I would have dated you longer before asking you to marry me, but these are not normal circumstances."

He looked away and stared at the ground while trying to regain his composure. When he looked up there was moisture in his eyes. "I wanted to get you away from all the things back home that constantly remind you of him, so that you could see *me* for a change. I wanted you to know that I'm serious about us; to realize where I stand." He gently reached for my hand. "I only have a few weeks left, and it kills me to think I might lose you. I *love* you, Eliza."

I turned away from him, feeling the tears burn my own eyes. I hated to see the suffering he was going through; I hated that I had caused it, and I hated that I still didn't know what to say. A small part of me wanted to accept his proposal and throw my arms around him.

Why?

"I never wanted to hurt you, Sawyer," I said with my back still turned to him. I had my arms folded around my chest, as if to hold myself together. "I've never even told you that I loved you—how could you propose to me when I've never told you that?"

He came around and lifted my chin until my eyes met his. "Because you didn't have to. I've seen it in your eyes. You love me, Eliza—*admit it*." His voice was low and his chest heaved with emotion. "You may not accept my proposal right now, but at least admit that it's true." He grabbed my shoulders and his face was mere inches from mine.

I wanted to look away, but his steady gaze held me. There was a tightness in my throat as a tear rolled down my cheek. I was tired of holding back.

"I do," my voice broke. "I do—I love you." I pressed the back of my hand to my mouth to keep from sobbing as my heart finally released the truth.

The frustration in Sawyer's eyes quickly melted into joy. He reached his hands up to my face and kissed me.

I surrendered to his kiss and could taste the salt from my tears as they continued to stream down my face. There was no one else around, just the two of us and the waves as we kissed. I wanted to stay in that moment; the moment where there were no obstacles and no complications between us.

He buried his face in my neck and continued to hold me tight as if afraid

I would disappear. "I know you don't know what answer to give me right now," he murmured, "but will you at least think about it for a few days? I'm willing to wait until after . . ." his jaw tightened, "until you know where things stand, before you answer me. I want you to keep the ring until then."

I pulled back and looked at him for a long moment. I couldn't believe he was willing to make that sacrifice, and I wasn't sure I could function with a proposal rolling around in my head for the next few weeks. This whole thing was crazy! I was only eighteen; I had just graduated high school for crying out loud! I wasn't ready to get married. Yet as I looked at the ring again and thought about becoming Sawyer's wife I realized that I didn't want to tell him no—but I couldn't say yes either.

I shook my head and gave him an exasperated look. "Okay . . . if you're sure?"

He grinned and placed the box in my hand. "Just think it over. That's all I ask."

I looked at the velvet box in my palm and sighed. "I am *so* going to fail finals."

He laughed and then pulled me tighter.

CHAPTER

twenty-five

It was early Sunday evening by the time we were driving back to my apartment. Sawyer and I had attended church with his family, and I'd met his dad
for the first time. He was friendlier than any of the other members of the family
had been, but when we were saying good-bye after church he'd called me Emily.

Awesome.

I wasn't sorry to leave the Murdock residence. It was an impressive house,
but a far cry from being an actual home. The place was so gigantic that each family member could carry on their own lives without ever having to interact with
each other; and sadly that seemed to be exactly the case.

I thought about what Grandma had said about the importance of family
spending time together. I'd often considered my parents' house small by most
standards, and had sometimes been embarrassed by that fact, but now I thought
it was just about perfect. It was cozy, and more importantly—filled with love.

"So I was thinking," Sawyer began; snapping me out of my thoughts. "It
would be really funny if you wore the ring when you walked into your apartment, you know . . . just to see your roommates' reactions."

I laughed and shook my head. "No way."

"Why not?" He pressed. "Think how hilarious it would be to see their faces. I could even record it and put it on YouTube or something. I bet it would get a ton of hits."

I grinned. "It *would* be pretty funny . . . but there's no way."

"Oh come one, just do it. You can take it off again and tell them it's a joke after I leave."

"Oh, so that's what this is—a joke? You weren't serious about asking me to marry you?" I teased.

"You know I was." His eyes narrowed. "You could just tell me yes right now and it wouldn't be a joke at all—*and* you could leave the ring on, permanently. Total bonus."

"*Sawyer.*" I sighed in exasperation.

"What? I have a point, don't you think?" he smirked.

I shook my head and smiled. Ever since I'd agreed to take the ring from him he'd been scheming up ways to try to get me to put it on. Of course I was tempted, but it just didn't seem right when I didn't have an answer for him.

"*Or* . . . we could wait until Lacey took a drink of milk and you could hurry and slip it on. That way we could watch to see if she'd snort the milk out of her nose. The video would go viral for sure."

I tried to look severe but couldn't stop the giggle from escaping. He was such a tease! I knew he really wanted to see that ring on my finger and wouldn't let up until he did.

"Look, if I wear the ring when we first walk in, will you be satisfied and stop bugging me about it?"

"Yes."

"Promise?"

"Scout's honor."

"Were you a boy scout?"

"No."

I laughed again as he pulled into the parking lot. Suddenly my heart was beating at a furious pace. I couldn't believe he had talked me into this and secretly hoped my roommates weren't at home. I'd promised to wear the ring inside; nothing more. If no one was home Sawyer would just be out of luck.

He put the car in park and turned off the engine. "So are you going to do it?" There was a challenge in his eyes, mingled with excited anticipation.

I took the ring box out of my purse and slowly opened the lid. The diamond caught the sun and a dozen tiny lights reflected around the car as I pulled it out of the case.

"Here, let me do it," Sawyer said as he reached for the ring. He held it in his hand a second before slipping it on to my left ring finger. The light in his eyes communicated too much and I worried this was a mistake. I let my gaze travel to the ring to distract my thoughts.

"It really is beautiful." I held my hand up to inspect it closer. "You have good taste."

He stared at me for a moment. "I know." I blushed as he leaned over and kissed me before grabbing the door handle. "Come on, I can't wait to see this."

After Sawyer's proposal yesterday I'd decided to fast today. I wanted the Lord to know I was serious about seeking an answer, but now the lack of food combined with the summer heat was making me feel dizzy.

Sawyer wasted no time getting my bag and carrying it up to the apartment, holding my hand tightly the whole way. I was about to chicken-out and slip the ring into my pocket before he opened the door, but he was too fast. He threw it open and said loudly, "Guess who's back?"

All three of my roommates were sitting on the living room couch when Sawyer pulled me into the room.

I tried to hide my left hand behind me, but he brought it forward and dramatically began swinging our hands back and forth.

"No. way . . . Is that a *ring* on your finger?" Bree exclaimed.

I felt a blush run from the top of my head all the way down to my toes. This was definitely a bad idea.

"Eliza, you're *engaged?*" Lacey squealed as she jumped up from the couch to look at my hand.

Charlotte and Bree were close behind as everyone crowded around to look at the ring. It seemed like all three girls were talking at once and Sawyer never let his hand drop from mine. He wore a huge grin, but I couldn't return his smile.

What had seemed like a funny idea now made me feel like crying. I was going to have to tell my roommates the whole story and explain the complicated mess that was my life, when I couldn't even explain it to myself.

In all of the commotion no one had bothered to close the door. A shadow moved and I turned to see what had caused it.

I almost sensed his presence before I saw him.

Luke. *My* Luke was standing in the doorway.

I dropped Sawyer's hand as I felt the breath being sucked from my lungs.

Luke's golden brown eyes met mine and I felt like I was staring at him through a tunnel. This couldn't be real . . . Luke wasn't getting home for a few more weeks.

The air around me began to swirl as our eyes stayed locked together. I saw the pain and confusion that filled him as he looked down at my ring and then back to my face.

"Liza, you're engaged?" he asked quietly.

Someone said his name, and I watched his features twist in concern. The voices behind me were dim and hollow. I saw Luke reach out, and then my body folded into blackness.

Intense pain was the first thing I felt; a writhing ache in my chest that wouldn't let up.

"Eliza . . . *Eliza!*" Sawyer's voice echoed through a haze as his face slowly came into focus.

I was lying down and tried to sit up, but Sawyer gently pushed me back. I had to move; had to get rid of the burning in my heart. It was unbearable; consuming every part of me with pain.

As the fog began to clear from my mind, I looked up at the concerned faces above me: Sawyer, Bree, Charlotte . . . my heart pinched sharply.

"Luke," I breathed. I sat up, ignoring Sawyer's protests. "You're here?" I couldn't believe what I was seeing.

"Yes." He stood a few feet back from the rest of us, letting Sawyer remain the closest to me. His eyes had taken on a hard, flat look, but there was concern underneath. "Are you okay?"

"I'm fine." I stood somewhat shakily, pressing against my forehead for a moment to still the throbbing. Sawyer insisted that I sit back down but I brushed him off.

I had to see Luke, had to explain about the ring. I looked at him and watched as his face transformed from concern to a mask of indifference.

He straightened his shoulders. "There was a change in the flights and they ended up sending me home early. I wanted to surprise you, but I can see now that it was a mistake."

It was Luke's voice, accentuated by the language he'd been speaking for so long, but this wasn't the Luke I knew. He wore an expression I'd never seen on him before.

I stood there speechless, completely mesmerized by the sight of him: He was older now; more mature, and if possible, even more handsome. His dark hair was cut short, and a deep tan was evidence of many days walking in the Mexican heat. He wore a suit, but no missionary nametag.

"You've been released?" I was still trying to make sense of the situation. For two years I'd imagined waiting at the airport when Luke got home. I'd pictured him coming down the escalator in his suit and nametag; pictured what he would look like. I'd never imagined our first meeting like this.

"Yes." His mask was crumbling; I was beginning to see the pain behind his eyes. "It was good to see you again, Liza." He glanced at me and then quickly away. "I wish you all the best." He turned, and for the first time I noticed the long-stemmed rose he was holding. He placed it on the back of the couch and disappeared.

"Luke, wait!" I started after him but Sawyer caught my arm.

"Just let him go," he said, gripping tightly.

I yanked my arm away and turned on him. "No! I have to explain. He's so hurt—and it's your fault."

Sawyer's head reared back. "You don't mean that."

I felt tears coming to my eyes and I knew I had only spoken in anger. There was no one to blame but myself.

"You're right. I'm sorry," I whispered and then rushed out the door. I reached the banister outside and saw that Luke was already getting into his car.

"Luke!"

He didn't stop or look up, just got in and drove away.

I dashed back into the apartment and straight past Sawyer. My roommates were all standing like statues, each of their faces completely awestruck, but I didn't care. I rushed back to my room and grabbed my car keys.

I had to get to Luke; had to find him and explain that I wasn't engaged. I couldn't lose him over this. I would find a way to make everything right again.

Tears were streaming down my face as I reached my car and unlocked it. I opened the door, but suddenly Sawyer was there, slamming it shut.

"I don't think you should drive right now."

"Sawyer, I'm fine. Please leave me alone." The tears were coming faster and I dashed them away as I reached for the handle again.

"Eliza, don't do this." He grabbed my hand and forced me to look at him.

"Luke needs time to think things over. He probably hasn't even been home twenty-four hours yet, just let him go."

"Stop saying that!" I snapped. "I can't just 'let him go'. I've been waiting for *two years* to see him again. He thought I was faithful to him, and I've completely shattered his trust."

"He knew you were going to date while he was gone," Sawyer argued.

"*This* looks like a little more than just dating," I held up the ring. "He thinks I went and got engaged just days before he was coming home." I shook my head in disgust and forced my hand out of Sawyer's. I took the ring off and tried to hand it to him, but he wouldn't take it.

"Don't . . . you're not thinking clearly." His blue eyes were filled with torment. "Just keep it until you've had a chance to really think things over."

I shook my head and continued to hold the ring out to him, my tears flowing faster than I could stop them.

With both hands he took my fingers and closed them around the ring, gripping my hand into a fist. "Please." His eyes were pleading and I wondered how many people I would hurt before this was all over.

We stood there, staring at each other. Neither one of us wanted to yield. The pain in his eyes was eating me alive and I didn't have it in me to fight anymore. I had to find Luke.

I nodded my head and slowly drew the ring back.

Sawyer's shoulders relaxed and he gave me a solemn look before opening my door. "Promise me you'll be careful; no running red lights or anything."

"I will." I put the ring in my pocket and climbed into the car. Sawyer closed my door and stood back, his face grim. I couldn't bear to look at him so I forced the car into gear and drove away.

I must have hit every red light in the city. My tears had stopped, replaced by a hollow numbness. I was still in shock. Luke was home. Luke was *home*. And I had given him the worst welcome imaginable.

I wanted to scream as I waited for yet another light to turn. My mind was racing in a thousand different directions; impossible to grasp onto any one thought to try to make sense of it.

Ugh. This had to be the longest light in existence! I glanced out the side window and something in the distance caught my attention: the temple.

Without thinking I flipped on my blinker. When the glaring red light finally changed, I turned instead of heading for the freeway.

The parking lot was almost empty, aside from the few cars that belonged to families out for a Sunday stroll. I found a spot far away from everyone and shut off the engine. It was dusk, and the sun was setting just as it did every night. The world was rolling along as if something monumental hadn't just occurred—something that had knocked my entire universe out of orbit.

I closed my eyes and pressed my forehead against the steering wheel. I needed answers. I'd made a mess out of everything and I wasn't going to talk to Luke until I knew what direction I was supposed to take.

The lesson in Relief Society this morning had been about missionary work. The teacher in Sawyer's ward had done an amazing job and the Spirit in the room was undeniable. All day in the back of my mind I'd wondered if maybe this was my answer. Maybe that's why I hadn't received any inspiration about Sawyer or Luke—maybe I was supposed to serve a mission.

Just one more path to add to the many that branched out before me. How was I ever going to know which one was right?

I thought back to my dream with Grandma. She had been so certain that the Lord would answer my prayers. I wasn't sure exactly when that answer would come, or if I would even recognize it when it did, but I trusted her. If she said I would get an answer, then I had to believe it was true.

I said a humble prayer. I was emotionally, physically, and mentally spent.

I didn't have anything else to give; not even another tear to shed. I promised that I would follow whichever path the Lord wanted me to take. I would move forward and not look back—if I could only know which choice was best.

It started slowly, but before I'd finished the prayer a warmth began in my chest and spread until it flowed through every inch of my body. I didn't hear a voice or receive an answer about what I should do, but somehow I knew everything was going to be alright.

I opened my eyes and stared up at the temple. A smile spread across my face as I listened to the chirping of crickets and savored what I was feeling. I was at peace. I knew that my prayer had been heard, and for now, that was enough.

I was ready to find Luke.

CHAPTER

twenty-six

It was fully dark by the time I reached Luke's house. On the drive I had rehearsed over and over again what I would tell him: I would explain that I wasn't engaged, and then I would beg for forgiveness. That was the gist of it, at least. I just hoped he would be willing to hear me out after what had happened this afternoon.

I took a deep breath as I stood on the front porch. The lights were on inside and I could hear several people talking. Judging by the line-up of cars parked in the driveway, I surmised that the Matthews had guests over to welcome Luke home.

With a sick twinge in my stomach I realized that I should have been one of those guests. In fact, I should have been first in line to welcome him home (well, at least second—a missionary's mom always took first priority).

I hadn't planned on facing an entire group of people; all my thoughts had centered on Luke. I considered turning around and going to my parents' house instead, but the thought of waiting any longer to talk to him caused me physical pain.

I gathered all the courage I could muster and knocked on the door. I'd checked my makeup in the car before getting out. Although I hadn't cried since leaving the temple, my face had still been a bit blotchy. I hoped that the touch of powder and lip-gloss would suffice to hide the evidence of my emotionally strained day.

I heard footsteps and the door opened. "Eliza!" Sister Matthews said as she stepped out and immediately drew me into a warm hug. The lump in my throat throbbed at her tenderness. I didn't deserve it.

"Hi, Janet," I said shakily. "Is Luke here?"

She quickly pulled away and held my shoulders. "You mean he's not with you?" Her eyebrows pulled together as she glanced behind me. When she looked back she studied my face and her eyes filled with pity. "What happened, dear? Is everything all right?"

I thought there couldn't be any water left, but when I saw the sympathy in her eyes my tears started up again.

"Yes. I mean no . . . I just really—need—to talk to him," I managed to choke out before I fell apart.

"Oh, sweetheart." Janet took me into her arms and held me tight. "I'm sure whatever it is, things will be all right." She kept one arm around me and closed the door before leading me over to the porch swing. "You don't have to talk about it if you don't want to, but is there anything I can do?"

I loved the motherly way in which she consoled me, instantly making me feel like things were going to work out. She smelled like cinnamon and baked bread and everything homey. I could feel her love for me, and ached with the realization that she might not feel the same after she knew what I'd done to her son.

I sniffed and gave her a weak smile. "I'll be okay. I just *really* need to talk to Luke. Do you have any way of getting a hold of him?"

She frowned and shook her head. "He doesn't have a cell phone yet. I should have thought to have him take mine." She cast a worried glance back toward the house. "Someone spread the word on Facebook that he was home and there are so many people here that want to see him." Her eyes were still concerned as she looked back at me. "You're sure you have no idea where he's gone?"

"No." I wiped my tears away and took a deep breath. "We had a . . . misunderstanding when he came to my apartment. See, there was a guy with me and . . . well," I looked down at my hands, "I was just so surprised to see Luke. The whole situation was a misunderstanding." I omitted the fact that I'd been wearing an engagement ring and that I'd been so shocked to see him that I'd fainted. My cheeks burned.

"I *warned* him that it might not be a good idea to catch you off guard like that." Janet shook her head slowly. "I wanted to call and tell you that he was flying home early, but he was dead-set on surprising you. I'm sorry, Eliza."

"No, please don't apologize. I think it's sweet that he wanted to surprise me—I just wish things had happened differently, that's all."

A pair of headlights turned into the driveway and I held my breath.

"There he is," she said with a relieved nod as the car pulled to a stop.

My heart began beating frantically as I watched Luke get out of the car.

His mom gave me a squeeze and said, "I'll run inside and tell everyone that he'll be a few more minutes." She winked and gave my hand another squeeze. "Just take your time, honey."

"Okay. Thanks." I smiled in appreciation before she hurried away.

Luke had been walking toward the house with his head bent down, but he looked up at the sound of his mom closing the front door.

I slowly stood from the swing and he started, doing a double take as his eyes found mine.

"Hi," I said, taking a small step toward him.

"Hi." He stared at the banister and slid his hands into his pockets, making no effort to move.

"I need to talk to you. I didn't have a chance to explain back at the apartment."

"I didn't think an explanation was necessary. I was able to put two and two together." He looked down and kicked a rock in the dirt.

"No, you don't understand." I held up my left hand. "I'm not engaged."

Luke's head snapped up and he looked from my hand to my face in confusion. "You broke it off already?"

I shook my head. "I was never engaged. It was a joke . . . a stunt to get a reaction from my roommates. You just happened to walk in at exactly the wrong time." I smiled as I watched the light that suddenly filled his eyes.

"Liza, are you serious?"

"Luke, I would never tease you about something like this."

He took a step closer to me but suddenly stopped. "So then who was the guy holding your hand—and where did the ring come from?"

Ick. This was the part that would be harder to explain. "His name's Sawyer . . . and the ring sort of . . . came from him."

Luke's face darkened. "Eliza, *what* is going on? Just tell me straight up, is he your boyfriend—your fiancé—what? A guy doesn't just give you a huge diamond ring to play a joke. I saw the way he looked at you. There is something more going on here than what you're telling me."

His Spanish accent grew thick with his anger and I shook my head in frustration. "I've been dating him but I told him I wasn't going to commit to anything until you got home. I never meant for any of this to happen. He just proposed yesterday—I swear I wasn't expecting it. He asked me to keep the ring until after you got home . . . until I knew where things stood between us."

Luke's expression had turned to stone and I rushed on, "He convinced me to put the ring on to see what my roommates' reactions would be. It was stupid and I never should have gone along with it."

"So you love him." Luke's mouth was set in a firm line and I saw the muscle in his jaw flex.

"Didn't you hear what I just said?" I frowned in confusion.

"Yes. I heard you say that he proposed and you took the ring because you're thinking about it. If you didn't love him you would have just told him no."

"Luke, please . . ." I reached out to touch his hand that was gripping the porch railing, but he withdrew it.

"Why didn't you tell me, Liza? Why didn't you write and explain what was going on? I couldn't wait to see you and I was so excited to surprise you. Do you have any *idea* how much it killed me to come home and find you with another guy?" His brown eyes burned with pain and frustration.

My face crumpled. "I wanted to write you, but I couldn't find the words. I only started dating Sawyer less than two months ago and didn't think anything would come of it. I didn't want to distract you during your last few weeks. I knew I would be here when you got home, so I decided against it." I put both hands over my face and squeezed my eyes shut. "I'm so sorry, Luke." I had tried to protect him, but ended up losing his trust instead. I had ruined everything.

It was quiet for several moments as I continued to hide behind my hands, brushing the tears away with my palms. I couldn't look at him anymore. I hated seeing the anger in his eyes; the pain that I had caused him.

"Liza." I heard his footsteps on the porch and felt the warmth of his body as he moved directly in front of me. My senses exploded as he placed his hands on mine, gently removing them from my face.

"Don't cry." His eyes were soft as he reached out and brushed my tears away.

Goose bumps broke out all over my skin as he touched me. My breathing became unsteady and my legs trembled.

"I'm sorry I was upset. I was just scared that I'd lost you." He placed his hand under my chin and tilted it until our eyes met. "I'd had a feeling that you were dating someone else. For weeks now I've been having crazy dreams that made me wonder if that's what was happening. But I told you to date while I was gone, and what guy in his right mind wouldn't propose to a girl as beautiful as you?"

Heat touched my cheeks and I shook my head. "I'm just so sorry, Luke. I feel like I've messed everything up." I bit my lip and looked away.

"You haven't messed anything up. Some things are worth fighting for, and I'll fight to win your heart back—no matter how long it takes. I told myself that if you weren't married when I got home I would do whatever I could to make you mine. And that's what I'm prepared to do." His jaw was firm and his dark brown eyes took on a resolute look.

My heart melted at his words.

"You don't have to fight for something that's already yours," I whispered. "You have my heart, Luke . . . you've had it from the moment that I met you."

"Liza," he breathed; his eyes searching mine.

I smiled as I saw the affirmation of my love slowly enter his eyes. He grinned before he moved closer and suddenly pulled me into his arms, embracing me for the first time since he'd come home. My pulse raced and I sighed as I clung to him with all the strength I could muster.

This was what I'd been waiting for; this exact moment. The warm feeling I'd experienced earlier returned, confirming what I needed to know. I cried tears of joy as I felt something inside of me become whole again. I hadn't known how broken I'd been until now. All at once it felt like I was *home*.

We stood there for several minutes and I relished each sensation: the familiar smell of his aftershave, the way his arms wrapped around me just so, the beating of his heart as he continued to hold me tighter until I almost couldn't breathe, but I didn't care. I would rather pass out again than have Luke's arms leave me for even a moment.

I remembered every happy memory we'd shared together and every tender word he'd written in his letters. He owned my very heart and soul! He was my best friend, and I never wanted to let him go.

When he finally pulled back I noticed that there was moisture in his eyes. I reached up and held his face in my hands before brushing at the tear that slid down his cheek.

"I can't believe this is real," he whispered as he looked into my eyes.

I smiled. "I know what you mean. I feel like I'm still dreaming."

He buried his face in my shoulder. "I've waited so long to hold you again, Liza. I was worried that things would have changed . . . and they have."

I frowned self-consciously and pulled back to face him.

His eyes narrowed as he gave me an appraising look. "You're even *more* beautiful than I remembered, and now I can kiss you as much as I want."

I blushed, thrilled by his compliment and the implication that followed. He grinned at my blush and his eyes danced with anticipation.

Neither one of us spoke as our faces slowly drew closer together.

The front door opened, painfully breaking the spell.

Luke grabbed my hand. "Come on, let's go somewhere where nobody can find us," he whispered and began to lead me down the porch, but we were too late.

"Luke, Eliza . . . where are you two going?" It was Janet.

"Just give us a few more minutes, okay, Mom?" Luke said as he gripped my hand tighter.

"I would, but some of your friends have to leave and I thought you'd want to see them." She smiled sympathetically at us. "I know you're anxious to be alone with your sweetheart, but just give a few moments to your friends first."

"I'm coming," Luke said. He gave me a disappointed smile and pulled me with him toward the house. I loved the possessive way he gripped my hand, as if he didn't want to let me go.

We entered the house and despite the lateness of the hour, it was literally packed with people. Luke's family, friends from high school and the mission field practically swarmed us as we walked in.

Everyone wanted his attention. He kept a firm hold on my hand and pulled me closer each time someone threatened to separate us. The signal he was conveying was that we were already an "us" instead of a "him." I couldn't stop smiling.

More than one girl gave me the evil eye; obviously hoping that our relationship wouldn't have lasted through the mission. Olivia Chambers in particular seemed more than slightly disappointed to see Luke holding my hand. I caught her analyzing me when she thought I wasn't looking. Without the wet hair and green skin, I hoped I looked good enough to pose as a threat to her aspirations where Luke was concerned.

"Liza!" Jill called from among the crowd.

I turned and waved in unexpected joy at seeing her.

"I'm gonna go talk to Jill, okay?" I whispered to Luke as he stood talking to an uncle.

"Hurry back." He winked and gave me one of those crooked smiles that showed his dimple.

My heart stuttered. "I will." I smiled back at him before leaving to find Jill.

Right before I reached her, I felt small arms wrap around my waist from behind. I spun around. "Morgan!" I bent down to her level and returned the hug.

"I knew you'd be here," she said, grinning as she held me tighter.

I was about to try to explain about Sawyer, but just as quickly as she'd come, she vanished again. I laughed. That was typical little Morgan: sweet and unpredictable. Her hug had mended another place in my heart and I was grinning as I reached Jill.

"Holy cow! Were you so surprised that he came home early?" she exclaimed as she gave me a quick hug.

"You have no *idea* how bad that went down," I said quietly.

"Oh no—Sawyer?"

I nodded. "Basically the worst scenario imaginable when Luke walked in."

"You were *making out?*" she gasped, covering her mouth.

"No . . . *worse.*" I related the whole story and her eyes grew larger and larger with each detail. Finally she couldn't contain herself anymore and laughed out loud.

I put a hand on my hip and scowled. "Jill, it's not funny!"

"Sorry, Liza, I know I shouldn't laugh—but something like that could only happen to you. I can't believe you actually *passed out*. Who caught you when you fell?"

Up to that point I hadn't even considered who had caught me, but I realized it must have been Sawyer. I thought of his resigned expression when I'd driven off today and felt my heart pinch. What must he have been through since I left?

I glanced over to Luke and saw that he was watching me as he stood talking to a group of friends. Our eyes met and he smiled the special smile I remembered. The one meant only for me.

"So what are you going to do now . . . about Sawyer I mean?" Jill asked, pulling my attention away from Luke.

"I'm going to give him back his ring and end things for good," I said, feeling the piece of me that cared for Sawyer break all over again.

Jill nodded and gave me a sympathetic smile. "It's too bad, but you're doing the right thing. Sawyer is a great guy, but when I saw you and Luke walk in together tonight, it was like . . ." her eyes took on a faraway look, "like you were just *complete* together, you know?"

"Yeah, I know," I couldn't stop the huge grin from spreading across my face as I looked back over to Luke. He *did* complete me, in every possible way. I'd had my answer the moment I'd seen him in the driveway.

Sawyer was incredible and someone that I loved—but not in the way that I loved Luke. I couldn't believe I'd even considered that my feelings for Sawyer could compare with the way I felt for Luke. His long absence had made me forget for a time, had diluted the memory somewhat, but deep down I'd always known. It was the reason I'd tried to break things off with Sawyer so often; the reason it took me so long to tell him that I loved him. My love for Luke was on an entirely deeper level, and from the moment I'd seen him again I knew that I wanted to belong to him—forever.

"Well, call me if you need someone to talk to after your conversation with Sawyer, okay?" Jill smiled and put her hand on my shoulder. "You're doing the right thing, Liza. The sooner you get it over with, the better."

I reached down and felt the cold, pointed edge of the diamond ring in my pocket. Jill was right—the sooner the better.

CHAPTER

twenty-seven

I plan to go apartment hunting this week," Luke said.

The guests had all finally left and we were standing next to my car. The August moon was full and bright above us.

"Good. That means I won't have to drive up here every day to see you." I grinned, trying to fight the urge to shiver. I wasn't sure if it was standing so close to him, or the night breeze that had caused the reaction.

Luke smiled as he leaned forward and wrapped his arms around me. "Better?" he whispered. His body was strong and warm, and I could feel the firm contours of his chest beneath his white shirt.

"Much better, thanks." My legs began to feel wobbly. He held me tighter and I could hear his heart pounding.

After a few moments, he pulled back to look at me. The moonlight shone across his face and I saw a warm spark in his eyes. My heartbeat quickly picked up pace to match his and I drew in a breath as he leaned slowly in. I laced my hands behind his neck and reached in to meet his kiss.

A rush of emotions hit me like a tidal wave the moment Luke's lips touched mine. I felt an almost euphoric sense of bliss as bursts of light seemed to infuse my whole body. It felt like my bones had turned to liquid! His lips were gentle, caressing at first. He seemed to possess a healing quality as I felt all the pain and heartache of missing him the past two years melt into nothing.

Then, after a few minutes his kiss became deeper, more intense. Chills ran all the way from my neck down my back as I returned his kiss with just as much intensity. I moved my hands from his neck to his chest, gripping the collar of his suit jacket tightly.

Luke moved his hands from my waist to my hair, gently running his fingers through it as he kissed me. I sighed in delight and felt him smile. Then, just as I was aching for more, he pulled away.

"Wow," he breathed.

I nodded as I tried to catch my breath.

"Wow," he said again.

I laughed, feeling almost light-headed. I knew exactly what he meant: there were no words.

He took my keys and unlocked the car before opening my door. "I don't want you to leave, but I don't think I can handle another kiss like that. You better get out of here before I change my mind."

I smiled coyly and shook my head, reaching for him again, but he took a step back.

"Oh no you don't; and don't give me that look or you'll *really* be in trouble," he teased, but I could see the restrained passion in his eyes.

As hard as it was to tear myself away from him, I admired his strength. With Sawyer, *I* had always been the one who had to be strong. But with Luke it was different. I knew I could trust him and knew that he loved me enough that he would never put me in a compromising situation.

"You're right," I sighed and reluctantly got in the car. My heart felt light as air; a weightlessness I hadn't felt for two years. "Will I see you tomorrow?" I asked before he could close the door.

"You'll see me tonight."

I looked up at him in surprise.

"I'll meet you in my dreams, remember?"

My shoulders slumped but I smiled. "It's a date."

"But until then," he leaned in and kissed me once more. It was a perfect kiss and I felt deflated when he pulled away all too soon.

"Good night, Liza Lou," he said as he traced his thumb along my chin.

My eyes lit up at hearing him use my old nickname again.

"Good night, Luke."

I crept into my parents' house and quietly closed the door. I'd called my mom from Luke's house to let her know (in as few words as possible), what had transpired in the past twenty-four hours, and asked if I could crash here tonight. I would have to get up at the crack of dawn to make it to my first class on time, but it was better than risking a late drive.

I tiptoed up to my room, maneuvering around the creaky spots in the floor as best I could. Thankfully, I had some spare PJs and an extra toothbrush in my room.

I knelt by my bed and offered heartfelt thanks for the day. I hadn't been able to stop smiling since leaving Luke's house. I felt in my heart that he was the man I wanted to marry and spend eternity with—if he ever asked me. All the confusion and doubt I'd felt about Sawyer seemed to disappear now that I had my answer. I prayed for him and for the right words to say as things unfolded tomorrow.

After ending my prayer I hopped into bed and snuggled under the covers with a happy spirit. Everything was going to be okay. The Lord had heard and answered my prayers, just as Grandma had promised.

All I had needed was to be patient.

Seeking Out and Helping Those in Need

"Charity Never Faileth"

– I Corinthians 13:8

CHAPTER
twenty-eight

Ever so slowly, my surroundings came into focus. I was standing in a room, which was filled to the brim with women in dresses and bonnets. I wondered if in my sleep I'd been transported into an episode of "Little House on the Prairie." If so, my mom would be jealous. She was a fan of the series and usually ended up crying at some point during each episode . . . which I could never understand.

"Glad you could join me, dear," Grandma said, as she seemed to appear from nowhere.

"Hey, Grandma," I smiled at her. I had a feeling she would be here.

She beamed back and then gestured around the room. "So what do you think? I'll wager you never thought you'd get to witness *this* event. Very exciting, isn't it?" Her eyes twinkled and I knew she was back to playing our old guessing game.

"Actually, I haven't really had a chance to take it all in yet," I admitted as I followed her sweeping gaze. I noticed an excited hum in the room as the women talked and I began to study each face for signs of a clue.

A door opened and a tall man entered.

"No way," I breathed. An instant hush fell over the room. "Grandma, it's *him!*" I whispered, excitement causing my voice to strain.

Grandma chuckled. "Yes . . . and do you see Emma sitting there on the front row?" She pointed over to where Emma sat and I immediately recognized her. I was once again in the presence of the Prophet Joseph Smith and his wife Emma.

"So, any idea what this event might be?"

I didn't appreciate her smug expression. "I'll get it. Just give me a few more seconds." Scanning the room more carefully now, I began to search for clues. Two men I didn't recognize sat in chairs behind the Prophet Joseph as he stood to speak. I turned my attention back to the women in the room and saw yet another familiar face.

"That's Eliza Snow, isn't it?" Although Sister Snow had been older in the previous dream I'd seen her in, her features were unmistakable.

Grandma nodded, placing her finger next to her chin in amusement.

The pieces were all fitting together. I quickly glanced at the other women in the room, but didn't see anyone else I recognized. It didn't matter, because I was sure I had the answer.

"This is the Relief Society getting organized, isn't it?" I folded my arms across my chest and raised a triumphant eyebrow in Grandma's direction.

"Oh, fiddledee-dee! I made this one too easy for you," she huffed, though her eyes were smiling.

"I wouldn't say *easy*." I put a hand on my hip and raised an eyebrow. "Now if there had been a gigantic centerpiece or some green Jell-O with carrots, it would have been a given; but you gotta give me some props on this one."

She stared at me blankly; obviously missing the joke. "Yes . . . well, you're absolutely right about this event. We are currently standing on the second floor of the Smiths' Red Brick Store."

She cleared her throat and continued, "The story began when two women, Sarah Granger Kimball and her friend Margaret A. Cook, wanted to sew some clothing for the men who were working on the Nauvoo temple. They realized that their efforts would go much farther if they invited others to join the project, and they soon came up with the idea of organizing a ladies' society. They petitioned Eliza R. Snow to write some rules and regulations for the society, and then to submit them to the Prophet for approval."

"Eliza did so, but when Joseph read the documents, he said, 'Tell the sisters their offering is accepted of the Lord, and He has something better for them . . . I will organize the women under the priesthood after a pattern of the priesthood.'"

Grandma beamed. "I don't think those women realized what they set in motion when they desired to make clothes for the workers, and then *acted* on that simple desire. Can you imagine what they would have thought if they could see that over 5 million women are a part of this organization today?"

I shook my head in awe. "Are Sister Kimball and Sister Cook here?"

Grandma nodded and pointed to where they were sitting. "The woman in the brown dress is Sister Kimball, and the lady in the green next to her is Sister Cook."

My eyes widened as I looked at them and considered the amazing force for good that was in this tiny, crowded room. Generations upon generations had been, and would be affected by the people gathered here—and I was mere feet away from them!

"This first meeting took place on March 17, 1842. Twenty women were in attendance, and Joseph Smith, John Taylor and Willard Richards were all here presiding." Grandma gestured to the men at the front of the room.

It seemed like important people from church history were practically coming out of the woodwork. I supposed the next thing Grandma'd be telling me was that Moses was sitting somewhere on the back row.

She continued, "This is one of the most powerful organizations of women on the earth, and you are a part of that. In this meeting, the Prophet outlined the goals of the Relief Society. Essentially those three aims are: Faith, Family and Relief.

She smiled. "We've already discussed the first two. What better way to talk about seeking out and helping those in need, than by showing you the creation of this organization—this Society whose motto is: Charity Never Faileth."

I nodded in understanding as I continued to gaze at these faithful women from the past. Wouldn't they be amazed if they could know what I knew? If they could see how many women were a part of, or had been blessed by, Relief Society. And it had all started here.

"Well now that you've seen the beginning, allow me to show some of the experiences that have taken place since then." Grandma's blue eyes flashed in anticipation.

C ✄

It was as if a slideshow of events were unfolding before my eyes, blindingly fast—yet I could clearly see and understand each circumstance. Beginning from the pioneer days, up through the decades to the present, I saw women performing acts of charity.

I marveled at how my mind was taking it all in so rapidly. Not only could I see the events, but I could feel the emotion connected with each one. I watched as births were aided, children were tended, meals were taken, houses were cleaned, funerals were organized, illness was cared for, burdens were lifted, lessons were taught, donations were raised, and emergency aid was given.

I saw women from almost every country, performing these quiet and simple acts of service in their own sphere. I watched faithful visiting teachers going out in pairs, bringing comfort, hope and inspiration to those they taught. I saw as faith increased, families were strengthened and generations were blessed by acts of service—both large and small.

My eyes were opened to the true purpose and grandeur of this noble organization and I felt my heart swell with pride as I realized that I was a part of it. I had my role to play in building the Lord's Kingdom on the earth; to counteract the darkness with a flood of light and charity.

I felt the warm and overpowering witness that this was a remarkable work. Women of all ages and walks of life were united by this inspired Society, creating a powerful force for good.

As the vision slowly came to a close, I turned to Grandma with tears streaming down my face. My body felt weak and overcome by the things I had witnessed.

Her eyes met mine and she nodded in understanding. It was as if she'd been keeping this last great secret and had finally been able to share it.

"Eliza, *now* you know," she said, her eyes bright and piercing. "The question is . . . what are you going to do with this knowledge? Relief Society isn't just something you join when you turn eighteen; it's something that you become. A way of living which—if you'll allow it—is woven into the very fabric of your soul."

Her voice grew soft. "Charity is the pure love of Christ. These acts you have witnessed are the things He would do if He were still on the earth, yet it's up to you to be His hands. You must feed His sheep."

I nodded, unable to find my voice through the thick emotion. But it was all being recorded in my heart. I understood that this was the final dream. My Great Grandma Eliza Porter wouldn't be back to teach me any more lessons, but this dream had impacted me far greater than any I'd had before. It had opened my eyes and instilled a burning conviction that I would never forget—I would work daily to make sure of that.

"Grandma, this is the last time, isn't it?" I said quietly.

"Yes. You're ready now; ready for all of the wonderful adventures and opportunities that lie ahead of you." She smiled in her cheerful way and her entire being seemed infused with light. I loved her so much in that moment it hurt.

"I love you, Grandma."

"I love you too, Eliza. Never forget that." Her eyes sparkled as she looked at me tenderly.

I wanted to reach out and give her a hug, but the dream pushed against me as everything began to fade. I felt the tears fall afresh as I watched her slowly disappear.

"Thank you," I whispered in the empty space.

"Remember . . . Charity Never Faileth," her voice echoed one final time before the dream ended and she was gone.

CHAPTER

twenty-nine

When I crept into the kitchen the next morning it was still dark outside. I would have to leave soon in order to get to my first class on time.

If I could just make it through finals with a passing grade, I would consider myself lucky. Once I talked to Sawyer and the drama of my personal life simmered down, I would be able to focus more on my studies.

The thought of facing Sawyer today diminished what little there had been of my appetite. I decided to skip the quick bowl of cereal I'd been planning on and just head out to my car. I stepped into the brisk morning air and was a few feet down the front steps when the porch light suddenly came on.

"Eliza, are you leaving already?" Mom's groggy voice called from the door.

I turned and faced her with a guilty smile. "Yeah, sorry, Mom. I wish I had time to stay and talk, but I have to get to class."

She nodded in understanding and tightened the tie on her robe. I felt terrible for having awakened her—I'd never seen her look so tired before.

"Alright, but are you sure I can't make you a quick piece of toast or something?"

"I'm fine; promise." I smiled at her again before continuing to my car.

"Well call me after you're done with classes. We have a lot to talk about."

"I will." I gave her a thumbs-up and then jumped into my car. I knew she wanted to hear all about Luke—and my weekend with Sawyer.

It was August, but I shivered and turned the temperature knob all the way to hot. I was so nervous it was making me shaky. I waved at my mom as I backed out of the driveway and headed down the street.

I tried to think about my night with Luke last night and the dream with Grandma, but no matter how hard I tried to ignore him, Sawyer was always in the back of my mind.

How was I going to tell him?

I walked to my history class with trepidation weighing down each step. When I'd gotten back to my apartment and re-charged my dead cell phone, there had been two missed calls and one text from Sawyer: *I hope you're ok. I love you.*

The sweet message had caused me to burst into tears. It had taken me a while to calm down and convince myself that I wouldn't cry anymore. I had never been such a bawl-baby in my entire life, and I was determined to buck up and face things like an adult—but I still felt a burn that threatened at the back of my eyes.

My roommates had all been home this morning. They hadn't pressed me for information, even though I knew they were dying to know details. There would be time for talking later, and (I hoped), the news that things were over with Sawyer and that he was totally and completely fine.

As I entered the hallway to class, I saw Sawyer waiting for me outside of the room. One look at his face told me that he *wasn't* completely fine—far from it. His face was strained and he looked like he hadn't slept at all last night.

As soon as he saw me, his features relaxed a little in relief. Without saying a word he walked over and pulled me into his arms. I felt the tears instantly begin to flow and decided I might as well give up the fight to stop them.

He pulled slightly back and lifted my chin to look at him. "Do you want to get out of here?"

I nodded. It would be pointless to try to hear anything the professor was saying today, and the last thing I wanted was an audience for my uncontrollable tears, which threatened to become sobs any second.

He gripped my hand and threaded me through the crowds of students hurrying to get to class. I kept my head down and angrily wiped at the tears that wouldn't stop falling.

This whole situation was awful. I could already feel little pieces of me shattering and trailing in my wake like broken glass.

I hated the fact that I was going to hurt Sawyer; that I couldn't make him smile and laugh the way he used to. I hated that I was the reason for the intense pain in his eyes. No one else had caused the pain there—it was all me. But hadn't I known that this would happen? Hadn't I told myself over and over again the past several weeks that eventually someone would get hurt? Why hadn't I stopped things after our very first date? Why hadn't I insisted on never seeing him again? Because I'd been selfish, that's why. Spoiled, self-centered and selfish. I had the sudden urge to yell and punch something.

Sawyer continued leading me across campus until we reached his car. The silence between us was growing thicker by the second, and part of me wished that silence would never have to be broken. I still didn't know how I would find the words I needed to say.

As Sawyer closed my door and walked around to his side, I reached into my pocket and fingered the diamond ring. It would have to be the Band-Aid method: ripped off as quickly as possible. I couldn't handle to stretch this out any longer.

He got into the car and turned to look at me; his blue eyes laced with a thousand unreadable emotions. "Where do you want to go?"

"I don't know . . . maybe just drive and we'll figure it out." I couldn't think clearly.

"Okay." He turned the key in the ignition and had scarcely pulled out of the parking space before asking, "So how did it go last night?"

He had tried to sound casual, but there was too much emotion in his voice to pull it off. I felt like my heart was suddenly in my throat. This was where the pain really became intense.

"It went . . . well." I felt my pulse speed up and my throat became dry.

Sawyer gave a short, hard laugh and his hand tightened on the steering wheel. "Really? So what does that mean, exactly?"

The pain and discomfort were at their peak. I was suffocating! I had to get it out and be done with it. The anger in his voice was easier to deal with than the pain I'd heard earlier. I wanted him to be angry with me; I deserved it.

I took a deep breath and pushed on, "It means that I can't see you anymore, Sawyer. I'm so sorry for everything I put you through—but this has to be the end." I reached into my pocket and pulled out the ring.

He continued driving. He glanced at the ring but made no move to take it. "So that's it? Luke's home for one day and you've already decided he's the one you want to be with?"

"Yes." It was barely a whisper, but firm.

"Eliza, the guy has only been home for one *day*. How can you know that already? How can *he* know what he wants? I wasn't in my normal head for the first few months I was home. I was in mission-mode for a long time; I didn't know exactly which direction I was going to take. It's a big adjustment, and neither one of you has given it enough time." Both of his hands were clenching the steering wheel now as he made a hard turn.

I bit back the anger that was suddenly rising within me like bile. What right did Sawyer have to tell me what was best for me or Luke? He was making me feel guilty for rushing things, but that's not how it had happened. Sure, Luke was different than he'd been when he left, but only in a good way.

There was something else to his words that stung. He had fed my long-held fear that I wasn't good enough for Luke. That if he stood back and took a good, long look at me, he wouldn't like what he saw. Luke could have his choice of any girl he wanted—so why would he choose me?

The car rolled to a stop and Sawyer turned off the ignition. I looked out the window and realized where he had taken us: the pond where we'd gone on our first date.

"Eliza."

I could feel Sawyer's gaze on me but I couldn't look at him. I wished I hadn't come on this drive. I should have just given him the ring back in the hallway and walked away. Without realizing it, I had agreed to remove the Band-Aid the slow and torturous way.

"Listen, I'm sorry about what I said." His voice was gentle, and I could hear the pain behind it.

The ring was still in my palm and I clenched my fist around it as I raised my eyes to his. We gazed at each other for several seconds. His eyes, so often warm and teasing, were now completely serious as they searched mine. I knew what he was looking for, and my tears flowed faster as I saw the exact moment when he received his answer.

He sat back in his seat and blew out a long breath. He shook his head and made a small, sad smile. "I guess I thought I had a chance. For a while there I almost thought . . ." his voice trailed off as he stared at nothing.

"Sawyer, I'm so sorry. I never meant . . ."

"No, don't do that—please. Don't apologize." He leaned back and placed both hands behind his head as he continued to stare out the window. "I knew the risk all along, and none of this is your fault, okay? You were honest and up-front from the very beginning." He released his hands and turned to look at me, one corner of his mouth lifting sadly. "I just had to try."

My lip trembled as I struggled to keep my tears in check. "Sawyer, I hope you know that I really care about you and I never wanted to hurt you. You are an *amazing* guy, and you're going to make some girl very happy someday."

He nodded quickly and looked away a moment before straightening his shoulders. When he looked back at me, he wore a smile that didn't reach his eyes. He held out his hand. "I believe there's something you've been trying to give back to me, but I was too stubborn to take it. I'm ready now."

I attempted a smile in return as I placed the diamond ring in his palm. My heart suddenly felt three times lighter and I knew I was doing the right thing.

Sawyer held the ring for a moment. "I was so close." He looked up at me and there was a trace of moisture in his eyes. "You were almost mine."

Twenty minutes later we were in the parking lot to my apartment. I'd asked Sawyer to drop me off here because I'd already missed my first two classes and had another hour break before the next one would start. I knew the apartment would be empty and I needed time to collect myself before I faced anyone in public.

Sawyer pulled up at the curb but kept the engine running. We both sensed the good bye that was coming and I knew he didn't want to drag it out any longer than I did.

I turned in my seat and tried to act casual, like we were just two friends parting ways for a time. "Thanks for dropping me off . . . .and . . . take care of yourself, okay?" It was a lame thing to say, but no words seemed to fit the situation. I held out my hand, only realizing after I'd done it how stupid it looked there, awaiting his handshake.

Sawyer ignored my hand and reached over, enveloping me in his arms. I hugged him back and breathed in his scent one last time.

"Good bye, Eliza. I'll never forget you," he whispered into my neck. I felt him shudder slightly. He cleared his throat and pulled back, placing a hand on the gearshift.

I gazed at him one final time before opening my door. "Good bye, Sawyer."

❧❦

It took me a moment to pull out my apartment key, fumbling with the key ring through the blurry vision of my tears. I finally found it and was about to unlock the door when I noticed that it was already open a crack.

I pushed it open, thinking that maybe one of my roommates had run home for something, but was surprised to find Drew and Paul standing inside.

"What are you two doing here?" I asked, frowning.

"Dude!" Paul spun around and smacked Drew on the shoulder.

Drew's expression of panic mingled with embarrassment was all I needed. They made as if to bolt for the door, but I was blocking the entrance. I quickly slammed it shut, closing them in like trapped rats.

"Okay, what did you guys do this time?" I folded my arms across my chest and gave them a fierce stare. "You may as well fess up, 'cause nobody leaves until you reverse whatever it is you've done."

My face must have looked worse than I thought, because Drew immediately asked, "What happened? Why are you crying?"

I blushed and wiped at my tears with the heels of my hands. "Don't try and change the subject Andrew Anderson. I know you guys have been up to something and you better tell me right here and now what you did and how you got in . . ." I paused as a strange sound came from the back hallway. "*Uh*—what was that?"

Drew put on a mask of innocence. "What was what?"

"That sound back there, what was that?" I turned to look at Paul but he stared at his shoes and scuffed a toe along the floor.

The distinctly inhuman sound repeated, only louder this time. It was getting closer.

I felt the blood drain from my face. "Oh man, whatever that thing is get it out of here. Now!"

"Eliza, I don't know what you're talking about," Drew persisted. He was putting on an act and I was in no mood to tolerate his games today.

"Listen to me, both of you . . . do I look like I'm in messing around here?" I gestured to my tear-stained face as my voice rose hysterically, "Get rid of whatever it is and get out, or so help me—!" My words caught as a chicken poked its feathered head around the corner of the hall. I screamed and jumped onto the couch.

Drew grimaced. "No, no, Belinda! I told you to stay in the back room." He waved at the bird in an attempt to shoo it back.

I had a hand over my mouth, trying to recover from the shock of seeing a barnyard animal in my apartment. Drew continued to lecture the chicken, which was now bobbing around the living room, completely heedless of his words.

I scowled. I should have been furious—I knew I should have been, but the hilarity of the situation suddenly hit me full force. Drew standing there, lecturing a chicken while Paul looked on in humiliation. It was too much.

A laugh escaped before I could stop it. And then another and another, until I was laughing so uncontrollably that I could hardly breathe. All of the tension from the morning seemed to roll off of me; cleansing from the inside out.

My laughter only escalated by the anxious glances Drew and Paul were giving each other. I was acting like a complete lunatic, but I couldn't help myself. I sighed between laughs as I slowly tried to regain control. It felt nice to be wiping tears of laughter away for a change.

Drew raised an eyebrow at me as he went over and picked up the chicken. He began methodically stroking her head. "So now that you've calmed down, will you please explain why you're in this condition?" He gave a small wave that gestured to my face.

I sighed as I wiped at the last of my tears. "Oh no you don't—just because I was laughing don't think you can change the subject and get off the hook." I did my best to look severe. "Why were you guys pulling another prank? We never even retaliated from the last one."

"Yeah right," Paul scoffed. "And I have the bruise to prove it."

Drew nodded as I looked from one to the other of them in confusion.

"You need to have your roomies fill you in on their escapades while you were out of town," he said. The chicken was clucking loudly in his arms as it sought to struggle free. Feathers floated down onto the carpet.

"*Nice,*" I said as I looked at the mess. "Well even if what you say is true, I'm sure it didn't warrant this kind of retaliation—A live chicken? You guys have taken things too far." I felt the anger simmering again. That chicken could have caused some serious damage to our apartment that we would have been fined, possibly even evicted for. The prank war had to stop here and now.

"Look," I smiled at Drew in an attempt at diplomacy, "What if I told you that I have some information pertaining to you that I know you'd find . . . useful."

"I'm listening." He casually examined his nails.

"Okay . . . but in exchange for this information, you guys have to agree to a truce."

"And let you girls have the last laugh? No way." Drew folded his arms as he shook his head, but Paul looked interested. I was willing to bet that Drew had been dragging his roommates through this prank war, just as Lacey had been fueling the fire beneath us.

"Paul," I turned and smiled at him next. "Don't you think that's reasonable? After all, I'd hate to have to turn you guys in for breaking and entering or some awful thing like that."

"It's not breaking and entering when you have a key." Drew bit his knuckle, realizing too late that he'd ousted their secret.

"A key? You guys have a *key* to our apartment?" I was horrified. "How?"

"Drew managed to steal Lacey's key and make a copy before she knew it was gone," Paul confessed as Drew gave him the evil eye.

"Well I guess that answers a few questions," I grumbled. I turned back to Drew. "So how about it? Are you willing to take me up on my offer or not?"

He sighed and rolled his eyes. "I guess so. Technically we got the last prank in," he gestured to the chicken, "so I'm satisfied."

I smiled and nodded. "I'm glad to hear you've come to your senses. Now listen up, 'cause I need to get to my next class so I'll have to talk fast."

CHAPTER

thirty

I left my last class feeling like I'd been run over by a train. After very little sleep last night, breaking up with Sawyer, and realizing just how much cramming I would have to do to have a prayer of passing my finals, I felt like a sponge that had been sucked dry.

I retrieved my cell phone, ignoring the headache that had persisted ever since the breakup this morning. I hit the power button to turn it on. There hadn't been much time to charge it earlier so I'd turned it off in order to save precious battery power.

As the screen flashed to life, I saw that I had several missed texts.

Bree: *Call me when you get a sec, k? I'm worried about you.*

Charlotte: *I'm praying for you! Keep your chin up & let me know what I can do.*

Mom: *Call me when you have time, honey. I want to talk.*

Courtney: *I heard Luke got back! What's the deal? Did u break up w/ Sawyer finally? I still can't believe mom & dad let u go to CA w/ him. CALL ME!!!!*

Lacey: *Eliza, call me!!! I can't take the suspense anymore.*

(An hour later)

Lacey: *Where are u?? Why haven't you replied yet?*

(Ten minutes later)

Group text from Lacey: *I'm calling an emergency mtg @ 4. You all know the place. Eliza, if you don't show I'm sending out search & rescue!!!*

Bree: *Eliza, I'll order you a double hot fudge sundae. I'm sure you need all the chocolate you can get right now!*

I glanced at my watch and saw that it was almost 3:40. Lacey had scheduled a time when she knew we'd all be done with classes. I had to admit, that hot fudge sauce sounded pretty darn good at the moment, and I was excited to finally unload to my friends. They always had the right things to say to make me feel better.

The text I answered first, however, was from a completely different source. I smiled as I read Luke's words again: *Liza, this is my new #. How did your day go? Are you doing ok? I miss you like crazy already. Call or text when you can.*

I appreciated that he didn't ask if I'd talked with Sawyer. He was giving me my space while still letting me know he was there for me. A tiny thrill ran through me as I tapped the screen to reply. It was so good to be able to communicate with Luke again! I wanted to jump in my car and drive home this second to see him, but I knew if I did Lacey would probably make good on her promise.

My phone beeped a warning and I hurried to reply before it died: *I miss you more!!! Phone's almost dead—I'll call in a bit. When can I see you again??*

I waited anxiously for his reply as I continued walking, but the Fates were against me. The screen went black in a matter of seconds.

Blah!

I kicked a rock with my shoe and then put the phone in my bag. I hadn't paid enough attention to Luke's new number to be able to call him from one of my friends' phones. I would just have to wait until after I got back to the apartment.

I glowered at the sidewalk; it shouldn't be so hard—considering I'd waited two whole years for him to come home. I had practically become the master of patience. But somehow all that waiting made the extra hour before I could talk to him all the more maddening.

The sweet aroma of fresh waffle cones was the first thing that hit me—a split second before I was tackled by my roommates.

"Eliza, you're alive!" Lacey shrieked.

"Are you okay?" Charlotte asked.

"Give her some space, guys!" Bree said as she elbowed her way toward me, holding out a sundae that was oozing with an obscene amount of hot fudge. "Here you go, Liza. Come sit down . . . relax . . . and give us all the nitty-gritty details." She grinned as she guided me to an empty booth.

I took the dessert and allowed them to herd me into my seat. I hadn't seen them this excited over anything since the last cliffhanger episode of *Mystery Falls* had ended. It was like they were waiting for the finale of the soap opera, and I was the leading star. Not that they didn't care about me, of course, but I couldn't help feeling a little dejected as I realized how dramatic the past few months of my life had been.

Everyone was asking questions at once as I scooped up the first delicious bite. The warm chocolate was like balm to my wearied soul. I looked from one to the other of my friends, not sure which question to answer first, when Lacey slapped her hands down on the table.

"Alright! It's obvious we won't get anywhere like this, so *I'll* ask the questions."

I had to stifle a giggle at Bree's crestfallen expression. She must have been itching for information because she didn't argue.

Charlotte nodded; smiling.

Lacey clasped her hands together in a businesslike manner. "So, Eliza— first things first," she paused and then leaned forward hungrily, letting go of all pretense. "What the heck happened on your trip with Sawyer? Why were you wearing that ring? How did things go with Luke and for pity's sake—*why* haven't you been answering your texts?"

"Lacey!" Bree objected, but we all started laughing. Lacey looked like she was ready to burst at the seams.

I took another bite of my sundae, knowing that it would probably be melted after my story had been told. I inhaled a deep, cleansing breath and started at the beginning—from the time I'd left the apartment Thursday night all the way up to my break-up with Sawyer this morning. My friends were hungry for every detail, and I realized that the process of saying it all out loud was somehow cathartic. I filled them in on the particulars, but I left out my encounter with Drew mid-prank. I had other plans in mind for *that* information.

Once I'd finished my end of the story, they instantly began with their own commentary. Lacey sat back in the booth and raised her eyebrows at me. "You know, you could totally write a screenplay off of your weekend, Eliza. Things like that just don't happen in real life."

I grimaced and stared down at the blob of fudge and melted ice cream in my cup. "Tell me about it."

"Well *I* think it's awesome—and so romantic!" Bree quickly interjected as she cast Lacey a dark look. "Liza, you totally did the right thing calling it off with Sawyer. I mean, we all liked him and everything, but when Luke walked into our apartment I swear I could hear choirs singing from above. He is one of the hottest guys I've ever seen in my life!"

"Bree!" Now it was Charlotte's turn to be shocked as she blushed for Bree's sake. "I'm pretty sure Liza didn't decide she wanted to be with Luke just 'cause he's better looking."

"No . . . but it doesn't hurt." Bree grinned impishly at me. "Am I right?"

I snorted on my spoon, which caused me to choke on my ice cream.

Lacey began slapping me on the back. "Quick, somebody get her some water!"

Charlotte darted off, and I was thankful when Lacey's cell began to ring, forcing her to stop the slapping which was only making me cough worse.

"What the . . . ?" she mumbled as she looked at the incoming number. "Hello?" There was an expression of surprise mingled with anticipation on Lacey's face.

Bree and I exchanged quick looks. My coughing fit had immediately subsided as soon as Lacey had stopped that infernal pounding. I took the Styrofoam cup filled with ice water from Charlotte with a grateful smile.

"Yeah . . . that sounds good to me, I mean . . . if that works for you." Lacey was nervous and completely un-Lacey-like as she continued the conversation.

Bree, Charlotte and I leaned in to try to get a clue as to who she was talking to. She waved an impatient hand and stood up from the booth, anxiously biting one nail as she walked away.

"What do you think *that's* all about?" Bree whispered.

"I'm not sure . . . but I have a pretty good guess." A sly grin stole across my face. I had distinctly heard a male voice on the other end.

Everything was going according to plan.

We all continued to watch Lacey as she paced around the ice cream parlor and then ended the call. She turned to face us, and her expression was exultant. "Holy smokes!" she squealed as she joined us back at the booth. "You guys will never guess who just called and asked me out!"

"Who?" Bree was practically bouncing with impatience.

"Drew Anderson. *Mystery Falls* Drew. Drew the prankster!" Lacey squealed again as if she couldn't believe it.

"Lace, that's awesome!" Charlotte exclaimed.

"Amen. Now maybe we can finally end the stupid prank war." Bree cast her eyes toward heaven and mouthed a fervent 'thank you'.

"About that . . . did you guys do something to them over the weekend while I was gone?" I asked as I remembered Drew's comments.

"Oh yeah! We totally forgot to tell you." Lacey's eyes held a fiendish gleam of delight. "We hadn't retaliated over the Kool-Aid incident yet . . ."

"And *I* never wanted to," Bree inserted.

Lacey waved her comment aside, "So we got some shortening and spread it all over their kitchen floor."

"Like varnish," Charlotte added.

"Are you serious?" I laughed out loud and shook my head. "That's sheer genius! No wonder they were—" I was about to blow my cover so I quickly changed the subject. "It sounds like Drew must have forgiven you though, right? I mean, since he's asking you out. What time is he picking you up?"

Lacey's face suddenly fell. "Do you think he's asking me out as a prank? I hadn't thought of that, but what if he is? That would be so humiliating!"

"No, no, no—that's not it at all," I assured her as I put my hand on her arm. "He likes you, Lacey. We all know that." I turned to Bree and Charlotte and they nodded. I looked back at Lacey and asked again, "So what time are you guys going?"

Her muscles relaxed. "I'm sure you're right. He's sneaky, but he wouldn't stoop that low." She smiled. "He's gonna pick me up in an hour so I need to bust it home. I haven't showered yet today." She covertly sniffed her armpit.

"Nasty." Bree wrinkled her nose. "Ladies, let's get this girl home so she can prepare for her hot date."

"Good idea." I glanced at the clock. I was eager to get back and call Luke.

"Wait—what about our study session tonight?" Charlotte said, placing a hand on the table. We had planned to do a late night cram-fest; the first in a series of cramming sessions this week.

"Don't worry; he's just taking me out to dinner. I'll be home early," Lacey said.

"Too bad you just stuffed yourself on that banana split," Bree chided, pointing to the empty dessert cup.

Lacey laughed and patted her stomach. "Plenty of room yet! Besides, when have you ever known me to turn down a free meal?"

"Good point," Bree said, raising her eyebrows.

We all laughed and made our way to the door. It felt great to be with my friends again. I had decided to keep my earlier conversation with Drew a secret for now. No need to mention that I'd hinted that Lacey would be agreeable to going on a date with him; or the fact that I'd recovered the key they'd copied; or that I'd sworn him and his roommates to a truce. That might all come to light later; this moment was for basking in Lacey's joy.

Now that I had Luke, I wanted everyone to feel as happy as I was.

As soon as we got back to the apartment, I rushed to plug my phone in. It seemed like an eternity before the screen flashed to life and I was able to retrieve my messages. There was one missed text from Luke: *I'd love to see you tonight. What's your schedule like?*

There was also a missed call from him, but no message. I quickly called him back. The line rang several times before reaching the automated voice mail. I guessed he hadn't had time to set that up yet. I tried to swallow my frustration as I waited for the beep and then left a message.

I ended the call and sat on my bed. Where could he be? The selfish part of me had hoped he would be waiting for my call. I'd half expected him to pick up after the second ring, begging to know when he could see me again (at least that's how it had played out in my mind). I knew *I* was dying to see him again. Now that he was reachable, my heart literally ached to be with him. After this long and emotional day, all I wanted was to be cradled in his strong arms.

I realized I was becoming borderline pathetic, but I sent him a text which basically restated everything I'd just said in the voice message—just in case. With that accomplished and after a few more minutes of staring at my phone, I finally decided that distraction was the best thing for me.

I sighed and made my way into the living room. Charlotte and Bree had already set up their study stations at the kitchen table. I was about to go back to my room and get my bag when the doorbell rang.

"Oh no—he's early!" Lacey wailed from the bathroom. She appeared around the corner with wet hair and a frenzied look in her eyes. "Liza, keep him occupied for a few minutes, okay?"

"No problem." I gave her a thumb's up before she disappeared again. Bree and Charlotte put their studies aside and watched curiously.

I grinned at them and then opened the door with a flourish. "Won't you come in, sir? Your date will only be a few—*Luke!*" I squealed in surprise and threw my arms around him.

He laughed and held me tight. "You were expecting someone else, I think."

"Lacey's date . . . but I'm so glad it's you instead." I pulled back and smiled at him.

His warm brown eyes were glowing. "I missed you."

"I missed you too." My heart began to race at the look he was giving me. He *did* feel exactly the way I hoped he would—the way I felt about him. A flutter ran through me in knowing that he had driven here to see me tonight. *All that worry for nothing*. But suddenly I remembered something and gave him a puzzled look. "I called you a few minutes ago; why didn't you pick up?"

He grinned mischievously. "I wanted to surprise you . . . and I was afraid you'd say you were too busy to see me tonight." He traced a hand along my cheek. "I know you've got finals coming up and if you're busy I understand, but it was worth the drive just to see you again." He raised a questioning eyebrow. "So . . . was it a good surprise?"

I smiled as I moved in to hug him tighter. "*Very* good." I breathed in the familiar scent of his cologne mingled with just a hint of wintergreen gum. It was Luke's smell, and I didn't realize until that moment how much I'd missed it over the past two years.

Bree made a small coughing sound and I remembered that my roommates had been watching our entire exchange. Luke seemed to realize it at the same time, and he reluctantly released me but kept hold of my hand.

I blushed as I turned to them. "Sorry, guys. I want to officially introduce you to Luke." I smiled as I pulled him into the living room.

He gave my hand a squeeze before reaching out to shake hands with Charlotte and Bree.

"It's nice to finally meet you," Charlotte said with a gracious smile as she took his hand.

When Luke turned to Bree, Charlotte had to poke her in the ribs to bring her back to reality. I stifled a laugh as Bree quickly closed her mouth and shook his hand. She blushed furiously as she mumbled a greeting, and the blush deepened when Luke told her he'd heard what a great roommate she was.

I felt for her; Luke was *that* good looking. I still found myself getting tongue-tied around him. I couldn't believe someone as handsome as he was could also be down-to-earth and personable. And I couldn't believe he wanted to be with *me*. Sometimes I was afraid I was still dreaming. That I'd created his presence from my innermost thoughts and desires and would wake up one morning to find out he wasn't real.

"Hey, anyone home?" Drew poked his head through the front door.

"Hi, Drew. Lacey will be out in a minute," Bree said.

The blow dryer was going full-blast in the back hall.

Drew nodded and walked in, his eyes instantly drawn to Luke. He cast me a brief, inquisitive look before he seemed to make the pieces fit together. "So you must be the missionary," he said as he gave Luke a head nod.

"Yeah," Luke nodded back.

"Luke, this is Drew. He's one of our friends." *And soon to be Lacey's boyfriend,* I wanted to add. A knowing smile played across my face as my eyes met Drew's. "Go ahead and have a seat. I'll tell Lacey you're here."

I gave Luke's hand a squeeze and left him to talk to Drew while I hurried back to the bathroom. "Better hurry, Lace," I whispered to her as she straightened her hair.

"I know," she whispered back in agitation. "What have you guys been talking about?"

"He just barely got here. That was Luke before."

She stopped with the flatiron mid-straighten. "Oh *really?*" She raised an eyebrow and smirked. "Good, then that gives me another minute to work on my makeup."

"Oo, me too!" I quickly grabbed a brush and worked through my hair. This was the perfect opportunity to spruce up a bit more before going out with Luke again. I did a quick touch-up to my makeup, but when I took a swig of mouthwash Lacey laughed.

"Big plans for tonight, hmm?"

I almost choked so I quickly spit the burning liquid into the sink. I laughed and then threw a bobby pin at her. "It doesn't hurt to be prepared, right?"

She laughed too, but then her face slowly straightened. "Here . . . give me some of that stuff."

We walked into the living room, still giggling over our private joke. My eyes moved first to Luke, and then quickly to Drew. I wanted to see his reaction to Lacey now that he knew her feelings for him.

I wasn't disappointed. Drew's eyes lit up the moment she walked into the room and there was a tangible something between them that hadn't been there before.

"Hey, Lacey," he said as he stood from the couch.

"Hey. Sorry I kept you waiting." She smiled shyly—an expression I'd never seen on her before.

"No worries. You look really . . . great tonight," Drew said with admiration in his eyes.

"Thanks."

She actually blushed! Wonders would never cease.

"Are you ready to go?" I could tell she was nervous, and eager to get away from our prying eyes.

"Sure." Drew took her by the arm and I heard Charlotte sigh happily before Bree kicked her under the table.

"Oh, wait," I interrupted, "Lacey, I want you to meet Luke before you go."

She turned and seemed to notice Luke for the first time. "We've met before—sort of—but it's nice to see you again."

"You too. Have fun on your date." Luke smiled at her and then nodded at Drew, "Good to meet you, bro."

"Yep," Drew nodded back before the two of them left the apartment.

My cheeks hurt from grinning. I was so happy for them! Bree and Charlotte whispered excitedly as soon as the door closed.

"So, how long do I have you for?" Luke asked quietly as he held up my hands and laced them with his. My pulse stuttered at the kindling spark in his eyes.

"As long as you want me," I whispered back. He seemed to read my thoughts as he pulled me toward the door.

"See you guys in a while," I called over my shoulder, not once taking my eyes from Luke's.

"Bye!" my roommates called back just before we closed the door. The sound of their giggling followed us down the hall.

Luke smiled as he led me down the stairs and toward the parking lot.

"Where are we going?" I asked, though I didn't really care. As long as I was with him, we could go sit in a gutter and I'd be in heaven.

"I don't know. Are you hungry?" He stopped in front of an old pickup and opened the door for me. The hinges squeaked a bit in protest.

"Whose truck is this?" I was momentarily distracted from his gaze.

Luke smiled. "Mine. I bought it this morning."

"You bought it? Already?" I turned and looked at it more closely.

"Yeah, do you like it? A guy in my ward was selling it. It's not much to look at now, but it runs awesome. With a bit of work and a new coat of paint I could sell it for a decent price . . . if I wanted to."

He looked at the vehicle with the pride of ownership that only a guy can have for his truck. He had sold his Jeep to help fund his mission and I loved the fact that he'd used his own money to get this truck. Sure, it was nothing in comparison to the car that Sawyer drove, but the fact that Luke had bought this himself made it all the more special.

"I love it." I grinned before hopping into the cab.

He nodded in satisfaction. "And you haven't even seen the best feature yet." He closed my door and then climbed into the driver's side. With a roguish smile, he reached over and pulled me next to him. "The bench seat. Now I get to have you right next to me while I drive."

I giggled and looped my arms through his. He turned to me and his eyes searched mine intently. "So how did your day go?"

I looked at the floor and blew out a long breath. "Let's just say I'm glad it's over." I felt a twinge of sadness as I pictured Sawyer's face before he drove off this morning. "I gave Sawyer back his ring and ended things for good."

"How did he take it?" Luke studied the steering wheel.

"Pretty well, all things considered. Break-ups are never fun, but I'm glad it's all behind me now so that we can move forward." I gave his arm a reassuring squeeze.

"You're sure you're okay about it, Liza?" Luke's brows were knit together as he continued to stare at the wheel.

"Of course!" I felt a little hurt that he even had to ask. "There's no doubt in my mind that you're the one I want to be with, Luke. I'm sorry for the drama and confusion I've caused."

He turned and gave me a half smile. "You don't need to apologize anymore. But if it's okay with you," he paused and a muscle flexed in his jaw, "can we not mention his name again for a while? Maybe after we've been married for fifty years it won't bother me, but right now I hate to think how close I came to losing you."

"Deal." I smiled back at him and there were a million thoughts flying through my head. Had he been teasing when he talked about our being married? Just hearing those words on his lips set the butterflies in my stomach into a frenzy.

"Thanks." His smile turned cajoling as he leaned closer to me. My heart thudded loudly in my chest and chills bathed my skin as he softly traced his hand along my neck, and then up to my jawbone, gently tilting my chin up. The air around us became electrified as we both leaned in for the kiss.

I knew I needed to study for finals tonight, but the moment his mouth met mine all thoughts of school and tests completely fled my mind. My senses were overcome to such a degree that I drew in a sharp breath.

Luke quickly pulled away. "Are you okay?" His eyes were filled with concern.

I blushed. "Yes, I just . . . can't believe how amazing it is," I breathed a moment before I leaned in to kiss him again.

"I know what you mean." He smiled as he took my face in his hands and drew me in.

The kiss was gentle and warm. It was comfortable and exhilarating all at the same time. I felt emotions that I didn't know had existed within me before.

Sawyer's kisses had been passionate and always pleasant, but solely on a physical level.

While kissing Luke I felt all of the physical joy and desire, yet there was something more. I felt a connection to his soul, melding with mine. Our hearts were entwined, which made his kiss all the more meaningful and overwhelming. It felt like my very core was going to melt into a puddle of pure, undiluted bliss!

Our kissing gradually evolved from slow and caressing to a more intense, driven exchange. My thoughts were growing harder to control, and as if reading each other's minds, we pulled away at the same moment. I saw the harnessed passion in Luke's eyes that I knew was reflected in my own.

He smiled and kissed my hand as he struggled to regulate his breathing. "Let's go get something to eat."

"Yeah." I smiled back at him and then put my head on his shoulder. It was dark outside, and he reached over to turn the radio on as he pulled out of the parking lot.

I sighed in contentment as I listened to the music and snuggled closer to Luke. I loved that I could feel safe with him. I loved that I could just be me, with no worries about how I was dressed or what I should say. I was completely comfortable with him; like being home.

Luke's cell phone rang, breaking me out of my reverie. He reached into his pocket and handed it to me. "Here, you answer it."

I smiled as I took the phone from him. I appreciated the little ways that he showed he trusted me, like taking his calls. I was so busy trying to figure out how to answer the phone that I didn't notice the incoming number. After a few moments of fiddling I finally answered, "Hello?"

"Liza, is that you?" my mom's voice asked.

"Mom! How did you get Luke's number?" I was caught off guard hearing her voice, but then I remembered that I'd once again left my cell phone behind in the apartment—as well as my purse. When had I become so scatter-brained?

"I tried calling your cell and Bree answered. I told her I needed to reach you and she found Luke's number on your phone." Mom's voice sounded strained and my heart stopped as I suddenly remembered.

"Your appointment. How did it go? What did the doctor say?" I reached over and gripped Luke's knee, already sensing that something wasn't right. He had gathered enough from my words to know something was up and gave my hand a squeeze.

"Honey, are you sitting down?"

"Oh no . . . it's something bad isn't it?" Tears began to choke my voice and I gripped Luke's leg harder. He pulled the truck over and stopped.

"Honey, I don't know how to say this," her voice sounded small and vulnerable. I felt a nervous sweat form at the back of my neck. I didn't know how to react to that tone. I subconsciously began to say a silent prayer, pleading for help. I held my breath as I waited in silence for her to continue; to say the words that I knew would change my life.

"Eliza . . . I'm pregnant."

CHAPTER
thirty-one

The words were not the words I had been expecting.

"Mom, that is *so* not funny." I couldn't believe she was trying to pull a joke right now. "Whatever it is, it's okay; you can tell me. We'll get through this." I pulled my hand away from Luke and bit my thumbnail, bracing myself for the news.

She gave a short, shaky laugh. "Sweetheart, it wasn't meant to be funny. It's the truth—I'm going to have a baby."

There was a long pause as I tried to wrap my brain around her words. A baby? At *her* age? I simply refused to believe it.

Luke was watching me and there was a crease in his forehead where his brows were furrowed. He put his arm around my shoulder and gave me a supportive squeeze.

"Mom, there must be some mistake. Did the doctor actually *tell* you that you were pregnant?"

I heard Luke take in a surprised breath. I turned to him and nodded, raising my eyebrows in disbelief. He looked as shocked as I felt, but there was the unmistakable hint of relief in his eyes.

I was relieved too, of course. After thinking the worst, the fact that she was pregnant was very welcome news compared to what I'd been imagining. It would take me a few days to recover from the shock of this, but I felt relief wash over me as she spoke.

"Eliza, of *course* I heard it from the doctor. I wouldn't have believed it otherwise! With all of the strange things happening lately, I thought maybe I was going through menopause . . . or something worse. This was the absolute *last* thing that had crossed my mind." She sounded as if she was still trying to process the information. "Sweetheart, I know this is shocking news for you, but . . . I . . . could really use your support right now," her voice broke and my heart instantly went out to her.

"Mom, I'm so sorry I reacted like that. I just wasn't prepared—I mean, how do you prepare for something like this?" I smiled, hoping she could sense it through the line.

She gave another uncertain laugh. "You can't. Your poor father has been in a state of paralysis since this morning. He keeps staring at nothing saying, 'I can't believe it.' To tell you the truth, I'm a little concerned about *his* health at this point."

I laughed. "Oh c'mon. You talk like you guys are ancient; you're both only forty-one . . . just a couple of young 'uns!" I grinned wider as I heard mom laugh—a real laugh this time. "But he's happy about it, right? I mean, this is pretty exciting news."

"Oh yes, he's happy. We just have to recover from the shock of it all first. We always wanted to have one more but it never worked out that way. I'd given up hope long ago that it ever would, and I was at peace with that. Now . . . it's like we're starting all over again and we're almost old enough to be grandparents! It just doesn't make sense, but I guess the Lord has His reasons."

"Have you told Courtney? How is she dealing with it?"

"She has taken the news better than anyone else; you know how she always wanted a little brother or sister. Of course she was surprised, but I think she's happy that all of our focus won't be on her anymore—especially now that she's almost sixteen."

I laughed. "That sounds like Court. I'm glad she's there to help you though." A wave of guilt swept over me. "I wish I could be home to help out. How are you feeling?"

"Don't worry about me. There are some higher risk factors because of my age, but the doctor said there's no reason why this can't be a perfectly healthy baby. Fortunately I was keeping up an exercise routine, so other than the morning sickness and fatigue I'm fit as a fiddle!" She was starting to sound more cheerful now. "To be honest, Liza, I debated whether or not to tell you so soon. You've got enough on your plate with finals and boy troubles—which I want to hear more about, by the way."

"Absolutely . . . but it will have to wait." I glanced at Luke. "We're on our way out to eat," I said, reminding her that I wasn't free to talk about it now.

"Oh, I see." I heard the smile in her voice. "Well then I won't keep you, but promise you'll call tomorrow? A mother can only stand to wait so long for details—and in my condition, you don't want to put me under any undue stress."

"Oh boy, here we go already!" I teased, happy to hear her sounding more like herself.

She chuckled. "Someday you'll understand that one of the few perks of pregnancy is getting special treatment, and I'm not about to revoke that privilege. After I make it through this, I'll have your father frame the birth certificate and hang it on the wall as a badge of honor."

We were both laughing now. I looked again at Luke, who had been patiently waiting throughout our conversation. He still had his arm around me but was staring out the window as if deep in thought. I wondered if he was thinking the same thing I was. A lead ball seemed to settle in my stomach.

"Well, I better get going, Mom. I promise I'll call you tomorrow, okay?"

We expressed our love and then I hit the end button. I turned to Luke as

I handed him back his phone. "Sorry that took so long, but . . . I guess you already know what that was all about."

He nodded as he smiled at me. "Sounds like you're going to be a big sister again. How do you feel about it?"

"It's totally crazy!" I shook my head and looked out the window a moment before continuing, "It's going to take me a while to get used to the idea. I'm worried about my mom, but she seems happy. I'm just so grateful that it wasn't something worse. I never wrote you about it, but she hasn't been herself for the past several weeks and we were all getting nervous."

"I bet." Luke looked at me again before placing his hand on the steering wheel. "So how far along is she?"

I slapped myself on the forehead. "I completely forgot to ask! Let me see your phone and I'll text her."

He nodded and handed it back. "I'm pretty clueless about this stuff, but she'll probably have the baby sometime this spring, right?"

"Probably," I finished the text and looked up at him. There was that look of concentration in his eyes again and I felt my heart jump. Could he possibly be considering what I hoped he was? Or was it just my wishful thinking?

Ever since I'd seen Luke again my mind had only been able to think of one thing: marriage. If he ever asked me I would say yes and marry him the next day if it were possible. But now that my mom was going to have a baby, what did that mean for my potential wedding plans? I couldn't ask her to help plan my wedding while she was pregnant. And she would need time after the baby was born to recover and adjust before she could even think about a wedding. I felt almost sick as I saw months and months pass away before my dream of marrying Luke could become a reality . . . if he ever asked me.

I knew I was being ridiculous. If he proposed it wouldn't be the end of the world if we had to wait a while to get married. But as he turned to look at me with his golden brown eyes and his crooked smile, I felt like my heart would literally burst if I had to be separated from him any longer. Just knowing that after our date tonight he would leave and be an hour away was painful.

The cell buzzed and I glanced down to read Mom's text.

"She's due on March twenty-first," I said. "So you were right—a spring baby. She's a little farther along than I thought, but I guess she has been acting tired for several weeks now."

Luke nodded thoughtfully and his eyes met mine. We stared at each other for a few seconds, and then he placed his hand on the gearshift and slowly pulled back into traffic.

"Penny for your thoughts," I said as we drove for a few moments in silence.

He smiled slyly. "I was wondering where you wanted to go out to eat."

I shrugged, entirely disappointed by that response. "You choose. You haven't been able to eat American food for two years, so we'll go wherever you want."

"Are you sure? Because I heard there's this really good Mexican restaurant down here. Does that sound good to you?"

I cast him a disbelieving look. "Of course . . . but are you sure you want Mexican food?"

"I know it sounds crazy, but I've been craving Mexican food ever since I got home."

"I don't think that's crazy at all." I smiled at him and shrugged. "Maybe I can learn some good recipes so I can make you an authentic Mexican meal sometime."

He glanced away from the road for a moment. There was that look again. The intensity in his eyes sent shivers down my back. "I'd like that, Liza—a lot."

Forget the penny! I would have handed over my entire savings to know what he was thinking that very moment.

☙

The next few weeks seemed to soar by. I managed to pass my finals and actually did well enough to give me hope of earning a partial scholarship.

Luke moved in to his apartment, and we spent every moment possible together. Our biggest challenge became dealing with the powerful physical attraction we had for each other, but we made a goal to go to the temple once a week to do baptisms. This way we were focused on keeping ourselves worthy to hold a recommend. I knew Luke also went to the temple fairly often on his own, which was yet another aspect I admired about him. He didn't make any fanfare about what he did; he just quietly went about doing good things.

We also decided that we had to keep up our personal scripture study every day. Our attraction was so powerful we needed all the help we could get. We avoided being alone too frequently, and kept to a strict curfew. It was an uphill battle and never easy to keep myself away from Luke, but I loved him enough to do it. I wanted to show him that I would honor his priesthood and his temple covenants.

He, in turn, always treated me with love and respect. I knew I could trust him, but I also knew it wasn't for lack of his attraction toward me. There was no doubt between either of us about that. I simply knew that he loved me and would protect me from anything that would cause me hurt or pain. He loved me enough to put my best interest before his own personal desires.

He got a job unloading trucks for a delivery service. The hours were early, but the job offered good pay as well as health benefits, which was almost unheard of in a college town.

I'd also looked for another job (one that didn't require a hairnet), and found a position as a receptionist that worked with my class schedule.

As fall semester began, Luke and I were busy with classes, but spent every moment possible together.

My roommates frequently teased me about floating around on a cloud, but that was exactly how I felt. It seemed like heaven had been brought down to earth, and each moment spent with Luke was a divine gift. My only fear was that it was too good to be true and I would suddenly have it all taken away from me. I saw the way girls stared at him everywhere we went, and I worried that eventually he would notice them and decide he deserved better than me.

One day I finally voiced my fears but Luke just laughed. "Liza, do you even realize how many guys stare at *you*? If I let every guy who checked you out bother me, then I wouldn't be able to enjoy just being with you. I trust you, and I hope that you return that trust."

Just another reason why I loved him. Those reasons seemed to be adding up more and more every day.

I ran into Sawyer twice after our break-up. The first time I'd been in the library with Luke, holding his hand as we were leaving the building. Sawyer came through the doors and I saw him tense the same moment that I felt Luke's hand grip mine tighter. It was an awkward encounter, charged with emotion. Sawyer glanced at Luke with a look full of loathing before his eyes traveled to mine. The pain I saw there made the breath catch in my throat.

He continued walking without saying a word and Luke led me out the front doors. The exchange had only lasted seconds, but it had been enough to leave me feeling sad for the rest of the day.

Thankfully, the second encounter had been much smoother. I'd been taking a shortcut through the science building when I saw Sawyer coming down the hall, holding the hand of a pretty blonde. He started a bit when he looked up and saw me, but then he smiled. I smiled back. The girl looked at me curiously as they walked by and I smiled at her too. She seemed like she would fit in perfectly in Sawyer's family.

He was moving on, and I wished him all the best.

CHAPTER
thirty-two

Almost before I knew what had happened, it was Thanksgiving. Luke and I spent half of the day with his family, and the other half with mine. I loved everything about this holiday, but mostly I loved being able to spend the entire weekend with Luke without classes or work getting in the way.

I spent a good deal of time in the kitchen, insisting that my mom take it easy while the rest of us prepared the meal and cleaned up. Luke stayed by my side through all of it. I couldn't help but daydream about what it would be like to have our own kitchen and prepare meals together someday.

Courtney helped out a lot too. She had turned sixteen a few weeks ago, and I was surprised by how much she had seemed to mature since last summer. Maybe it was because she'd had to step-up helping around the house, or maybe it was getting her driver's license and having more responsibility and freedom. Whatever the reason, I was beginning to feel like she was becoming a friend; someone I could talk to and confide in, rather than just my little sister.

"So, Court, Liza and I were thinking of going to Temple Square tomorrow night to see the lights. Want to come along?" Luke asked as he dried a dish and handed it to her.

"Tomorrow night? Are you guys nuts? Aside from being Black Friday, it's the night they turn the lights on. There will be like a million people downtown," she said as she took the plate and put it away.

"I know, but that's part of the fun." Luke grinned at her. "Besides . . . think of all the guys there will be to check out," he teased.

"Better not let my dad hear you saying that," I scolded him with a smile.

Courtney looked thoughtful for a moment. "Good point, Luke. I know you guys are just dragging me along so you'll have a chaperone, but I'm game. I'll call Alexis and see if she wants to come."

"That's a great idea. I haven't seen her for a long time. How's she doing?" I asked.

"Good. Did I tell you she signed up for seminary this year?"

Alexis was Courtney's best friend. She had taken the missionary discussions and was interested in getting baptized, but her dad had insisted that she wait until she was eighteen.

"That's awesome. How does she like it?" Luke asked. He still had the missionary zeal that so many newly returned missionaries possessed. I loved to see the excited spark in his eyes and hoped it would never wear off.

"She thinks it's cool. She has Brother Richards, who's one of the best teachers. I can tell she's learning a lot." Courtney stopped helping with the dishes for a moment to send a text message. "I'll see what she's doing tomorrow night. She just broke up with a guy so I bet she'll want to come."

"That would be great. And Court," I looked at her until she made eye contact with me, "We're not just bringing you along to play chaperone; we *like* when you come with us."

"Uh huh." She rolled her eyes and smirked.

"Seriously," Luke said, giving her his famous crooked smile that showed his dimple.

She blushed and looked at her phone. "Okay."

Luke and I exchanged smiles and he winked at me. "I might bring Morgan along too . . . if neither of you would mind? She loves seeing the lights."

"That's cool with me," Courtney said. Although there was a six-year gap between them, Courtney and Morgan got along really well.

"Of course." I dried my hands on a dishtowel and gazed at Luke. He looked adorable drying dishes with his shirtsleeves rolled up to the elbow.

I liked that he was including our little sisters on our date tomorrow night. He was so thoughtful, and by including them it made me feel like our two families were already blending together.

Chills prickled the back of my neck as Luke suddenly met my gaze. There was so much emotion behind those captivating eyes of his that I forgot to breathe. It was in these small moments that I gained insights to his soul. I felt my heart swell even bigger to make room for the feelings I had for him. Just like any muscle, I could literally feel my heart stretching in that moment. I loved him so much that it hurt—in a good way.

"Looks like Lexi can come," Courtney said as she read her text. "Do you guys mind finishing up while I go ask mom if it's okay?"

"Sure. Why don't you get Monopoly set up too? We'll bring out the pies in a minute," I said.

"Okay. And remember, Luke," she said, pointing a finger at him, "Boardwalk is all mine."

"Don't be too sure." He wound his dishtowel and playfully whipped it at her, missing intentionally.

She squealed and darted out of the kitchen, leaving the two of us alone. Luke walked over to where I was standing by the sink. He unwound the dishtowel and wrapped it around my waist, pulling me in until our lips met.

I sighed and ran my fingers through his dark hair. Dishes could wait. We only had a few minutes and I had been longing for his kiss all day.

Using the towel, he pulled me closer and deepened the kiss until I was blissfully unaware of anything else.

Approaching footsteps on the creaky floor caused us to break apart. Seconds later my dad entered the kitchen. "You kids need help bringing in the pie?" he asked.

"Sure, Dad. Thanks." I cast a quick, sly glance at Luke. "But you better go find out what kind Mom wants first, don't you think?" This was my attempt at getting a few more seconds of Luke's undivided attention.

"I already asked: pumpkin." Dad walked over to the freezer and removed the vanilla ice cream.

"Oh. Well what about Courtney?"

"Chocolate cream."

Luke grinned at my dejected expression and I shrugged. I ached to have him hold me again, but it would just have to wait. He continued to smile at me and I saw a cunning gleam rise in his eyes. "Oh, Liza . . . I forgot. I brought a few games from home. Would you mind helping me bring them in?"

My face instantly broke into a smile. "I would love to! Be back in a sec, Dad."

"Okay, but hurry up or this ice cream will be melted," he warned.

"We will," I said cheerfully. I took Luke's hand and he led me out into the chilly November dusk.

"Did you really bring some games?" I whispered as we walked to his car.

"Yeah; lucky break." He grinned rakishly before grasping me in his arms again. "I just wanted one more kiss. If I remember right, you have a bit of a competitive streak and may not let me kiss you after I school you in Monopoly."

"I do *not* have a competitive streak!" I pulled away from him, crossing my arms and stomping my foot.

He laughed, entirely amused. "See? I've made you upset already." His eyes narrowed. "I guess I'll just have to steal that kiss from you then."

He lunged forward, throwing his arms out to grab me. I shrieked and darted around the car, laughing hysterically as he chased me. We circled the vehicle a few times until he finally caught me, wrapping both arms around from behind and holding me captive.

I squealed and wiggled fiercely to break free, managing to slide down to the ground before he tackled me again. We were both breathless and laughing as the stiff, frost-covered grass dampened our clothes. Luke took my face in his hand and planted a kiss firmly on my lips.

"There!" He said triumphantly. "Now do you give up?"

"You may have won this battle, Luke Matthews, but I'll show you up on the game board," I said in defiance.

He laughed and kissed me on the nose before helping me to stand. "Would you care to back up that statement with a bet?"

"Maybe . . . what are we talking?"

A mysterious smile played across his lips. "I'm afraid I can't tell you what my terms are—yet. What do you want if you win?"

"Ooo, so secretive," I teased. "But I'm not worried, 'cause there's not a doubt in my mind I'll win."

He put his hands in his pockets and raised an eyebrow. The challenge in his eyes made me bold.

"I think I'll wait to reveal my terms too—you're not the only one who can be sneaky," I said, crossing my arms. I really had no idea what I would ask for, but all sorts of fun possibilities began to take shape in my mind.

Luke gave a low chuckle. "You're on. Now we better get in there before the ice cream melts and your dad blames me. I need to stay on his good side, you know."

"Why?"

He gave me a withering look and I grinned before helping him retrieve the games from his car. He could have easily brought them in by himself, but hopefully my dad wouldn't notice.

Luke took me by the hand and led me back to the house. I loved the way his hands were warm even when it was freezing outside; the way his broad shoulders moved as he walked. I loved the dimple in his cheek that appeared when he smiled that special smile reserved solely for me.

In short, I loved Luke Matthews more than anyone or anything else in the whole world.

CHAPTER
thirty-three

O-kay, did you just see that guy?" Alexis turned wide-eyed to Courtney.

"Huh?" Courtney asked distractedly. She had been acting this way all night and I wondered what was up.

"No way did you not see him!" Alexis exclaimed as she turned and gestured behind us, "The one in the black jacket. He totally looked at you as he walked by . . . and his friend isn't bad either."

I exchanged smiles with Luke. He had been spot-on about the abundance of teenage boys here for Courtney to scope out, but to my surprise she didn't seem interested.

"Are you okay, Court?" I asked.

"Hmm? Yeah, of course." She shrugged but cast a nervous glance at Luke.

I was beginning to wonder if maybe my little sister had a crush on my boyfriend. I shuddered. *Oh the fun,* that *would be.*

"Look, it's the red tree! Can we go see it?" Morgan asked. She tugged Luke's sleeve, her ten-year-old eyes bright with excitement. I loved that she hadn't outgrown the magic of Christmas yet.

"Sure, let's go," Luke said as he smiled down at her.

We made our way through the crowds to the gigantic tree glowing with thousands of tiny red orbs. I tilted my head back to admire the meticulous placing of each strand and wondered, as I did every year, how long it took the workers to hang all of these lights. I wondered how much they got paid, and whether or not they enjoyed the task.

I turned and was about to voice these questions to Luke, when I noticed that he was a few yards off, whispering something in Morgan's ear. She was smiling and nodding while Courtney and Alexis stood by, also wearing big smiles. Luke stood and tweaked Morgan on the nose before she, Courtney and Alexis all walked off.

"Hey, wait a sec—where are you guys going?" I called, but they only turned and waved at me.

"Where are they going?" I asked Luke as he joined me.

"We'll meet up with them in a bit," he said with a cryptic smile. "I have a surprise for you."

He took me by the elbow and began weaving me through the crowds toward the south gates. "Do you think they'll be okay by themselves?" I continued to worry, "I mean, there are so many people here—what if we can't find them again?"

"I told them exactly when and where to meet us. And besides, you have Courtney and Alexis' cell numbers. They're sixteen; they'll look after Morgan. We'll only be gone for a little while." He gave me a reassuring smile, but there was something else behind that smile; an ember of anticipation.

"I guess you're right," I finally conceded as we walked through the gates. Butterflies filled my stomach as I wondered what surprise Luke had in store. "So where are you taking me?"

He grinned and led me straight up to a waiting carriage. "Right here."

"Matthews?" the driver asked. He wore a top hat and heavy cloak. The carriage was decked with sprigs of pine and holly. It felt like we were stepping into a Charles Dickens novel.

"That's us," Luke answered before taking my hand to help me into the carriage.

"Right on time," the man checked his watch and nodded.

"You reserved this carriage?" I whispered to Luke as he climbed in beside me and draped the blanket over our legs.

"Yep." He grinned and placed his arm around me. The driver gently slapped the reigns and we moved forward. "I knew it was going to be busy tonight so I wanted to make sure we would get a spot. I tried to get the same carriage we had last time, but to be honest I can't even remember the color of the horse. I was too busy watching you that night."

I tilted my head to look up at him. He was so thoughtful! The night he had taken me to prom we had gone on a carriage ride through the city. Only this time was much, much better. This time I didn't have to worry about him leaving for two years, and this time there was a good chance he would kiss me sometime during the ride.

I smiled at this private thought and realized Luke was watching me. "Is this a good surprise?" he asked.

I couldn't bear it any longer; I reached over, placing both of my hands on his face, and kissed him. I felt him smile before he put his hand behind my neck and kissed me back. We were lost in our own blissful world until a horn beeped and someone made a loud catcall through their car window.

We laughed as we pulled apart, placing our foreheads together. The carriage driver glanced back over his shoulder and gave Luke a quick, sidelong wink, before facing the road again.

"To answer your question: yes, this was definitely a good surprise." I smiled at him a moment before I snuggled closer and put my head on his shoulder.

"Good, because I was kind of hoping to make it a tradition," he said quietly as he made slow circles in my palm with his thumb. Even with my coat on,

I was suddenly covered head to toe with goose bumps. I loved the implication behind that statement.

We continued to steal covert kisses as the Clydesdale plodded along through the city. My heart felt like it could float away at any moment, and I wished the ride would never end. I felt a little bad not having our sisters and Alexis along, but my selfishness won out. It was nice to have some time alone.

"Did you tell the girls where we were going?" I asked as I looked up at him. I tried not to frown as I realized we were almost back to the south gates again.

"Yeah," he said, that same mysterious light shining in his eyes.

"Did they feel bad you didn't invite them to come?"

"Nope. I told them I'd treat them some other time, but for tonight I wanted you all to myself." His warm, brown eyes smoldered and I thought I was going to melt into a puddle on the carriage floor.

The driver pulled the reigns to a stop and Luke helped me down before turning to pay for the ride. I watched as the man smiled at Luke and tipped his hat before greeting an eager family waiting for the next ride.

Luke took my hand and glanced at his watch. "Well, looks like it's time to go meet up with the others." There seemed to be a nervous agitation to his step as he pulled me through the crowds.

I wondered why he was suddenly in a hurry. We'd only been gone thirty minutes, but I hoped the girls hadn't minded waiting. They had all dressed warm so I wasn't worried about that. Besides, I knew they could always wait in the visitor's center if need be. I hoped that's where our meeting point was; I wanted to see the Christus before we had to leave.

Instead of walking straight toward the center, Luke turned right.

"Are we meeting them by the reflective pool?" I asked. Was I imagining things, or was his hand shaking a little?

"Yep. That's where I told them to wait for us." He gripped my hand tighter and I wondered if it was to hide the shaking.

I bit my lip as we walked swiftly toward the popular gathering place. Why was he acting so strange? It wasn't like Luke to be nervous.

We were making our way through the thick patches of crowd, when suddenly I heard a violin playing Christmas music. The delicate notes drifted above the din; soothing and peaceful.

"Where's that music coming from?" I strained my eyes to discover the source.

Luke was also searching. His eyes lit up as they rested on something. "Over there. C'mon."

He maneuvered us through the crowd until we were on the edge of the circle formed around the violinist. I waved at Courtney and the other two as they stood on the opposite side of the circle. Courtney and Alexis waved back enthusiastically with huge grins on their faces. I watched as Morgan turned toward the violinist and raised her hands in the air, giving him two thumbs up.

Completely baffled, I turned and watched him nod at her. He immediately switched from the carol he'd been playing to a new song. It took only a few notes into the melody for me to recognize it—"The Promise." He was playing our song.

I turned to Luke, my mouth hanging open in surprise. He nodded and smiled as he took both of my hands and pulled me to the center of the circle. A blush warmed my cheeks. Was he going to dance with me, right here in front of all of these people?

When he let go of my hands and got down on one knee, the crowd around us cheered. I was vaguely aware of cameras flashing, vaguely aware that the music was still playing. Everything was muted and dreamlike. The only thing I could focus on was Luke's face. His eyes were dancing with emotion and my hands trembled as he started to speak. The crowd hushed so they could hear.

"Eliza Marie Moore, you are the girl of my dreams. You're the only one I could imagine spending eternity with. I promise to love you unconditionally and to do my best to make you happy." His golden brown eyes were locked on mine.

We were the only two people there. My entire world was kneeling before me, holding on to my hand as he searched into my soul. I felt moisture fill my eyes as he reached into his coat pocket and produced a ring box. He lifted the lid, his eyes never leaving mine. "Marry me?"

Time stood still.

"Yes," I breathed, finding it hard to speak through the emotion. The crowds around us erupted into applause and cheers. I nodded and laughed, brushing away tears as Luke put the ring on my left ring finger and then stood and swept me into his arms.

We were both grinning as he spun me around and then continued to hold me tight.

"I love you," I said into his ear so he could hear me above the noise.

"I love you too." He pulled back to gaze into my eyes. I saw the look he'd held there for so many weeks, and all at once I realized what it meant. Eternity. He loved me in a way that was limitless; he wanted me for forever, just as I wanted him. There were no conditions, no bounds . . . just love.

He slowly leaned in and kissed me, causing the crowd to roar with approval. There were several catcalls, but we didn't break apart. In that moment, I didn't care who saw us. I loved this man and I wanted the world to know it!

The violinist began to play the wedding march and we finally pulled away and beamed at each other.

"Congratulations!" Courtney ran up and gave me a hug.

"I can't believe you were in on this!" I cried as I hugged her back. My cheeks already ached from smiling, but I couldn't stop. This was the happiest night of my life.

"Totally! Did you suspect anything?"

"I didn't have a clue!"

Courtney smirked and gave Alexis a fist bump. "We are so good!"

Morgan was next to give me a hug. "I'm so glad you said yes!"

We all laughed at that, especially when Luke nodded and pretended to wipe his forehead in relief.

"Let me see your ring, Liza." Courtney eagerly grabbed my hand.

Even in the darkened area, the diamonds on the band dazzled as they caught light from a nearby streetlamp. There were small stones lining the band, with a single, larger diamond in the center.

"Wow, it's *beautiful!*" Courtney gushed as Alexis and Morgan crowded around to see. I'd barely had time to glance at the ring, but that glance had been enough to know it was exactly what I would have picked out on my own.

Luke was watching me anxiously. "Do you like it, Liza? I wanted to take you ring shopping, but that would've ruined the surprise. I talked to your mom and she told me what styles you like, but if it's not what you want we can take it back."

I shook my head, reaching for his hand. "It's exactly what I want. It's perfect."

He kissed my hand, causing my heart to stutter wildly. I smiled at him and felt the moisture returning to my eyes.

I glanced up at the spires of the Temple and he followed my gaze. I couldn't believe it was actually going to happen. I couldn't believe I was going to marry the man of my dreams and be sealed to him forever.

Dreams really did come true.

CHAPTER
thirty-four

So I'm calling in that bet," Luke said.

We were sitting on the couch in my parents' living room. It had been an exciting night; we'd stopped by his parents' house to drop off Morgan and Luke's parents had insisted on hearing every detail of the proposal.

Afterward, we'd come back here and told the whole story again for my parents' benefit. I discovered that basically everyone but me had been privy to the knowledge that Luke had planned on proposing tonight. He had asked for my dad's blessing yesterday while Courtney and I had been busy making pies. I'd never known Luke possessed such a stealthy streak, but he knew how much I loved surprises. He had succeeded in pulling off what was, in my opinion, the perfect proposal.

While I had enjoyed reliving the glorious moment when Luke had proposed, it was nice to finally be alone with him now. The room was dark except for a fire in the fireplace and the lights that glowed warmly from the Christmas tree.

"I was hoping you'd forget about that bet," I said as I wrapped my arms around his waist and snuggled into his chest. Technically, my dad had won Monopoly last night, but Luke and I had tallied our assets and he came out ahead. Lucky break.

He put his hand on my back and played with the ends of my hair. "I want us to get married soon—before your mom has the baby."

"Wow, you *do* play for high stakes, don't you?" I teased.

"I'm serious, Liza."

I sat up and looked at him, the corners of my mouth turning down. "I am too." I sighed and turned my gaze away. "Luke, I don't want to wait any more than you do . . . but what choice do we have? My mom has been looking forward to planning my wedding since I was practically in diapers, and there's no way she could be up to that right now. I would rather elope than run her ragged because I'm too selfish to wait a few months."

"You would consider eloping?" Luke's eyes danced as he raised an eyebrow. "Well . . . that puts a whole new spin on things."

I laughed. "You make it sound like we should run off tonight."

"Don't tempt me."

My stomach did a flip, but I tried to ignore it. "What part of 'my mom's dream is to plan my wedding' did you not hear?" I smiled and traced the dimple in his cheek.

"What if I told you that I've already talked to your mom about this, and she agrees with me?"

"You did? She *does?*"

He nodded. "After asking your dad for his permission—which was absolutely terrifying, by the way—your mom came into the office and we all talked. She knew you would be concerned about her, but both of your parents felt that it would be unwise for us to have a long engagement. I happen to agree with them."

He ran his fingers through my hair. "I would never do anything to hurt you, Liza, but I have to admit that it's getting harder and harder to keep away from you. I think dragging things out would only be a mistake."

I felt as if a huge weight had been lifted off my shoulders. Instead of months on end, I could possibly marry Luke in a matter of weeks? The thought was intoxicating.

"So when are you thinking?"

"You know I'm game for whenever you're comfortable with. This is your wedding and I want it to be exactly the way you want it."

I felt the smile reach my eyes as I gazed at Luke. Would he ever cease to amaze me? How would I possibly be able to make him as happy as he made me? I traced his lips with my finger and smiled. "I don't care about having an extravagant wedding—I just want you."

Luke shook his head and searched my eyes as he leaned toward me. He stopped a breath away from my mouth and mumbled, "Liza, you are going to make me a very happy man."

His golden eyes reflected the flames from the firelight as he leaned in to kiss me.

✺

Although it was late by the time Luke left, the light was on in my bedroom. I opened the door to find my mom propped up with pillows on my bed, reading a wedding magazine.

"Mom, what are you still doing up?" I raised an eyebrow and my mouth twitched. "And when did you buy that magazine?"

She grinned as she closed the magazine and set it on the bed. "I bought it this morning at the grocery store. I've been secretly thumbing through it all day."

I giggled as she smiled and patted the bed beside her. "And how can I sleep with such exciting news? I thought Luke would never leave! I've been dying to talk to you."

I started walking to the bed and then stopped. "Can I get you anything? A late night snack?"

"No, no; I'm fine. I already had something." She gestured to an empty

Snickers wrapper and a bottle of Tums on the nightstand, which earned another laugh from me. She smiled and shifted her round belly in an attempt to sit up higher. I helped prop the pillows behind her back.

"So, did you and Luke have a chance to talk about when the big day will be?"

"Yes, and he told me that you had already talked about it." I reached out and placed my hand on hers. "Mom, are you *sure* you're okay to do this right now? I don't want you overdoing it and putting yourself or the baby at risk for my sake."

"Liza, trust me, I'm absolutely positive that this is the right thing. I'm thrilled for you and Luke and I promise not to overdo." She grinned at me as she picked the magazine back up. "And lucky for us, we've been talking for months about how you want your wedding. Now it will just be a matter of filling in the details."

I smiled at her enthusiasm. She was right; we *had* been talking about my wedding for months—just for fun. It was the reason why my mom knew my ring preference. She wasn't pushy or weird about it; she simply loved weddings. I often thought she'd missed her calling as a wedding planner.

"That's true, but what about the shower and the reception and the shopping . . ." I frowned as I thought of how taxing it would all be for her.

"Sweetheart, you're forgetting one very important detail."

"I am?"

"Yes. You're forgetting that I have an entire network of help at my disposal."

I looked at her in confusion and she glanced at me through her lashes. "I *may* have hinted to Rose that you were probably getting engaged soon. She's practically already sent out the invitations for your shower."

Rose Lawson was the Relief Society president in my parents' ward and one of my mom's dear friends.

"Really?" My eyes widened in surprise.

She nodded. "Even if I wanted to go overboard, the sisters in the ward wouldn't let me. They've already been so sweet and supportive about this pregnancy. I can't tell you how many little acts of service keep going on around here. I've told everyone I'm fine, but it doesn't make any difference." She shrugged and waved her hand helplessly before smiling at me. "My point is—the sisters will be there for me. They'll recognize any needs I have before I do; it never fails."

Mom wiggled back further into the pillows. "Would I be stressed if I knew I couldn't rely on them? Absolutely." A slow smile spread across her face. "But with their help, I guarantee we can pull off this wedding in two months. What do you say?"

Warmth flowed through me as I thought about the Relief Society. Because of the dreams I'd had with Grandma, I knew that Mom was right; the sisters would be there to help.

My face broke into a smile and I gave her hand a squeeze. "I say, let's do it."

It had been a long day but I was too giddy to sleep. I went into my room and opened Grandma's music box, listening to the familiar tune as I scanned through my texts.

News of our engagement had spread fast. There were several messages from my friends, all offering congratulations. I grinned as I read them, and then gasped as I opened a message from Courtney. It was a picture of Luke proposing tonight. I felt my heart swell almost to bursting as I studied the image. I still couldn't believe it was real.

Before climbing into bed I said a prayer of gratitude. My list of things to be thankful for had never been longer.

I realized that every good thing that had happened in my life was the direct result of trying to stay close to the Lord. He loved me, and truly did want me to be happy. I'd felt His love before, but never as powerfully as I did now. It was humbling.

After ending the prayer, I snuggled down under the covers. I was about to put my phone on silent when it buzzed. It was a message from Luke: *Good night, Liza. I'll meet you in my dreams . . .*

I held the phone to my heart and sighed. I was the luckiest girl alive. No, not lucky—blessed.

I was very, very blessed.

CHAPTER
thirty-five

That night I had a dream. It was a brisk winter morning, but the walls of the temple glistened in the sun. A group was gathered at the bottom of the stairs leading to the temple. As I walked closer, I saw that the group consisted of my family and friends.

Jill and my roommates were smiling and talking excitedly. Luke's family was there, standing at the base of the steps. Morgan was in the middle; grinning with importance as she held a bouquet of flowers.

I smiled as I saw my dad looking handsome in a tuxedo, holding on to my mom's arm. She was positively beaming from ear to ear, her round stomach just visible beneath her dress coat. Courtney stood next to them, wearing a dress similar to Morgan's.

I felt a gentle breeze blow across the back of my neck and turned to see Grandma standing several yards behind me. Her smile was as big as my mom's had been. She winked and waved at me. A small group of children stood around her.

I waved back and started toward her, but just as quickly as she and the children had appeared, they were gone. I wondered what it meant, and who the children had been, but my attention was drawn back to the group by the temple.

A photographer suddenly appeared from behind the wedding party. He gestured for everyone to move away from the stairs. The group parted, and for the first time, I saw the bride and groom.

I gasped as I recognized myself. I was draped in a gorgeous wedding gown, holding the hand of the most handsome man I'd ever laid eyes on. Luke looked so dashing in his tuxedo it was almost painful. His face was bent down, staring into mine as he held my hands.

The scene mesmerized me. It was as if we were in a world entirely our own. I hadn't known my face could hold an expression like that: alive and radiating joy. Luke's countenance also beamed with pure, unconditional love.

The photographer had to speak to us three times before we heard him, which caused the group at the base of the stairs to laugh.

I wanted to walk closer; to stand on the steps next to my dream-self and get a better look, but there seemed to be a wall pushing against me as I tried. I understood that this was all I was meant to see. Unlike my other dreams, which had shown me past events—this dream was my future.

Tears spilled down my face in gratitude for this final gift from Grandma. I realized now who those children were.

When Luke and I were sealed in the temple, we wouldn't just be getting married and starting our future together as eternal companions; we would be starting our eternal family. That was the beauty of the plan.

My gaze traveled up the temple walls to the engraving, "Holiness to the Lord; the House of the Lord."

I felt for my Young Women medallion. This was what it was all for: the dreams, the lessons and life experiences, the Relief Society and the Gospel— to draw closer to the Savior. To help others draw closer to Him, and to have an eternal family.

In short: to find joy.

I took one final look at my future, standing there on the temple steps. The dream began to fade.

"For time and all eternity," Grandma's voice echoed.

I smiled.

For time and all eternity.

ABOUT THE AUTHOR

Holly J. Wood is an avid reader. She attended Ricks College and Brigham Young University where she pursued a degree in health science. Holly has a passion for travel and has lived briefly in Israel and Mexico. True to her name, she enjoys watching classic movies and musicals. She currently lives in Mountain Green, Utah, with her husband and three young children.

www.hollyjwood.com

hollyjwoodauthor@gmail.com

SUGGESTED READING

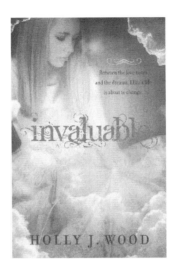

Eliza Moore's sophomore year of high school is turning out to be anything but ordinary. After only half-listening to her mother's lesson on Sunday about the importance of the Young Women values, something strange begins to happen. Eliza begins dreaming about her great-grandmother, who visits her with some important lessons taught by some very special people. Each time Eliza awakens, she finds herself on a treasure hunt of sorts as she begins to understand the significance of the eight Young Women values, and she finds her life changing for the better as she strives to live them. Invaluable is the fun and inspiring story of Eliza's journey of spiritual self-discovery that will have girls of all ages excited to be part of the Young Women program.